RECLAMATION

RECLAMATION

BOOK THREE OF THE LELAND DRAGONS SERIES

BY JACKIE GAMBER

SECOND EDITION

Published by Big Imagine 2023

ISBN: 978-1-7360238-4-6

Library of Congress Control Number: 2023931833

©2013, 2023 by Jackie Gamber

Cover art ©2023 by Ellen Kjiersten Gamber

Reclamation is a work of fiction. Names, characters, places, and incidents are the product of the author's imagination or used fictitiously.

First edition published 2013.

All rights reserved. Published in Atlanta, GA, USA.

Cover Art by
Interior Design by
Ellen Kjiersten Gamber

Written by
Jackie Gamber

To Robin
As true today as ever:
Friend to dragons, friend to me
Believes in who she knows she can be

RECLAMATION

Chapter One

Jastin raced. He dug his heels into Blade's ribs, spurring his mount along the Esra tree line. Rain turned dust into mud, and splattered his boots, his legs, even Blade's throat.

Thunder rumbled, just as he heard a sharp inhale above him. He yanked Blade's reins to shove the horse into the copse of pines they'd been skirting, and dodged. Still, his shoulders sizzled from dragon flame, spat from above. He only narrowly missed the full blast, and the pine boughs blocked the relief the rain might bring.

He glanced over his shoulder at Leesa, the mute servant from Riddess Castle who shared the wild ride. Her dark hair was glossy with water. The arms of her dress, where she hugged his waist, were flame-charred. But she met his gaze with her brown eyes. Steady.

"You should have gone with the others," he said.

If only Leesa had flown away with the wizards and their dragons; Orman Thistleby, Drell the black dragon, Layce Phelcher, and with Sela the human-girl-turned-red-dragon; Leesa would be safe with them. Long gone into the sky, and away from the war busting loose all around them.

Two hard days ago, dragon upon dragon had dropped from the sky over Riddess castle, led by Fordon Blackclaw, and attacked Esra Province, her castle, and her people. And while Sela and the others escaped, headed for the Leland border, Jastin couldn't—wouldn't—bring himself to step into Leland for any reason. Not even to avoid this fiery confrontation. No way. No how.

For two days, Jastin had been driven south, riding hard with dragons on his tail, and had wished, the whole time, Leesa hadn't chosen to stay with him.

And yet, even as he scolded her now, and she gave him a flat look that was her way of scolding him right back, he was glad for himself that she was here.

An elm tree burst into flame beside them. He tugged Blade's reins, veered him sharply right. In all his years as a dragon hunter, he'd learned to navigate a forest at high speed, but never with a passenger. His balance was off. His timing. But Blade knew the scent of dragon flame, too, and sensed it coming even before Jastin tightened his grip on the leathers. The horse leapt a fallen limb. Circled a fat oak. And banked a sharp left, just as another fire spout exploded into undergrowth.

The forest erupted all around them, trying to swallow them. "We need to get open," Jastin shouted. To Blade, or to himself.

Blade's hooves hit dirt, and kicked the stuff into

Jastin's eyes, already bleary from smoke. They'd found the road again, but the reins tugged out of Jastin's grasp. He struggled to capture them.

Then, behind and above, the dragon screeched. Not just angry, but in pain. Jastin blinked into focus, and spun at the waist to look. The Green had drawn up. It thrashed his head back and forth. Then Jastin spotted the arrow shot straight up through its jaw, locking its mouth closed.

Behind him, Leesa lowered his crossbow.

Jastin blinked again. He felt himself smile.

She slid the crossbow back into the latch on Blade's saddle, and hugged her arms around Jastin's waist. Then she smiled, too.

"Heyah!" Jastin called.

Blade raced on.

He recognized the feel of compacted South Morlan soil beneath Blade's feet when they crossed into it. The layers of gravel and hard clay gave his gallop a unique sound, even more pronounced with Leesa's weight. He couldn't keep pushing Blade as hard as he'd been, though. South Morlan ground would batter them all before they reached Jastin's home, at this pace.

With the Green off their trail, he risked reigning Blade in, just a little. He slowed enough to catch his breath. The loyal horse would need a long drink and good rub down tonight. He'd earned one, anyway.

As they loped along the afternoon, he felt Leesa's head rest against the back of his shoulder, and then grow heavy. Her arms slackened around his waist. He might have stopped before she had the chance to fall off, only he could see edge of his home's roofline just through some trees.

But... something felt wrong. Smelled wrong. He kicked Blade back into a quick trot. Leesa roused, and tightened her arms again.

Just as they reached the edge of Jastin's property, his house exploded. He galloped close enough to see flames belch through windows, and up the chimney. Roof tiles bubbled.

The home he built. The one he'd once shared with Rimin, his wife. The shed full of tools and weapons. The well he'd dug with his own two hands. Memories, wishes, regrets. All of it, food for the furnace that raged so hot that even at this distance, even beneath the pattering of rain, he felt his cheeks scorch.

He eased Blade under the cover of a tall sycamore. Two gem-colored dragon bodies, disfigured through heat waves, blasted a final flame spray. They ascended and abandoned their work.

Then he let Blade's reins drop. And he watched the fire.

He felt Leesa's hand press gently to his back. He shook his head. "It's just as well," he said. He turned his head to regard her dark eyes, and the flames reflected in her irises.

"It's just as well."

§

Sela remained in her dragon form since she'd escaped Esra Province, and Fordon Blackclaw's attack. For two days, she'd slept, hunted, and eaten as a dragon. She shared home once again with her parents in Leland Province, and the mountains she loved. The land welcomed her, fed its magic up through her scaled feet and throughout her veins. This was the life she was meant to have, all along, and each and every little nerve ending in her strange and comfortable shape knew it.

And yet, as a human, she'd experienced things she couldn't have otherwise. A view of the species at ground level. At empathy level. She'd seen the darkness in a human soul, and the dawn of understanding in another. She'd witnessed the worst of betrayal, and the best of loyalty. Friendships broken. Promises kept.

And then there was Bannon Raley, and their kiss.

Now that the scramble of the first few hours here had settled, and her human and dragon friends had been given food, rest, and what first aid had been needed; now that the Dragon Council had been alerted to Blackclaw's attack and had been called to a meeting; now that all Sela had to do for the next few hours was wait to find out what happened next, she had time to think.

To remember Bannon, and his kiss.

She ran her tongue across her ruby-scaled mouth. No, a kiss in this form wouldn't feel the same as human lips. Maybe her mouth was the only physical change she might actually miss. But she could carry the memory and the feel of his kiss in the place where her dragon self and human self shared everything. Her heart.

She heard the ponderous footfalls of her father cross the wide expanse of carved, marble steps at the gaping mouth of Mount Gore Manor, home of the leader of the Dragon Council. Home of Sela's family. And now, Sela. For real. For good.

"And here I thought I would be the one to greet our council," said her father. He sat on a wide landing tread beside her, and curled his crimson tail around her rump.

She smiled at the contact. "It will be the first time they have seen me since I was a child," said Sela.

Since she'd discovered how to become a dragon again. That thought hung in the air between them a moment. Then her father stroked her tail with the tip of his. "They will be happy for all of us. They have missed you, too."

He rose to his feet, and rippled his strong wings along his back. He squinted up into the vibrant morning sun, focusing on two bronze shapes that dipped and rose, gracefully echoing each other's movement as they drew near.

"Hale Brownwing, and his daughter, Vaya," said her father. "Early, as usual."

Sela didn't even know Drell was awake yet, but he appeared at the mouth of the manor, and slowly strode forward to join her on the steps, as well.

Drell, the black dragon who had come from the desert, but seemed so at home in the mountains. The black dragon without a tribe name, without a history. He lifted his chin, silent, as he watched the Brownwings land.

Then even Sela's mother, Riza Redheart, emerged from the manor.

Her mother continued down the steps, her ruby scales refracting the low, bright sun shining through pine needles. She watched Vaya, and when the Brown came close, she paused. Vaya and Sela's mother exchanged a nervous smile. A knowing nod.

"No more secrets," said Sela's mother.

Vaya glanced at Hale, and then at Drell. She released a long breath, stippled with sparks. "No more secrets," she said to Sela's mother.

Then Vaya climbed two manor steps. She faced Drell. Her amber eyes settled onto his own golden gaze. "No more secrets, Drell," she said. "We must fly, and I will answer questions you have always wanted to ask."

Drell's eyes softened.

Hale Brownwing snorted. "I thought we were called for a council meeting. What is going on here?"

"*You* are called to a council meeting, Hale," said Sela's mother. "To discuss Fordon Blackclaw's attack on Riddess Castle, and his plans to destroy humans, and whichever dragons get in his way. Reason enough to join Kallon in the manor hall and get started."

"But the other council members—" Sela's father began to say.

"Will be here soon enough," Sela's mother finished. "Take Hale into the manor. His daughter has business of her own to deal with right now." She looked again at Vaya, and Drell. "Once and for all."

Drell seemed unaware of the discussion around

him. His eyes remained fixed on Vaya, nervous and hopeful.

Vaya and Drell peeled away from the group, and strolled along the mountain path that led down and away to privacy. Hale watched them, his face taut, until Sela's mother nudged her chest against his ribs, urging him inside the manor. "Much to discuss," she said.

Her father's face was tight with something, too, as he regarded her mother, but he simply turned, and led Hale inside.

Other council members began to arrive, bringing warm mountain breezes on their wings. Min Greenscale, one of the eldest mountain dragons, brushed his feet across the carved statues outside the manor entrance before he swerved around to land. He gave Sela a faint nod before lumbering into the manor, although, just before his head passed through, he glanced back.

He must have noticed the difference, after all.

Shera Yellowfang's feet barely touched ground before she smiled at Sela. "Look at you! When your mother's message of your change reached me, I could scarcely imagine you any other way than your gangly little self. But here you are, all grown and as lovely as your mother."

Sela took that as the highest compliment.

Lin Orangepaw touched down beside Yellowfang, and the two oooh'd and ahhh'd. "Her father's topknot horns," said Orangepaw. "But her mother's eyes."

Not sure what else to do, Sela just smiled. Until she caught a flutter of motion from the corner of her eye.

A golden eagle caught a low pine branch, and bobbed, watching. *zz* golden eagle. The one that stopped a soldier from swinging a sword at her head during the Esra fight. The one who had followed her and the group here, to Mount Gore. The one who regarded her from the trees yesterday afternoon. And last night. And who, she was sure, knew her.

"Sela?" called her mother.

Yellowfang and Orangepaw had already ascended the stairs and were chatting as they passed through the manor's gaping entrance.

"We are starting," said her mother.

Sela climbed the steps. When she looked back over her shoulder into the trees, the eagle was gone.

§

Drell landed onto a rocky path between Mount Gore and the dragon village he was never before allowed to visit. Habit made him slow his flight before he reached the village, but the conversation made him have to pause entirely, and set down. He couldn't seem to keep his wings moving and process what he'd just been told at the same time.

Vaya lowered to her back feet, and then dropped to all fours beside him. Her tawny brown forehead creased. "Drell, are you all right?"

"Yes," he said, a little breathless. "I have wondered. Suspected all along, I think." His mind formed the word before his mouth tried to speak it. "Mother," he said.

"You are my mother."

She smiled, but it held back a conflict of emotions in her eyes. "I should have told you a long time ago."

"I would have liked that."

She slowly nodded, and gazed down toward the rubbled path. "I was not brave enough to face the walls of deceit I had already built." She raised her head to regard him. "I have asked others to participate in my charade, and I see the price they have paid. And I have denied you a tribe, and a birthright." Her throat clenched. She drew in a long breath. "But things have changed. With everything happening now, my personal concerns hardly seem worth protecting anymore."

He'd already worked through these thoughts for himself. He'd even had conversations with her, in his mind, over the years. He practiced what he would say and do if this moment ever really came to pass. All those rehearsals were lost now. He just watched her, and her eyelashes that rimmed her eyes with dark lines as they fluttered with each blink. He tried to see her differently, tried to feel something more for her than a warm, mysterious bond of companionship. He cared for her, of course. They had spent many long hours together, talking and flying, and being friends. But she hadn't raised him. Whatever matronly connection he'd thought would spring into place between them, it wasn't there.

"You must be very angry," she said.

"No," he said. "I am not angry. You have taught me the ways of Leland, as much as you could, and the Ambercrest tribe has taught me well, too. Tay is as good a father as I could ever hope to have. You chose him well for me."

Her eyes filled with moisture. It was the closest thing to crying he'd ever seen from her.

"We can go to the village another time," said Drell.

"I promised to show you around," she said. "And I will."

Drell laid his digits over her paw. "I know you will. But perhaps today is not the right day."

She closed her eyes. When she opened them, they were clear, and her expression was tight around the edges. Familiar. She nodded once. "Yes, you are right. I should be with my father now, and supporting the council. Thank you for understanding."

With a quick push, she lofted, and hovered. "Will you come?"

"I will be along," Drell said.

She nodded again. And then she darted forward with a strong wing thrust, and soared off toward Mount Gore.

It wasn't really what he was hoping she'd choose, but of course, Drell did understand. It's what he did best; understand not to pry, not to ask, not to want anything more than what he was offered.

He'd always thought that's where his loneliness came from; his never asking, never quite knowing. But now, with the words directly from Vaya's mouth, and the riddles to his heritage finally solved, his emptiness was still there, still rumbling like hunger in his heart.

§

Orman Thistleby hunched over a stack of parchments in his quarters in Mount Gore Manor. He pulled a candlestick closer, and slopped wax onto his beard that sprawled over his desk, and over a word on the scroll he was trying to read. "Blast it all!" he complained to the shadows. "Carnsarned dragons can't carve a few windows in this place?" he muttered.

The door behind him squeaked open. Layce Phelcher, seer and self-proclaimed wizard, stuck her head in. "It's a cave, what do you expect? The deeper inside the mountain your room is, the less the chance for a window."

"It's not just a cave, it's a home," he said. "Some visitors around here like a little sunlight for studying."

Layce crouched beside Orman's chair. She gripped his beard and scratched her fingernail at the cooled wax bump. "Fancy cave, I'll give you that. Have you seen the tapestry in the Great Hall? Did you know dragons could weave?"

"Of course they can weave."

"And the statues of the council leaders through the ages, all carved around the entrance. As beautiful as any sculptures I've seen in any chapel."

Orman tugged his beard out of her hands. "You've been the Esra dragon liaison for how long? And yet dragons still surprise you?"

Layce shrugged, dislodging a swatch of blue silk draped around her shoulders. "Esra hasn't liaised with dragons in years. They're spread out, and wild. I only ever really got to know Fane Whitetail, and that's not saying much." She held up the wax she'd rolled into a tiny ball. "Can I keep this?"

Orman snatched it. "With my whiskers in it?" She was flat out barmy, asking something like that. He tucked the misshapen little wax blob under the belt around his trousers.

Trousers. That's what he'd been reduced to. Borrowed clothes and borrowed papers, in a borrowed room with no windows.

"Oh, plenty of wizards forgo robes for trousers," said Layce. "I think you look fetching."

"Bah." He had far too much on his mind to be playing at Layce's love games. He didn't trust them anyway. He didn't trust her. Last time she tried to distract him with her feminine charms, she'd paralyzed him and left him for dead.

"I knew you weren't dead!" She stood abruptly. The blue silk uncoiled from her neck and snapped off, its edge trapped under Orman's chair. "And what do you mean, 'tried'? It worked well and good, didn't it? Or did that solidifying crystal pop into your mouth all by itself?"

She reached down to recover her scarf, but Orman leaned his weight sideways and pinched it tight beneath the chair leg. She tugged.

"And I've said I'm sorry." She grunted lightly, and yanked again at the fabric. "Ease up, would you?"

Orman obeyed. He leaned the opposite way.

Just as she gave it another hard pull.

The fabric suddenly came free, too fast. Layce squealed, ran backward trying to keep up with her momentum, and tripped over Orman's bedroll. She dropped back with an "oomph."

She pushed up on her hands. "Bully," she said.

"Wanna-be."

She crawled to the edge of the puffy, woven mat, and knelt there. "You know you're not cross with me. You're cross with yourself."

Orman scowled at her. Then he spun in his chair and returned his attention to the papers spread across his desk.

"You feel it too," she said. "This unrest. Not just here in Leland, with the violence and all that, but farther and higher, as though all the earth has a bellyache. And you don't know what to do about it."

"I could figure out what to do if other people would leave me to my studying."

"You're not going to find the answer in those wrinkled parchments," Layce said.

Orman laid his hands on the desk, fingers splayed across his meager pages. "They're all I've got." He shook his head, dragging his beard back and forth across his lap. "I've lost everything now. All my crystals. My books. Even my robes."

He heard the soft steps of her bare feet. Then she was beside him again, kneeling. She laid her hand over his wrinkled knuckles.

"A wizard is nothing without his tools," he said,

regarding her hand. He flipped his hand palm up, and captured her fingers, then turned out her hand to make sure she hadn't pilfered anything. She hadn't.

"I'm old, Layce," he said. "And getting more useless by the day."

"Feeling more sorry for yourself, you mean." She nudged her fist into his ribs. "There are plenty of things you can do without crystals. Or are you conceding I'm the better wizard than you?"

He hopped to his feet, glared down at her. "You're not a wizard at all!"

She stood, too, slowly. And then walked toward the door, her gaze on the carved ceiling. "But I know how to talk to the wind, and how to call for a dream. I don't need crystals for that."

"Nobody needs crystals for that!"

She turned. Smiled. "Nobody but you."

Orman balled his fists. He could have struck her, if he was the woman-striking type, but, as far as he knew, he wasn't. So instead, he pressed his fists together, knuckles to knuckles, and shouted "Alaxiamon!"

A breeze fluttered in, as though the room did have windows after all, and someone had just flung them open. It brought the scent of apple blossoms and fallen leaves and a soft whisper that used no words. But Orman heard it. So did Layce, judging by the way the smile collapsed on her mouth.

"Torn?" she asked, her aging face going pale. "What does it mean?"

"The fabric," said Orman. "The material that

formed this world, and the dragons in it. It's been ripped."

Layce took a step toward him, her jaw slack. "Blackclaw has done much more than start a war, hasn't he?"

"I'll need to dream before I really understand the wind's message." Orman lowered his hands to his sides. "But I think the brute has really done it. I think he's brought on the end of the age."

At Orman's words, the wind rose again, and whirled dust and secrets around their shoulders. A strand of Layce's hair rustled against her cheek. She didn't seem to notice.

"I'll dream, too," she said quietly. "I'll find out what I can between Avara and me."

Orman didn't think the sisters could be much help. What could a couple of seers tell him than his dream wouldn't reveal? But if it made them feel better to keep busy, all the better. Give them something to do, they'll stay out of his way.

"She's fine, by the way," sniffed Layce. "The venur, too. Since you asked."

"Did I?"

"He's aging fast. As though all those years spent sleeping are catching up to him. But he's stronger today than he was yesterday."

"Fine. Fine." Orman shuffled toward his desk.

"The three of us are going to that forest library you're always bragging about. We want to do some studying of our own."

Orman spun. "What business do you have there?"

Layce slowly wrapped the blue silk around her throat, and then pulled her long, dark locks free to spill down her back. "Same as anyone."

"You'll not go without me," said Orman, pointing his finger.

"Suit yourself." Layce turned for the door. "Meet us on the manor steps after the council meeting."

"I'll be there," he said. Then he scuffled toward her again. "Oh, and Layce, dear?"

"Hm?" She peered over her shoulder.

He held out his hand and glowered at her. "Give me back that bit of wax."

She screwed up her face. "Oh, fiddle." She slapped the smudge to his palm. "I had wonderful plans for your whiskers, Orman Thistleby." She closed his fingers, and then leaned against him, and whispered toward his ear. "And in the end, I don't think you would have minded very much."

"No?" he asked, gazing down into her blue, blue eyes. They really were lovely to look at, with pleasant little crinkles in the corners. Whether from age or smiling, it didn't matter. Her hair was soft and where it tickled against his arm. He reached for it, and fondled it between his thumb and fingers.

She grinned. "Or maybe I don't need your whiskers."

He nudged her away. "Be off with you and your feminine ways," he said. "I have work to do."

"For the life of me, I can't figure out what I see in

you." She gripped the door handle and pushed it open. "If you're not at the steps when we're ready to go, we'll leave without you."

"Be off!"

She slammed the door.

Orman held up his hand and triumphantly studied Layce's long, black hairs he'd stolen. Then he hurried to his desk, pulled open the drawer, and set them inside it. For safekeeping.

Just in case.

CHAPTER TWO

The chime of birdsong outside the Great Hall archway conflicted with the dour shadows on the faces of the Dragon Council members. Min Greenscale sat against a far wall, on a flax rug that was as worn at the edges as his tired expression. Lin Orangepaw was bright-eyed, but leaned forward toward Sela's father, as though anticipating bad news. Shera Yellowfang and Hale Brownwing touched shoulders where they stood near the wide serving table, the one carved from a single trunk of a giant marrwood tree. Sela's mother was proud of that table, but she used it now as a brace, with both paws on the smooth, dark surface while she gazed up at Sela's father.

Sela, as she sat quietly and awaited her re-introduction to the council, felt the weight of their collective weariness. For two days, she'd been looking forward to this meeting. She was ready for a fight. She wanted her Dragonkind to rally into warriors for justice; to be as incensed at Blackclaw's treachery as she was.

She'd spent years knowing and respecting these dragons from a distance, and now was her chance to get an up-close look at their righteous anger and formidable power.

Except the meeting didn't seem to be working that way.

"You're certain Fordon Blackclaw was the leader of the Esra attack?" asked Brownwing.

"My daughter was witness," said Sela's father. "She is here to give a full account." He opened his paw toward her.

"Your daughter?" asked Min Greenscale. "Then, this *is* the Sela who has been a child on this mountain? A human child?" He turned to regard Sela's mother.

Everyone else looked at Sela. She shifted uneasily, feeling their gazes like tiny pinpricks. "I am," she said.

"You know Fordon Blackclaw by sight, then?" asked Brownwing. "You would recognize him from other dragons?"

"I recognized him," Sela said, sensing something behind his question, but not quite what.

"And we are meant to recognize you?" Brownwing asked. "A stranger among us, wearing the scales of a Red and claiming to be the daughter of our leader?"

Sela felt heat rise from her throat and spread across her face. She opened her mouth to speak, but her father beat her to it.

"That I claim it is enough," he said, advancing angrily toward Brownwing. "She is Sela Redheart, daughter of the Herald of the Reds. She is here to bear witness to Blackclaw's threat, not to be interrogated as some sort of outsider."

"I think what Hale means to say, Kallon," said Yellowfang, easing in front of Brownwing, and between them, "...is that your daughter's transformation is sudden to the rest of us. The timing appears coincidental to this alarming news that Fordon Blackclaw has surfaced, and is attacking human establishments."

"It is not a coincidence," said Sela.

All gazes swung to her. She felt them as an oncoming wall of ocean water. She cleared her throat. "I mean, many things happened at once while I was in Esra. That is where I met the Gold, and he showed me how to be whole."

The flat expression on Brownwing's face made Sela's words feel empty and ridiculous.

"What do you mean, whole?" asked Orangepaw, gently. "Maybe it would help others understand if you explained it a bit." Orangepaw smiled, and nodded in encouragement.

"Well," she began. "I met the Gold at the well in the desert—"

"The well? *The* well?" asked Brownwing, his face contorting in amusement. "In the legendary garden that gave birth to dragons?"

"I have not heard my daughter say anything humorous, Hale," said Sela's mother.

Brownwing's smile disappeared.

"Go on, Sela," said Orangepaw.

"It is a long story," she said. "But it is all true. In

meeting the Gold, he showed me how to be whole again. That is how I am able to meet you now in the dragon form I was born with."

"The Redheart tribe seems to have an affinity with the Gold. So many encounters, when so many others have never even seen him," said Greenscale.

"Many of us do not believe it is actually possible to meet him," said Brownwing.

"Nevertheless, I have no reason to lie." Sela found it too difficult to maintain eye contact with Brownwing, so she said it to Orangepaw, instead.

"Of course you are not lying," said Orangepaw.

"At first she came home, to our mountains," said her father. "But she returned to Esra to rescue a friend."

"Orman Thistleby," said her mother. "Among others."

"And that is when Fordon Blackclaw, Fane Whitetail, and the other dragons attacked Riddess Castle," her father continued.

"That is why I say it was no coincidence," said Sela. "I think my interference there set it all off."

Her father put his paw on her shoulder. "You have no blame in any of this, Sela. If there is blame, it is on me, for not stopping Blackclaw before you were even born."

Min Greenscale stepped forward. "The blame is on Fordon Blackclaw himself," he said, settling his pale, yellow gaze onto each dragon, in turn. "He is a dragon of free will. He has let his greed for power destroy everything he has ever touched." Then he spun to face

Sela, and looked down into her face. "I, for one, am proud of your loyalty in all this." He looked, then, to Sela's father. "Not all of us can say that about our young."

A silence settled into the room. It turned uncomfortable. Sela looked from her mother, to her father, searching for meaning behind Greenscale's words. Then to Min Greenscale, himself. She sensed nothing concrete in his thoughts, only his deep, abiding sadness and an emptiness where memories of his offspring should be.

Orangepaw broke the lingering silence. "This returns our discussion to where it ought to be. Our reaction to Blackclaw."

Dragons shifted positions. Greenscale lumbered back to his place on the rug. Her father inched backward from Brownwing and took his place near the interior arch, where the Great Hall funneled off into a hallway. Yellowfang released a long breath, and Brownwing's face went flat. It was as if someone had thrown a pail of dirt over the last embers of a dying fire in the room.

Where was their indignation? Their moral outrage?

"Is there any reason to believe he will bring the violence to Leland?" asked Brownwing.

"Every reason," said her mother. "Blackclaw will take his violence wherever it leads him."

"But he has not openly threatened our mountains," Brownwing said.

"I met his followers at our border," said Sela's father. "They made it clear Blackclaw will attack all those who resist him."

"Our numbers are not what they once were," said Yellowfang. "I am not even sure we have the power to resist him."

Brownwing nodded. "Agreed. Our best course for now is to wait and see."

"Wait and see?" Sela said, standing to all fours.

"I call a vote," said Brownwing, his heavy gaze on Sela. "From those council members who have the right to do so. Non-voting attendees may see themselves out."

Her father stepped once again toward Brownwing. "I will call the votes here, Herald of the Browns. And I will dismiss whom I wish, when I wish it."

"It is all right, Father," said Sela, through clenched teeth. "I believe I am addressing the wrong council, anyway. I am happy to leave."

And she was, for the moment. It felt good to stomp out, her chin up, and the tip of her tail swishing defiantly.

But outside, on the steps of the manor, while the murmurs of the meeting continued behind her, without her, she deflated. Her show of temper wasn't enough to stir them out of the apathetic mud they were trapped in. Even Blackclaw's cruelty didn't rouse them to action.

What, then, would it take?

Vaya Brownwing appeared at the crest of the mountain trail. Sela moved off the steps as she approached. "They are voting," she said.

"Voting? On what?" Vaya asked.

Sela shook her head. "On which way to not do anything, I think."

Vaya frowned, then bounded up the steps, pulled

in her wings tightly to her back, and continued into the hall.

Apparently not all daughters were disallowed from the voting process.

She stood for a time, wanting to fly, but not knowing if she ought to abandon the manor altogether. Temper was one thing, but disrespect was another. She still hadn't decided when a shadow enveloped her, and grew across the earth at the base of the manor steps. She looked up to find Drell descending, looking very much like a shadow himself as he thrust out his legs for a landing beside her.

"Meeting adjourned, then?" he asked.

"Only for me."

He tossed his head, and rippled his scales from his crown, across his spine, and down his rump, before he pleated his leathery wings to draw them in. Her eyes caught on the flickers of sunlight that reflected as a wave of his movements.

"Your wing is healing nicely," said Sela. She poked her claw at a sealed wound at the edge of his wing, where an arrow had struck him during their escape from Esra.

He winced at her touch.

"Oh. Sorry," she said.

"It's fine. Just tender."

She nodded. She looked out at the trees, scrambling for something else to say.

"She's my mother," said Drell. "Vaya. She finally told me, after all these years."

Sela swung her gaze back to him. "Vaya is your

mother?"

That explained a lot. Her own mother must have known. It was a secret her mother had kept from everyone, all this time. Sela would have thought that sort of thing was impossible, with the way her Kind shared thoughts and feelings without even meaning to, so much of the time.

"That's amazing," she said quietly. She found herself admiring her mother in a way she probably wasn't supposed to.

"I fantasized about it a lot," said Drell. He lowered his head, and examined the tip of his foreclaw that was clotted with dirt. He dragged the claw against a marble step, trying to scrape it clean. "But now that she's said it, nothing feels any different." He gave up on the dirt, and just regarded Sela with golden eyes. Sad eyes, full of disappointment and confusion.

"I thought it would feel like coming home," said Drell.

Sela looked toward the manor, and into the darkness just on the other side of the archway, where dragons discussed official matters about Leland, and the mountain, and the future.

Without her.

"So did I," she said.

In time, Sela heard the shuffle of feet, and the low murmurs of dragon voices drawing closer to the arch. Either the vote had happened quickly, or as Sela suspected, they hadn't decided on anything.

Yellowfang and Brownwing exited first into the

sunshine. They each blinked at the light, and parted to descend on either side of the manor steps. Behind them, Greenscale emerged, but lofted instantly, without so much as a nod of goodbye.

Then hands of mahogany, as wrinkled as the bark of the same tree, reached around the entrance wall, gripping it. Ebouard Riddess, elder venur of Esra Province, pushed off from the wall and made his way down the manor steps. His aged skin seemed to drink in the sun's rays, effusing it. Strengthening him from inside.

Orangepaw, just appearing at the same time, shifted aside.

Layce Phelcher hopped down the steps two at a time, passing the venur, and Orangepaw. Then Layce's sister, Avara, appeared, and hurried to the venur's side and offered her arm to steady him. He smiled at her. She smiled back, in a way that warmed Sela's heart, and made her think again of Bannon.

Sela's father and mother came next, followed by her golden-haired friend Gladdis, who hadn't often left her room in the manor. Or she hadn't spent much time in her room, maybe, now that Sela thought of it. The door was always closed, and Sela assumed her friend was on the other side, but Sela had been so busy, she now realized she'd been neglecting Gladdis.

Gladdis sidled along the wall, and crept down the steps as though she was afraid of being seen. She stepped into place beside Sela, her hand resting gently on Sela's foreleg. "Look at them all," she whispered.

Dragons, she meant. Considering Gladdis had

only just seen her first dragon some weeks ago in Esra, and now was among one of the only humans on Mount Gore, surrounded by dragonkind, she was coping pretty well.

The venur paused to take the final step, and glanced up. Dragon gazes were trained on him, in surprise. Or curiosity. Sela thought she read disapproval in Brownwing's eyes, but maybe that was just the Brown's usual look.

The venur's gaze fixed on Sela's father, and then on each dragon, in turn. He drew himself up. "I am Ebouard Riddess. Those of you know who know my name will have thought me dead these many years."

Murmurs rippled through collected crowd. Sela's mother moved closer to Sela's father.

"May I speak?" asked Venur Riddess, turning again to regard Sela's father.

Sela's father nodded.

"Then allow me to thank your leader, Kallon Redheart, in providing me and my supporters refuge in your province during this treacherous time," said the venur.

His dragonspeak was impeccable. Sela was impressed. And so were the others, judging by their half-smiles and nods.

"It has been a confusing few days for me," the venur continued. He turned to Avara. She took his hand. He seemed to draw strength from that; his shoulders straightened.

"I have woken up from some sort of dreamless

sleep," he said. "I should have died, but survived all this time because of a linking stone."

Sela's father and mother exchanged a long look, their expressions soft. Sela hadn't seen that sort of affection between them in a long time. The other dragons nodded, and quietly rumbled in understanding, urging the venur to go on.

He did. "I should have died by my own son's hand. He thought he was ready for leadership; that he would succeed where he thought I, as venur, had failed. It is difficult for a father…" His voice trailed. He looked again at Avara. "It is difficult," he whispered.

She tightened her grip around his hand.

Sela's father turned his soft gaze now to her. She felt his heart ache to explain things to her even his mind couldn't communicate.

The venur drew in a breath, and collected himself. "I thank you all, once again, for shelter and refuge. It is beyond your responsibility to provide, but in the end, when the wrongs are righted, this kindness will be remembered."

"You are welcome here until you have a home to return to," said Sela's mother.

The venur smiled.

Yellowfang and Brownwing broke off to continue whatever topic they'd been discussing previously.

Avara turned to Layce. "Your Orman didn't show. Should we go without him?"

Layce looked back at the manor. "I told him we would, if he wasn't here."

"Go where?" asked Sela.

"To the library," said Layce. "In Wren Meadow."

"Oh," Sela said, smiling. She hadn't been there in ages. It was one of her favorite places. "Is it a private outing? I'd like to tag along."

"No need to be a tagalong," said Layce, raising both hands. "You can be our ride! The venur isn't strong enough to walk the whole way."

"I wouldn't know it if I did try to walk it," he said. "Considering I've never been there."

"But will we all fit on Sela's back?" asked Avara.

"I'd like to go, too," said Drell, stepping toward them. He looked at Sela, then. "If you don't mind, that is. I've heard so much about the place."

"Of course I don't mind," Sela said. "Why would I?"

Drell smiled. She hadn't often seen him do that, and it curled his face pleasantly, turning his eyes into crescents.

"Would there be room for me?" asked Gladdis, who looked so hopeful and frail, even mixed in with her human companions, that Sela didn't have the heart not to include her.

"Drell will take you," she said.

"Let's be off, then," said Avara. "Before the day gets away from us."

"Not without me! Oh, no you don't!" Orman came running, then, his gangly legs looking all the more gawky in those trousers that were several inches above his ankles. His beard wagged along behind him, over his shoulder, as he pedaled his legs down the manor steps.

"Not without me," he called again, reaching for Drell's leg for a step up.

Sela thought she caught a flicker of a smile on Layce's face, just before the rest of the group shimmied up into their seats.

CHAPTER THREE

Jastin dropped an armload of firewood beside Leesa. She knelt, blowing a sliver of kindling flame into an orange fan for a breakfast campfire. He squinted down at her work, and then up into the glint of morning sun. They'd traveled east from his ravaged home; at first, without realizing it, and then, purposefully. Further from Esra, the better. Into territory he recognized and could navigate. What they were going to do next, he didn't know. He was oddly uncomfortable at the thought of confessing to Leesa that he had no friends, no family, no place which could shelter or help them.

She fed the campfire into a crackling glow. She'd dug up some tubers earlier, and now she laid them all around the fire's edge, and watched them roast.

Jastin crouched beside her. "I wish there was some other way of making breakfast. I've had my fill of fire for a while."

She nodded slowly. She turned her brown eyes to regard him.

"You're good in the wilds. A natural."

She nodded again, and smiled.

"That's good," he said. "Because we might be spending a lot of time—"

The campfire exploded into a fireball. Jastin felt the heat as much as saw it. He leapt at Leesa, pushed her to the ground and covered her.

Only then did he realize it wasn't the campfire that had inflamed, it was a wall of scorching fire that sliced the scrubland and cut them off from Blade, a few yards away. Above them, two dragons, a Green and a Brown, flapped in a wide circle, turning around to come at them again.

Had they happened across them, or were the beasts tracking them? *Why* would they track them?

Jastin didn't have time to puzzle out any answers. He rolled off Leesa to help her to her feet. "Run," he said. "Run west. I'll lead them away."

She didn't hear him, or she ignored him. She looked up at the dragons, and then at the flames between her and Blade.

"Leesa," Jastin said. "You have to run."

Blade whinnied. His dark shape drew near to the fire wall, and then broke through. He galloped toward them, his mouth spitting foam, his eyes wild with fear.

Leesa grabbed at Blade's reins and swung up into the saddle. She reached down to Jastin.

He gaped.

Then the crack of a burning tree broke through his surprise, and he took her hand. In a fluid move, he became the passenger behind the saddle. Blade pawed briefly, and then shot off across the scrubland, headed for the nearest tree cover.

§

Drell followed Sela and her riders up and over the scratchy pine boughs and prickled tops of fir trees. Wind chirped past his ears, and kissed cool hints of frost against his throat and chest. He tasted autumn, playing hide and seek in invisible places in the air, so unlike the dry and relentless summer of his Esra home.

His Esra home. Did his foster tribe think of him while he was gone? Would they wonder if he was coming back?

And then, another thought that drew the autumn air into his lungs, and deep into his bones, chilling him. Would Blackclaw's war come to the desert caves, too?

"I think Blackclaw won't be satisfied without total control," said Orman Thistleby, who perched on Drell's neck so lightly, he might have guessed the wizard to be a bird. A tall, bearded bird. Behind him sat Gladdis, who had grown so quiet and ghost-like at Mount Gore he kept forgetting she was even there.

"He asked me to join him," said Drell to Orman. "In Esra. At the castle. He saw me, and knew me, somehow."

"He's not the sort to share anything, son." Orman's grip tightened around Drell's top horns. "You made the right choice."

Drell knew he had. Fordon Blackclaw was a

stranger to him. He'd given Drell the color of his scales and wings, but nothing more. When others talked of Blackclaw's greed and treachery, Drell could see it, too, and wasn't compelled to defend his father, or to identify with him.

And yet, Drell did feel something. Shame, maybe. Or something else he couldn't name. When others' faces filled with hate for his father, did they hate that part of Drell, too?

He followed Sela through a canopy of abundant green. Soft, fernlike fronds tickled past his ribs when he cut through and down. The temperature shifted to a warm spring morning, and he felt moisture collect against the ridges of his face scales. He heard, and smelled, the dance of clear water somewhere nearby.

Wren Meadow. His mother had never allowed him here before, either.

Orman slid off the moment Drell's feet touched spongy ground. Gladdis took more time to scramble down his ribs. The wizard stalked off, snapping orders to the others before they had a chance to climb down Sela's back.

Sela just smiled at Orman. Drell didn't think she even knew she was doing it. It seemed an unconscious expression. Whenever Orman spoke, either to froth at some minor infraction, or to chastise, or to counsel because the wizard did have wisdom to share—Sela's crimson face would betray such a deep joy that it oozed out into a grin that brightened her green eyes and made Drell think she'd swallowed a sunbeam.

It took his breath when she smiled like that.

He became aware of Gladdis, standing beside him. She regarded him, and then looked at Sela, and back. Drell wasn't sure what his expression betrayed, but it must have been something. Gladdis patted him sympathetically on the side of his face.

"Take care with these scrolls, all of you," said Orman. "They aren't originals, mind, but it's taken years of blasted hard work to copy them."

Layce Phelcher swept down Sela's back in a waterfall of blue fabric, followed by her sister, Avara. Avara waited for the venur, who seemed sturdier than yesterday. More than a few minutes ago, even.

Wren Meadow's healing magic was a good idea, even if not for the scroll library.

"Where are the prophecies?" asked Layce.

"Prophecies," Orman sputtered. "You think the work is just going to pop out of a cubby hole and unroll itself for you? You have to read, woman." He opened his arms and passed under a stone-carved arch, and then circled slowly in the center of mound after mound of granite slabs, carved into the shapes of the mountains, with hollowed pockets stuffed full of rolled parchments. His eyes blazed with pride. "Nothing like it in any province," he said. "Organized by century, and then by leader, and then by—"

"Here's one!" called Avara, opening a scroll from a mound under a broadleaf tree. "A prophecy."

Orman stomped his foot, sending a puff of grass and dirt into the air. "It doesn't work that way!"

"Here's another," said Layce. She held up a roll by its neatly-tied green ribbon.

Ebouard Riddess caught a fluttering stalk of grass dislodged by Orman's foot. He stuck it between his teeth, and smiled.

"Bah!" Orman waved his hands. He strode off on his own.

Sela and the women murmured together, and collected armfuls of papers before they all sprawled into the grass and began to read on their bellies. The venur crossed to them, lowered himself to his back, and rested his head on the back of Avara's thigh. He stared up into the trees, his skin fairly glowing, and his countenance growing heartier by the moment.

Gladdis watched them, still standing beside Drell. Then she walked around in front of him to grasp at a scroll in the nearest granite slab. She unrolled it, and frowned at it.

"What's wrong?" he asked.

"I can't read it."

"Let me see." He held out his paw.

She set the parchment in his grasp, and he shook it open. "It's dragonscript," he said. "A history of the hunting lands to the north." He shook his head, and offered it back to her. "Pretty boring stuff."

She unrolled it again, and gazed at it, anyway.

"Would you..." he began. Hesitated, for some reason. Then tried again. "Would you like me to teach you?"

She pulled in a sharp breath, her brown eyes bright.

"You would do that?"

"I'd be happy to." If for no other reason, than to at least feel of some use these days.

Gladdis plopped to a seat, and unrolled the paper across her lap. "Where do we start?"

Drell knelt, and then settled onto the grass beside her. "I guess the beginning is as good a place as any."

Hours later, when Ebouard had roused from his nap, and the day had stretched into what felt like evening, although Drell couldn't tell if it was, judging by the way the sunlight continued to stream through the canopy like mid-day, and Drell's throat was dry from talking and teaching, Orman appeared in the center of the group, holding a clay mug of stream water. He offered it to Layce, who sipped, and passed it on.

Orman was subdued; more than usual. "I'm convinced, now," he said. "I know what the wind tells me."

Layce stood, and brushed soil from her knees. "Avara and I see it, too."

"We'll have a doozy of a time convincing the others," said Orman. "But we'll do it anyway."

"Convincing them of what?" Gladdis asked.

"We have to do more than defeat Blackclaw's uprising," said Orman. "Leland is dying. Esra is dying. All the magic, everywhere around the earth, has been shriveling up like winter leaves beneath our noses, and we haven't seen it happening."

Avara rose to her feet, and took Layce's hand. The sisters spoke quietly in unison, their voices a single sound with breathy echo. "The fabric of this world is worn threadbare. As stone against cloth, conflict chafes against magic."

"And Blackclaw has struck a tearing blow," said Orman. "Our world is unraveling into pieces. As it stands, he'll win this blasted war, and his triumph will shred it into nothingness."

"There must be a way to stop him," said Sela.

"Heal the land and heal the rift," said the sisters, together. "Heal the rift and heal the land."

A long silence followed.

Then Orman moved to action. "Collect all the scrolls you've been reading. All of them. Bring them." He bobbled across the grass toward Drell. "We'll have to convince the leader of the Dragon Council before we'll convince anyone else."

§

A spray of dirt hit Jastin's cheek. He tasted it, along with sweat, and a strand of Leesa's black hair. This time, he had his arms around her waist and gripped his legs around Blade's ribs with all his strength, while Leesa rode Blade like an oncoming storm; wild, unrestrained.

He didn't know Blade had it in him.

"We can't just keep running," he shouted. "Slow down. Let me fight."

Flame spat at Blade's hooves. The horse stumbled, recovered. Jastin used the off-kilter momentum to swing himself around behind Leesa, and face backwards. A

Yellow swooped low, nostrils spewing steam. Behind the Yellow, a Blue closed in fast.

Jastin kept his eyes on the Yellow, and reached for his crossbow. He nocked a bolt, and then raised the crossbow, aiming between the Yellow's eyes. He held his breath to minimize his movement, and waited just long enough for Blade's running gait to sync up with Yellow's pumping wings, until the dragon's forehead hovered along his sight.

Then Blade missed a step. Jastin wobbled; one arm lashed out for balance. And from the open collar of his tunic, his dragon scale, the one he wore always, since his encounter with the Gold, flashed a dazzling glint of sunlight.

The Yellow yelped, blinded, and pulled up. The Blue stuck out his legs to brake, but not in time. Dragons collided, and wings flared, and then wrapped, entangled. The blue and yellow ball of scales and gnashing teeth fell like a boulder to the ground. Hard.

At the tremor and screaming, Leesa looked over her shoulder. Blade slowed, just a little. At first, Jastin thought she'd tugged the horse's reins, but no, they were still slack in her grip.

"They won't stay down for long," said Jastin. "But we've got to catch our breath."

Leesa looked back over Blade's head, and drove the horse toward the horizon. Jastin hooked his crossbow back onto the saddle edge, and then hoisted up and over, walking on his hands to spin round and settle back onto Blade's hips facing forward.

"I take it you know where we're going," he said into Leesa's ear.

She nodded, and pointed.

Just over the curve of the earth, Jastin saw trees. At first, they shrugged together like tiny broccoli heads. Jastin squinted. As they drew nearer, the trees grew in his sightline into a thick, green line of what looked like an impassable wall. A forest barrier? East?

"Eh, Leesa? Is that what I think it is?" he asked.

She nodded.

"You're taking us to Murk Forest on purpose?"

She nodded again.

For a moment, Jastin considered turning them all around. Better to fight the monsters he knew. The ones he'd been fighting his entire life. Besides, the dragons would soon tire of chasing them around the countryside, wouldn't they? What was he to their in-fighting? Esra Castle, Leland Mountains, what was any of that battle to him?

They'd destroyed his home at the order of Blackclaw, no doubt. Just the lashing out of a ranting bully. He guessed the dragon might even feel betrayed, if Blackclaw had enough emotional depth for that. But whatever the dragon's ire against Jastin, he'd tire of it soon enough. The Black had more important battles to face. Didn't he?

Jastin looked ahead to the trees. And then behind himself. In the distance, two glittering shapes of blue and yellow bore down on them. Then, a third. A White.

"Are they serious?" Jastin said.

Leesa answered him by nudging her heels into Blade's ribs. Blade lurched into a tired gallop.

CHAPTER FOUR

Lestir Grimmin stared out through a crenel of the Shornmar Castle parapet surrounding the west tower. He'd taken residence there lately, watching and waiting. His boots had worn fresh indentations into the wooden planks over the past several days, while he clasped his hands behind his back and rocked forward and backward, toes to heels, toes to heels. A nervous habit he thought he'd broken years ago.

But then, the news he waited on was no ordinary announcement.

Years of patience had culminated here. Planning, and cautious execution of those plans. In recent months, he'd seen so many of his desires scribbled out onto pieces of paper, as though a man's hopes and dreams could be filtered down into mere words, to be signed and sealed. Yet, that was all he had to rely on, now. Letters of ink and parchment, sealed with wax promises.

He couldn't help but watch out across the Leland landscape, past the ramshackle farmlands and stone piles citizens called homes, out onto the horizon, and a road that should be bringing him news. Any moment.

Water slapped his nose.

Lestir looked up to find gray clouds pricking at the white sky like a hunched blueberry bush, crawling its thorny legs toward the castle. Didn't matter. Rain or not, he would watch.

A door in the tower floor rattled. "Lestir," called the venur's voice. "Do we go to the garden glade today? Lestir?"

Lestir groaned. How had the fool found him up here? The venur—even in Lestir's mind he used the term loosely—was afraid of heights, afraid of ladders. Spiders. Dead trees. Lestir had known Moras Shornmar the Second since the lad was nine years old. He'd had the brain of a rump roast then, and, as far as Lestir could tell, hadn't managed to learn any new thing as a grown man, either, except how to find more things to be afraid of.

The door shook against its latch. "Lestir! You said we could paint the glen today!"

Oh, yes. And paint. The one thing that kept Moras distracted and quiet for hours, once he got settled into it. But the hours leading up to, and then after? He just wouldn't shut up about it.

Lestir tapped his foot on the door. "It's raining, venur. No glen today."

Quiet.

Lestir eyed the door, narrowed his eyes.

Iron clattered. And then the door swung up and

open, and slammed against the floor on the other side.

Venur Moras Shornmar the Second stuck his wide, round head through the floor and grinned. The fringed point of his sleeping cap hung over one eye. He clutched his stubby fingers into a wrinkled, pointing fist. "Found you."

"You aren't even dressed," said Lestir.

"I didn't know if I should wear trousers or riders," said Moras. A blotch of rain hit the venur on the forehead, and he went cross-eyed, trying to find it.

It might have made Lestir laugh, a long time ago. Back when Lestir was young, too, and found his venur's son a source of amusement, like a jester in a traveling minstrel show. Back then, their fathers were friends, and Lestir had no brother, so it seemed a natural relationship.

Moras had been protected by the castle, and by his father's position, and so as long as Lestir lived in the castle, too, he was mostly unaware of the townsfolk's opinions of the last surviving Shornmar heir; born to weak and elderly parents and a surprise that he survived to adolescence.

But then Lestir moved out and on to his own dreams of leadership. Mayor of Simson, for a while, with his eyes on Durance. And he heard the talk. Vicious talk, and laughter. And Lestir realized he'd considered this idiot a brother, and felt such deep shame he'd still never quite forgiven Moras.

Even after Lestir returned to Shornmar Castle as Lord Grimmin, appointed custodian of Leland affairs for an ailing venurship. Even as venurship passed from father to son, ensuring Lestir's long-term leadership. Even now, as Moras grinned up at him through the tower floor, with his crooked teeth and slanty eyes, wanting nothing more from Lestir than a hug and a day in the glen, Lestir was ashamed of him.

Resented him.

"Mollee," Lestir called.

"I'm here," called Moras's nursemaid, her voice muffled through the tower floor. The girl was nearly an idiot herself, from what Lestir could tell so far. Gave Moras the run of the place.

"Why is Moras still in his sleeping gown?" Lestir asked. "And how did he manage a ladder to this tower?"

"I'm sorry, Lord Grimmin," said Mollee, from down below. "He wanted to find you."

"But I don't want to be found."

"She's holding the ladder so it isn't so wobbly," said Moras, pointing downward.

"Moras, go with Mollee. Go on, now."

Moras frowned. He shook his head. But then he sighed, and climbed his way back out of sight.

From the corner of his eye, Lestir saw movement. He spun toward the horizon. Sure enough, a small dot worked toward him, raising dust from a distant road. Finally. The news was here.

"Oh, Mollee," he called then through the tower door.

Her youthful, dirtied face peered up at him.

"Moras Shornmar may bear the title of venur," said Lestir, "but when it comes to who's in charge around here? That's me."

Mollee swallowed. "Yes, Lord Grimmin."

Then Moras's hand grabbed at her arm, and she was yanked out of sight.

Lestir looked again at the road, squinting through rain just beginning to turn insistent. The black dot formed into a horse and rider. At a fork in the road that could take him south, the rider held direction toward the castle.

"Yes," he said under his breath.

He crouched, dropped down onto the tower ladder, and closed the door above his head. Then he wound down and down the tower's circular stairway. Near the base, he caught up to Moras and Mollee, and pushed past them.

"Lestir!" he heard Moras call after him.

"Not now," said Mollee.

By the time he reached the main bailey, the rain turned hard and pounding. He sprinted across muddy grass to an inner wall with a door that led to the courtyard. He ducked inside, scraped water from his face, and then charged back into the weather.

He guessed the timing right. The messenger and his horse were just reaching the courtyard. He sat hunched, a hooded cape drawn over his face. He didn't even give the man a chance to duck under an arch, or to dismount. He ran to them, and thumped the rider's leg. "Well?"

Marck, the messenger, startled. He yanked the horse to stop, and the horse whinnied and bucked.

"Well?" Lestir asked again, through the rain and the

splat of hooves on mud.

Marck pulled back his hood. His sandy ponytail wrapped his neck like a snake, and the mud on his face looked like freckles. His eyes were puffy from exhaustion. He took several short breaths before he could speak. "It isn't signed."

Lestir took a step back, and blinked up through the rain. "What?"

"Or it's lost." Marck's horse shied, and he had to tug the reins to get it to settle. "There was a wedding. I was waiting for the final word, and the papers."

"And?"

"Then, dragons. A hundred, maybe."

"Dragons?" Lestir went cold, deep in his soul. Deeper than the rain could chill him.

"I don't know what happened, or why. But they attacked, inside and out. I think a black dragon, and Riddess's white one were in it together." Marck shook his head. "Riddess is dead. I barely escaped."

Riddess dead. Dragons in Esra. The great and clever plan to combine lands and leadership, and to get out from under Moras Shornmar, castle fool, had evaporated before it ever had a chance. "What does that... where does that leave Leland?" asked Lestir.

Where does that leave me, he asked himself.

Marck shrugged. He shivered, his cloak and clothing soaked through.

"Go on," said Lestir. "Find a warm fire and hot wine." He patted the horse's haunch.

Marck clicked the horse forward, but then drew

him up again, and turned sideways in the saddle. "Something else, though," he said. "The elder Riddess, Ebouard. The one that was dead. He isn't."

"What are you talking about?"

Marck pulled his cloak under his chin. "I saw him with my own eyes, the day of the attack. He walked out of the castle. There was a group of people who were helping him, I think. And a couple of dragons."

"I thought you said dragons attacked the castle," said Lestir.

"They did. But these others were fighting back, from what I could tell. And then I saw Ebouard Riddess, and a wizard and a red dragon, and a black one, smaller. And they all flew off. North."

Lestir trudged closer to the rider, to read his lips as well as to hear him better above the pounding of hard rain. "Are you saying Vorham Riddess, who we thought was alive, is dead? And that Ebouard Riddess, who we thought was dead, is alive?"

"That's what I'm saying," said Marck.

"And Esra has been attacked, and is without a venur in residence at all?"

"It's a shambles, Lord Grimmin. People were dead, dying, or being herded together when I got out of there."

Lestir stood still for a long time, letting the sky batter him with water, and letting grass turn to muck around his feet. He was thinking, and couldn't be bothered to be annoyed by trivial things just now. "Any ideas on why Esra? Something personal?"

"I don't know, my Lord," said Marck.

"And this black dragon, the one you think leading them. Does he seem reasonable?"

"Hard to say," said Marck. "But he did speak to the others. He let them escape, as best as I can figure."

"I see. Well done." Lestir patted the horse's flank again. You've earned that wine, Marck. Thank you."

Marck nodded, and trotted his horse toward the alcove in the hallway grounds toward the stables.

Lestir continued to stand in the rain, thinking. Thinking. Black dragon, white dragon, and dead and absent venurs. Now seemed an opportune time to get what he could out of this situation: no more waiting and hoping Vorham Riddess would come through for Lestir's fair share of money and rank in the land bride union. Instead, Lestir just might come out with more land and rank than he dreamed possible. If he played this right.

He was nothing, if not adaptable.

CHAPTER FIVE

"**B**lackclaw damages the very fabric of this world," said Orman to Sela's father. "It's more than just war. He brings more danger than any confounded earthbound war could ever threaten."

In the Great Hall, Sela stood with her friends before her mother and father. Drell had been silent since their return to the manor, as he usually was around her father. Avara and Layce still wore their glazed expressions, hands clasped as they'd been at Wren Meadow. Venur Ebouard Riddess remained wherever Avara was, and so he lingered there in the giant space, but didn't speak.

Beyond them all, just in the next room, platters and dishes clattered. Sela's mother had called for dinner the moment everyone arrived, and dragon staff was seeing to it now, along with Gladdis, who had slipped off to help them. Sela could smell buttered hare and boiled wine. Her mouth watered.

Orman didn't even seem to notice the promise of incoming food. His focus was on Sela's father, awaiting some kind of acknowledgment.

Sela watched her father's face, watched his silence. As shadows grew along the walls of the Great Hall, tiredness expanded over his features. He shifted his massive weight to the side, and drew his legs against himself as a woodland creature about to nap. His wings lagged to the floor. "Dragons have fought each other before," he said.

"On behalf of humans," said Orman. "For land. For friendship. For principal. But dragons have never fought each other for control. Not like this."

"I understand your words," said Sela's father. "What I don't understand is your meaning."

"The land's turned against us, Kallon." Orman stepped closer, his wrinkled face bunched up into fear. "She's been trying to tell us for years. With the drought. With the way the mountains suffered—you remember?"

"There's no more drought," said Sela's father. "And the mountains are strong again. Ever since Riza and I..." He looked at Sela's mother.

"Since our love used magic to make it rain," said Sela's mother.

Orman shuffled closer to Sela's mother. "You understand what the land is trying to tell us, don't you, Riza?"

"Yes," said Sela's mother. "I think so."

"Even back then, she was ill. Starving. Your magic fed her, healed a symptom. But didn't cure her." Orman shook his head. "I've been a fool, confound it. I haven't seen it. I haven't even been looking."

"It isn't just Leland," said Ebouard Riddess.

Sela and the others turned to the Esra venur.

"It's the desert," he said, his face solemn. "It grows by the day, devouring the green earth around it. My father's father warned against it, and marked its expansion each year." Ebouard withdrew a scroll from beneath his shirred jacket, and held it out. "I even found a parchment in your library about it."

Orman took the scroll, but kept his eyes on the venur.

"My father taught me about balance, and nature, and the things of man and beast. He knew the desert had the power to consume us, and made me understand it before he would pass the venurship to me." Ebouard's gaze turned toward the floor. "I could never seem to get through to my own son. Not about his greed, and his impatience. I withheld the venurship from him until he could understand."

"He never did," said Orman.

Ebouard shook his head. "I can only imagine how the land has distorted while I've been sleeping."

"Heal the land, heal the rift," chanted Layce and Avara.

"Does it have something to do with the well?" asked Sela's mother. "In the garden where dragons come from?"

"The legend of the well?" asked Drell, startling Sela with the sound of his voice. "You've heard of it?"

"More than just heard of it," said Sela. "I've been there."

Drell's expression clouded over with something Sela couldn't interpret. His thoughts were blank to her, too, and she could tell he was doing it on purpose. "You've been there?" he asked. "Could you find it again?"

"I think so." Sela looked from Drell to the venur, and back. "I was... there was a sandstorm. I sort of stumbled into it."

"I knew it was there," said Drell. He drew in a deep breath. "The desert dragons thought I was mental, but I knew it was there. You'll show me, some day?"

"I can try."

Orman tapped Drell's chest with the parchment in his hand. "You may be seeing it sooner than you think," said Orman.

"There's more," said Drell. "I haven't said anything, because I wasn't sure it had anything to do with this..."

"Go on, son," said Orman.

"Murk Forest is dying," said Drell. He looked at Sela, but she wasn't sure why.

"Murk?" asked Orman.

"Murkans say the magic has turned against them. Just how you've described it, Orman."

Orman's eyes narrowed. He leaned into Drell, and peered closely into his face. "How do you know this?" asked Orman. "No one has contact with Murkens."

"I do," said Drell. He looked again at Sela.

"You," said Orman. He followed Drell's gaze to Sela.

Sela shrugged. "I don't know what he's talking about." Then she moved toward her father. "But I do know that something is very wrong here, right here in these mountains. Look at you, Father! Blackclaw is attacking just outside our border, and Orman is telling you our lands are dying, and you lay there. You haven't said a word!"

"No one has asked me a question," said Sela's father.

"Here's one," said Sela's mother, circling around to stand beside Sela. "What are we going to do?"

Sela's father regarded them both, in turn. "What is there to do?" he asked. "I hear you saying you're worried. You believe magic is dying, and the world is coming apart, but I don't hear anyone offering suggestions how to fix it."

Orman raised up the venur's scroll. "It's all here, clear as mud. Blasted warnings and prophecies always have to be so mysterious. Takes time to figure the answers."

"Prophecy?" asked Sela's father.

"Heal the rift, heal the land," Layce and Avara droned again. "Heal the land, heal the rift."

Orman pointed at the women. "That's all we've got. And we're not even sure which does which."

"May I see that scroll?" asked Sela's mother.

Orman offered out the parchment, and Sela's mother wrapped delicate claws around it. She unfolded it, and began to read.

Avara and Layce blinked and looked around as though they were awaking from a dream. Avara went pale and droopy. Ebouard lunged and caught her just as she swooned.

Layce turned to Orman. Her eyes fluttered, and her

knees went soft.

Orman scowled at her.

Layce frowned and stood straight. She crossed her arms.

"So where does that leave us?" asked Sela's father.

"I know this much, Kallon," said Orman. "If Blackclaw wins this war, his gluttony will consume the last of what holds this world together."

Sela's father sighed, then. He was quiet for a long time, his head bowed toward his paws. "And I must tell you something I have dreaded saying since this whole thing began." He raised his head, and his brown eyes were as dark with sorrow, and as weak with age as Sela had ever seen them.

"We cannot hope to defeat Blackclaw," he said. "Not as we stand now. Our numbers are too few."

"We can recruit from across the sea," said Sela.

"We can try," said her father. "But Blackclaw has already been there, scraping together his own loyalists. He's gone ahead of us everywhere, doing the work of collecting dragons to his cause. The work we should have been doing, as well."

"They'll come," said Orman. "They'll come when they understand we're all in danger now."

"Will they understand better, if they see Esra and Leland already joined together?" asked Ebouard. "By venurship, between myself and Venur Shornmar, if he'll have me. And by leadership, between myself and the Dragon Council, if you will have me."

Sela's father studied the venur. Then he rose to

his feet. "Are you offering alliance to Leland dragons, Venur Riddess? As an entity separate from human governance?"

"That is what I have witnessed here, in these few days. Dragons who move and decide and administer unto themselves with highest of moral reasoning. It would be an honor to ally with you and serve in whatever capacity I have left to offer."

"Unprecedented," whispered Orman.

Sela's father smiled. He extended his paw. "Then as Herald of the Reds and Leader of the Dragon Council of Leland, I accept."

The venur placed his dark hand into the crimson paw of Sela's father, dwarfing it, before enclosing it completely in a grip of union.

Sela felt goosebumps prickle beneath her scales.

"Will this help?" she asked Orman, quietly. "With everything we have to do, in whatever time we have left to do it in, will this alliance make a difference?"

Orman watched the venur and the leader, and smiled. He crossed his arms, nodded his head slowly, and then looked up and around at the ceiling, or at something invisible in the air around them. "I believe, my dear," he said, "It already has."

"Who's this 'champion'?" asked Sela's mother, looking up suddenly from the scroll. "The one with the key to the boundary?"

"Eh, what?" said Orman.

"It says right here," said Sela's mother. "A champion of fire and a champion of flesh. With a key to the boundary, together they shall open the heavens to rain down righteousness."

"Does it mean a dragon and a human?" asked Sela. When all eyes in the room swept toward her, she startled. "I mean. That's how it sounds to me."

Then all eyes moved back to Sela's father, and Venur Riddess.

"I'm afraid I don't know anything about a key or a boundary," said the venur.

"Maybe it's a dragon who *is* a human," offered Gladdis, who was suddenly standing at the end of the long feasting table, holding a platter of simmering meat.

"Maybe," said Sela. "But it isn't what it sounds like."

"Just as I said," said Orman. He took the parchment from Sela's mother, and waved it in the air. "Clear as mud."

"What it sounds like is folk tale," said Sela's father. "I don't think it's possible the boundary would have a key."

Orman puffed up, and stuck a finger in his face. "Just like it's not possible for a dragon to cross into the boundary and survive? Eh?"

"I just don't think—"

"Bah!" said Orman. "What it sounds like to me is dinner time." He stuck the scroll into the beltline of his trousers, and then clapped his hands together, hungrily eyeing Gladdis's platter. "We can't very well be deciphering mysteries, and saving the world on empty stomachs, can we?"

Sela felt her stomach grumble. That mound of rabbit meat did look delicious.

Gladdis set the platter on the table, and backed away, going ashen. Apparently Sela wasn't the only dragon who looked her fair share of hungry.

§

They reached the edge of Murk Forest, just as the sky belched rainwater.

Murk Forest. The land Jastin had never trespassed, had never dared to enter. The land no one went to, and if myth were truth, no one came back from. Murk was the place of mystery and magic even dragons avoided. Feared.

But Jastin heard, and felt, the air behind them being buffeted by dragon wings. He smelled the acrid burn of their breath. Blade was long exhausted. Jastin had spent his last crossbow bolt.

Leesa hurried Blade without hesitation, past scratching trunks, like razor teeth. Into the damp and sunless depths, like a hungry mouth. Jastin felt himself tighten against the sense of being eaten.

Behind them, dragons roared.

Several feet in, even the rain didn't penetrate the canopy. Blade slowed to a walk. Jastin slid from his seat. He crept back across Murk's dank forest floor as close to the edge as he dared, and peered up and out. The dragons circled each other, dipped above or below each other, layering and churning, just where he, Leesa, and Blade had entered. He half expected one of them to blast a flame at him from sheer frustration, but then the

White dropped low enough to meet Jastin's gaze.

Whitetail. Jastin should have guessed.

The dragon glared through the rain into the trees. "The forest will spit you out, Armitage. We will wait. Whatever is left of you, once the forest has had its fill, we will scoop up and finish off."

"Why wait? Come in now and get me."

Whitetail slowly exhaled hot breath into Jastin's face.

He felt a tug on his arm. Leesa pulled at him. He let her drag him into walking away, but he felt Whitetail's eyes on his back, boring into his skin.

And then he felt new sets of eyes. Several, all around, and the sensation bristled his skin.

A cocoa-mottled feline the size of a pony crept from around a gray tree trunk, and examined him. Then another. And another. Blade faltered back, panting. Jastin's hand shot toward the saddle, and the empty crossbow.

Leesa calmly laid her hand on his arm. Then she knelt, hand outstretched. The largest of the three cats sauntered forward, sniffed her knuckles, and then lowered to its haunches.

Leesa hugged it tightly.

Then she stood again, and in one hand, took Jastin's fingers. In the other, she took Blade's reins. The three cats bounded forward, deeper into the trees.

"Where are we going?" he asked.

Leesa nodded toward the disappearing cats.

"Why do I get the feeling you've brought me to

meet your friends?"

Leesa smiled.

Jastin hadn't quite meant it funny. He stood in a forest he'd never seen, surrounded by a kind of magic— he shuddered at the thought of the word—he didn't like, being led by a woman he didn't really know. What was going on?

Blade seemed eager enough. And Jastin was tired, thirsty, and had been running from the dragons for days. For now, he followed Leesa. Once he rested, and rummaged some food, he'd think again.

But for now, he walked.

CHAPTER SIX

Gladdis sat on a stone outcrop on Mount Gore, just outside the dragon manor. She stared out through an open expanse between pine trees, with her knees pulled to her chest. She rested her chin on her kneecaps, and, although she was tired from sleepless nights and too much confusion, she didn't want to close her eyes. The sight of the sloping mountain against a field of peaks, draped with sunrise and sinewy mist, and was too beautiful to miss, and she didn't know how many more chances she'd get to see it.

Never in a hundred, million years would she have guessed she'd end up where she was, smack in the middle of an adventure like this. On a magical mountain. Surrounded by dragons. Who spoke. And were at least tolerant of her, if not welcoming.

Not that she understood what they said, most of the time. Whenever they collected, they spoke a rumbling, almost musical kind of language. Or, sometimes, they seemed to know each other's words without saying anything at all. She tried not to pester them to explain; she didn't want them to lose what patience they had with her. She was already wondering why they hadn't delivered her home yet, and didn't want to rush them into it.

She had managed to understand the seriousness of this war the black dragon stirred up, and she knew he'd tried it before, back before Sela was born, before she turned human. And then, back to a dragon.

Gladdis had also figured out that Sela's mother had been human at some point, but never changed back. Maybe she couldn't. Maybe Sela was the only one who could choose it.

She would have liked to ask Sela more questions, but her friend had been awfully busy with meetings, and council discussions, and all sorts of official and family business. Layce and Orman, the wizards, were spending a lot of time reading scrolls and arguing in whispers about them. Meetings were being planned between the visiting venur and the dragon council, and she thought she'd overheard he would also be going to Shornmar Castle in Leland, where Gladdis and Sela had first met for the bridal census.

Was that really just a few months ago? At the beginning of spring, when the roads from Cresvell to Shornmar Castle had been thick with mud and runoff from Reacher's Pass. She and Emlee had just arrived at the castle, when Sela Redheart arrived at the same time. Almost too late.

They almost didn't meet.

But they did. And here Gladdis was, staring down from mountains she'd tried to see so many times from her bedroom window.

At least she was used to solitude. In Cresvell, her sister, Emlee, had always drawn the attention, and Gladdis had become pretty good at watching and learning from conversations she didn't quite understand. A skill she was putting to good use here.

And her sister was safe, so it was something she didn't need to worry about just now. That's what she kept telling herself. After Sela was chosen as the bride-elect in Esra, the other maidens had been sent home, and, as far as Gladdis knew, Emlee had been one of the first to leave. Emlee was long gone before all those dragons dropped from the sky and started hurting everyone.

She wasn't so sure about the other girls.

And Cresvell was so far away from everyone else most folks kept forgetting it was even part of Leland. Surely the black dragon wouldn't attack a drowsy little village full of farmers and fisherman. Surely. Or, at least the others would stop him before he had a chance.

She hung on to that hope.

She was just getting dozy, despite her resolve to keep her eyes open, when a rustling sound startled her wide awake. She craned to listen. Somewhere to her left, in fallen elm branches, something moved.

She pushed to her feet and crept toward it. Another burst of scrambling noise. Too loud for a snake, and the sound didn't run off, like a rodent. She paused, let the creature settle. And then she inched forward again.

A bird. A pigeon, actually, that strained and fluttered in a panic. It wore something around its neck.

"Sssh," Gladdis soothed. "I won't hurt you."

The bird calmed. She cupped her hands around its soft body, but it only blinked its pebble eyes and waited for her to save it. She saw then that the pigeon wore a pink crystal shard affixed to a slender, copper chain, and the chain was what tethered the bird to the branch. She untangled it gently.

But when the bird was freed, rather than fly off, it sat itself onto Gladdis's palm. Gladdis smiled. "I guess you can come with me, if you like."

She pulled the bird closer to her face to give it a good inspection. No missing feathers, no blood. The pigeon seemed unharmed, if a bit thin; hard to tell how long it had been trapped in the underbrush. And it was no wild thing, it was too groomed and accustomed to handling. It wouldn't fare well on its own out there. "Well, Feather Face, let's find you some food."

The crystal shard suddenly sparked, and glowed red, stinging her eyes. She winced, and covered the brightness with her hand. The bird just watched her. Then, slowly, the crystal faded back into a pale pink, and she lowered her hand.

"Did you do that?" she asked the bird.

The crystal flared again. What was happening?

She didn't know the first thing about magic or crystals, and anyone she might ask was already overwhelmed with concerns. And the pigeon didn't seem keen to help.

Maybe Drell? No, he was off flying with his mother, that brown dragon. Or Layce, except she was always with Orman Thistleby, and that grumpy old wizard frightened her. Sela was definitely too distracted.

Gladdis returned to her seat on the rock outcrop, and set the pigeon on her kneecaps. Then she squinted at the intense, red glow from the crystal, and reached a finger to poke at it.

But she felt a whoosh of wind against her back, and felt a cool shadow engulf her from behind. She twisted to find Drell, and then his mother, dropping into a soft landing.

She instinctively covered her hands over the bird. She didn't manage to douse the light, though. It shone red through her fingers, and onto her knees and the ground.

"What do you have there?" asked Drell.

The crystal blinked off.

"Oh, um…" she said. "I found a bird."

"Injured?" asked Drell.

"No, it seems fine."

After a minute, she wondered what she was doing, hiding it, and so she slowly lowered her hands. The brown one walked toward the manor, but Drell was watching her, his wide, glossy head cocked.

"It's wearing something," she said, offering the pigeon toward him. The crystal brightened again. "A necklace. It keeps turning red."

"May I see it?" Drell asked. Once again, the crystal went dull and pink.

"Is that a messenger crystal?" asked the brown dragon.

Gladdis struggled to remember the dragon's name. She stood up, wobbling the bird in her hands, and the feathered creature startled, resituated itself, and peered disapprovingly up at her.

"What is a messenger crystal?" asked Drell.

Vaya! Gladdis finally remembered.

Vaya sidled closer, her golden eyes on the bird. Drell followed closely behind.

"Speak again," said Vaya to Gladdis.

"What should I say?"

The crystal flared red.

"Say your name," said Vaya, as the crystal went dull. "And then, say 'open.'"

Gladdis looked between them, at their eyes, which both reflected the rays of the morning sun in gold flecks. Then she held up the bird, and regarded it. "Gladdis," she said. The crystal threw such red light at them all that Gladdis had to squint. "Open."

And, just like that, the bright crystal split open at the place where it joined the chain, and dangled. It wasn't just a piece of stone, it was a locket! And something was wedged inside.

"That message is for you," said Vaya. "The crystal reacted to your voice."

"For me?" asked Gladdis. "But no one knows I'm here." She dug out a wisp of parchment from the necklace, and unrolled it. She couldn't quite make out the markings at first glance.

"What's wrong?" asked Drell.

"It's dragonscript."

Drell arched his scaly brows. "Do you need me to help you read it?"

Gladdis shook her head. "No, I'd like to try on my own."

"You read dragonscript?" asked Vaya.

"She does," said Drell. "I've been teaching her."

Vaya lifted her chin in surprise. She nodded. "Well done, Drell."

He smiled. The tips of his long, white teeth poked out between his lips, and his nostrils pulled upward. But it was a nice smile, anyway.

"If you reply to the message, just say 'close' to the crystal, and it will lock itself again," said Vaya. "The bird should know what to do, after that." She began a sinewy walk toward the manor, but paused, and turned her head over her shoulder. Her long, dark eyelashes lowered, regarding Gladdis. "I'm curious now, who would be sending messages to this mountain?"

Gladdis looked at the paper again, and studied it. "I don't think there's a name."

Vaya's snout leaked a curl of gray smoke that filtered up and across her face, and split into strands on the edges of those long lashes. "These are extraordinary days, human," she said. "Be on your guard."

"Gladdis," she said. "That's my name. And I will."

Vaya curved her neck to look into Drell's face. "Watch her, won't you?"

Drell looked away from his mother, but he nodded.

When Vaya finally pushed off and around the path, and became obscured by limbs and boughs, Gladdis released a breath. "She doesn't like me very much."

"It's not personal," said Drell. "She has a suspicious nature. For the most part, it's served her well."

"It's all right. I understand."

Drell nodded, and his smile returned, faintly.

"I do, though," said Gladdis, thinking he might be laughing at her. "I'm a stranger here."

"It's just, usually I'm the one saying 'I understand.'" He cocked his head again, with a serpent-like curiosity. "Let me know if you need help with your note."

Gladdis nodded. She waited until he, too, disappeared around the path, before she sat down, set the bird on her kneecap again, and uncurled the paper.

CHAPTER SEVEN

Blackclaw shot into the air, and roared down at Whitetail, while the sniveling dragon perched on the Esra Castle wall like a cornered mouse. "You lost them where?"

"Murk," said Whitetail, his snout lowering. "In Murk Forest."

"How did they get that far?" Blackclaw circled Whitetail, fanning his wings to stalk his cohort. He loved the show of the rebuke as much as the rebuke itself, with his tiny human prisoners staring up from the castle grounds in terror. People huddled against the castle rubble, hugging each other, probably defecating themselves every time he raised a yell against his dragon kin.

Most of the castle itself had burned through the night and day of the dragon takeover. Even now, smoke tendrils still curled now and again upward as humans cleared away charred wood and stone, making paths through the grounds and opening whatever rooms were left for their use. The entire upper floors had toppled on the east side, but one exposed stairway left a lower and upper floor accessible.

Blackclaw liked the upper floor for himself. Reminiscent of his leadership days at Mount Gore and its manor. And he'd long wearied of skulking around in the old dragon tunnels beneath the Esra grounds, hidden away as he was for years. Recruiting his dragon followers in secret, flying only at night or under cover of stormy weather.

No, enough lurking for him. He was a creature of the sun and the sky, and at the dawn of this new age, this new dragon age, he would conduct his affairs boldly, loudly, and for all to see.

Especially the affairs that turned his captured humans into frightened little bags of mulberry jelly.

Blackclaw landed beside Whitetail on the castle wall, and took a deep breath to really give his shout resonance. "Tell me how you managed to let them get that far, Whitetail!"

The stones beneath Whitetail rattled, and some gave way. Whitetail leapt upward, wings suddenly beating, as pebbles and dust scattered to the ground.

"Jastin Armitage is skilled in dragon battle," said Whitetail, watching the people below run from the wall rubble. "He anticipated and out-maneuvered us."

"That human has been a nit under my scale for years."

"Agreed," said Whitetail, settling back onto the wall.

"Well, now he is the nit under your scale." Blackclaw

leapt from the wall to the ground, outside the gate, just as a slender Green appeared over the distant treetops. "Go back and get him. And don't come back here again without him."

"Your Eminence?"

Blackclaw paused, and turned to find the White's eyes churning with fear. He might have laughed, except he knew people were just on the other side of the wall, listening in. "Don't worry, Whitetail. Murk Forest isn't the dangerous place myth would have us believe."

The Green landed smoothly beside him, and he drew in a deep sniff of appreciation. She smelled of ash and anger, and regarded him with jaundice eyes hardened by determination. She'd proven herself a strategic ally of highest regard; so unlike the simpering Whitetail, who failed at his own thinking and would be nothing in this war if Blackclaw hadn't carried him along all these years.

The Green had yet to submit to Blackclaw's mating overtones, but she was softening. Time would make her his own, and in the meanwhile, he would scour her brain for tactical wealth. In that way, she would serve him twice over.

"You remember Jia Greenscale," Blackclaw said to Whitetail. A Leland dragon. One of the few he'd managed to impress to his point of view. And the daughter of Min Greenscale, a Leland council member, to boot. Ah, but the coup did taste as fine as tenderly aged venison.

Whitetail paled moreso, if such a thing were

possible. His nostrils flared. "Jia," he greeted.

The Green nodded once in return. "It is good to see you again, Fane."

"Be off, Whitetail," said Blackclaw. "I want that human by tomorrow."

"If I may, your Eminence," said Whitetail, opening his forelegs and bowing low over the wall edge. "I respectfully ask that if you find the human Armitage so important, and the forest so inconsequential, why do you not retrieve him yourself?"

Blackclaw whirled on him. "What did..." He caught himself, quickly, with a glance toward Jia. Blustering was for humans, or other dragons he wished to intimidate. He'd already learned it didn't play well for Jia. He cleared his throat. Controlled his response.

He would throttle the White's neck later.

"Not that I owe you explanation," said Blackclaw, "But Jia and I have important strategies to discuss concerning Shornmar Castle, and the taking of Leland."

"You do not feel I should be a part of this discussion?" Whitetail asked.

Jia stepped toward Whitetail. "I would welcome your counsel. You have been in the service of Fordon Blackclaw longer than anyone."

"Yes," said Whitetail, his pale eyes on Blackclaw. "It is a good thing to remember."

"Whitetail has other duties to attend. He is not one to question my authority," said Blackclaw, returning Whitetail's gaze, hard. "And *that* is a good thing to remember."

"Retrieving the human Armitage," said Jia. "From what forest?"

Whitetail lifted his chin. "His Eminence has ordered me into Murk."

Jia gasped, and looked between him and Whitetail. "Murk Forest? To the east?"

"Is there another?" snapped Blackclaw. "What is all this fuss about a simple task? Armitage is only a human. A forest is only trees." Blackclaw spun on his feet, and then launched upward. "A fledgling could do this, and with much less discussion."

He swooped low across the castle wall, nudging bits of stone to send them rattling toward a group of humans collected near a thatched shed. "Maybe that is who I should send," he shot over his shoulder.

§

Maybe you should, Whitetail shot back, confident the egomaniacal leader wouldn't sense it. Couldn't sense it. Fane Whitetail had been thinking loudly around Blackclaw for years without detection. Blackclaw had been doing the same around Whitetail, but the leader was so deeply entrenched in himself it made him obtuse to the fact Whitetail could sense it. And now, Whitetail seethed. Again.

Simpering. Failed at his thoughts. Only a part of this war because Blackclaw had carried him along. Whitetail felt Blackclaw's thoughts bounce around inside his mind while the Black puffed off toward the ruined castle. And he burned.

"He undervalues you," said Jia's voice.

Whitetail startled. He'd been so focused on Blackclaw's retreating form he'd forgotten about the Green. He looked down at her from where he sat on the stone wall. Then he dropped to the ground beside her, and drew in his wings against his ribs.

He studied her. Sinewy neck. Wide, yellow eyes. Head cocked, just so. She would be a challenge, this new adversary; but Blackclaw had considered replacing Whitetail before, and always Whitetail had managed to win back the day. This time would be no different.

"I have no intention of replacing you," said Jia.

Again Whitetail startled. "Too many years in conversation with Fordon Blackclaw," he said. "I have dropped my guard against my thoughts."

"You have no need to guard them on my account," she said. "I do not believe service to anyone should be mindless obedience."

"That is what attracts him to you," said Whitetail. "Once he has had you, he will be bored, and return again to my counsel."

Jia smiled faintly. "You quite took me at my word when I said not to guard your thoughts."

Fane opened his mouth to explain, but she raised a paw. "I take no offense. I agree with you." She lowered her paw to the ground, and resettled herself onto her haunches. "I have no intention of being 'had', though. So you will have to bear with me until he tires of me in some other way."

"Or you could simply stop impressing him. Fail to show to your meeting, perhaps."

Her smile widened. "For the sake of your bruised ego?"

Fane regarded her smile. It raised too easily, lit her face too brightly. He eased back a step, suspicious.

"That would be very generous of me, considering all I have done to reach this place in his service." Jia rose up to her feet, and tipped her head, looking more fledgling than soldier in that moment. "To reach this place in your service."

"Mine?"

"Fordon Blackclaw may believe his leadership has come by his own design, Fane, but wise dragons recognize the white shadow beneath his wings." She lowered her gaze toward the ground, and he thought he saw the color in her scaled face darken, just across her cheeks. "At least, I do."

He was so accustomed to being unnoticed, unappreciated, that his first reaction was to disbelieve her. At the same time, he wanted very much to drink in her words, and the sincerity of her feelings. Craved it, even. But he resisted. "Perhaps you have sights on turning his shadow green."

"I tell you, Fane, that is not why I am here."

"Then why are you here?" he asked.

She raised her head, and smiled again. Reminded him of his suspicion. "I would like to answer that. I should meet with Blackclaw, though." She looked up at the twilight sky. "Will you be leaving for Murk very soon? Or wait until morning?"

"I have dragons posted, watching the forest edge for Armitage. I am in no rush."

"May we talk again, in that case? Later?"

Fane considered carefully. Already he'd had more conversation with her than with any dragon besides Blackclaw. He kept to himself that way on purpose. He kept his focus, his objectives always before him, and had mastered his impulses to reach out to others, ignoring those more banal needs of companionship or friendship other weaker dragons desired. He couldn't see a reason to change tactics now.

"I see," she said. Her smile vanished, replaced by a chill behind her eyes. "You are right, of course. You have not gotten where you have by trusting others. I have much to learn about that."

"I imagine you do." And a long way to go to reach Fane's level of disengagement. His persistent isolation didn't come naturally to most. "Still," he continued. "I did ask a question, and I would like the answer."

She nodded. "Of course."

"Boulder Bend. At first starlight."

"I will be there," she said. Then she pushed off, and swept her emerald wings into the morning light. She soared off toward Blackclaw's quarters in Esra Castle. She didn't look back.

CHAPTER EIGHT

Jastin and Leesa paused while Blade chewed on a succulent fern in Murk Forest. His horse seemed refreshed by the plant's nourishment, but Jastin needed more than a juicy fern to quench his thirst. He needed a river.

And he needed more than a handful of berries and a quick nap beneath a bush to feel refreshed. Leesa had kept needling him forward, hardly resting, herself. Throughout the night, she urged him, and Blade, to keep walking.

At least, Jastin thought they walked through the night. He tried to sense time by the darkness, but he couldn't tell if the sun had set, or if he was losing light just because they were moving deeper into the trees. Having no break in the canopy above left him disoriented, having no streaks of sunlight across the ground left him confused. Even the repetition of gray tree trunks and green foliage made every part of the forest look like every other part. For all he knew, they were going in circles.

The dark and mottled cats had long disappeared ahead of them. But Leesa seemed confident she was moving in the right direction, and her keen eyes seemed to see more than Jastin's. Although, now, as he watched her, he noticed for the first time she was wary, and watching the ground.

He paused. He searched the ground, too. "What is it you're looking for?"

Then he was yanked off his feet. He hit hard ground with his face, and felt it bounce. He dragged. Someone pulled at his ankle, he felt his boot pull off his left foot. He spun to swing a fist, and to clutch at the knife loosed from his boot. He found neither a face, nor the weapon.

Leesa was there, hacking at a vine enwrapping his foot. Just as he broke free, he felt more squeezing around his thigh. He clutched at greenery, tried to break it. Then a jut of vine shot out around his wrist.

"What the—"

He was yanked into the air. He kicked, fought against the bindings around his wrists, his waist, his legs. He felt the vines constricting, tightening around his chest. He struggled to breathe.

Leesa leapt at his legs, and clung. She reached up, cut at the trails around his wrists. Just as one vine broke apart, another came to replace it, and tighter.

A cat-like snarl erupted beneath him. He saw only a flash of fur, and then a large brown cat leapt from the nearest branches, mouth wide and spitting. Jastin would have flinched, and ducked, but he was helplessly immobile. All he could do was close his eyes, and wait for the bite of the feline teeth.

Then he hit dirt again. His breath knocked out. He panted, dizzy. And he was dragged. He twisted, trying to see who or what had hold of him, but he bounded across the forest floor, face down, or face up, bobbing like a stick on rough water. He felt his arms scratch and bleed. His leg seared with pain.

"Let me go," he yelled, when he'd finally managed to take a deep enough breath.

And then, just as he was pulled onto smooth ground, whoever had been dragging him did let go. He flopped, vines falling apart.

The forest cat skulked away, greenery in his teeth. He eyed Jastin as a meal, or at least, a nuisance.

Leesa knelt beside him, helped him clear away debris from his chest, and dirt and blood from his arms. He rolled, and pushed to stand. He grunted in pain; his left leg tried to give out. Leesa braced him.

"What in the hell just happened?"

His question froze on his lips, just as he spotted the three jaguar cats encircling them.

The largest studied him. Growled quietly.

And then it lowered its head, hunched its legs together, and swelled upward into a fur-covered man bent at the waist. The man reached for a loin cloth hooked onto a gray tree trunk, and wrapped and tied it into place. Then he lifted his chin, glared at Jastin, and slowly, deliberately, his brown fur receded to reveal a solidly-built man with olive skin, like Leesa's. His face was smooth, his eyes dark. His hair was the mottled brown of his jaguar fur.

Jastin stared. All he could do was repeat himself. "What just happened?"

"The forest knows trespassers," said the man. He turned his glare to Leesa. "She shouldn't have brought you here."

From behind him, two more men emerged, tying off loin cloths. One had sun-darkened skin; the other wore his hair in a long, brown braid. The jaguar cats were gone.

"I'm Faren," said the first man. "These are my brothers."

"Reev," said the man with the braid.

"Ivek," said the last.

Leesa shifted her weight against Jastin. He looked down at her, from her skin, to the man's, from his hair, to her smooth, black strands. "You're one of them," he said suddenly, and gave her a push, breaking contact. "Why did you bring me here?"

"We've asked her the same question, but she refuses to answer us," said Faren.

"She can't speak," Jastin said.

"Her throat doesn't work, but there's nothing wrong with her mind." Faren stepped closer, studying Jastin. Then he turned a quirked brow to his brothers. "At first, we suspected you were threatening, but you're definitely not."

Reev and Ivek chuckled.

Jastin rankled. But he didn't think it was very smart,

just now, to inform the group he could be as threatening as he wanted to be.

"You'll be safe in this clearing," said Faren. "Look around. You see where this large area is free from growth?"

From where Jastin stood, outward for several yards, was only flattened, leafy ground cover stabbed here and there with the same, monotonous gray trunks as the rest of the forest, except stripped completely of any green.

"For now, stay in the safety of this area. We will figure out what next to do with you once we've spoken to our Shepherdess." Faren began to move off.

Jastin limped one step. "I thought you said to stay put."

"I said to stay in this area. But to meet our Shepherdess, you must go up." Faren pointed.

Jastin followed his gesture. Swinging above them, built into the very branches of the gray forest trees, were woven nests of stick and thatch, lit from within by soft glows, and connected by a network of rope-and-wood bridges that went on and on, upward and outward for hundreds of feet. Some nests dangled like pendants with openings at the top, others mounded onto huge branches with mud around the entries.

"You live up there?" Jastin asked, wondering if he'd blustered into the home of felines or birds.

"Not all of us are ground walkers, but yes, we all live up there."

Blade sauntered in from the trees, casually chewing on a straggle of vine.

"Ah, Blade," said Faren.

Jastin had never told him the horse's name. He looked at Leesa, mute as ever.

Faren sidled over and spoke quietly toward Jastin's ear. "Blade is one reason we decided to help you back there. He speaks highly of you."

Blade nudged Jastin's hand, and Jastin scratched him between the ears. "Thanks, buddy," he said.

And then realized what he'd just done.

Braided ropes dropped from overhead, ends coiling on the forest floor. Faren and his brothers wrapped one ankle, and one wrist around the material. "I don't see you climbing with that leg, so we'll hoist. Grab on," said Faren. Then he tugged his rope, and drew up fast into the trees.

Reev and Ivek were next. Jastin looked up, searching for whoever manipulated the rope, but he couldn't make out any shapes from this distance.

He felt Leesa put the rope to his ankle, and he flinched at her touch. He hopped back, regarding her. "I don't like not knowing what to expect. I'm not the kind of person for surprises."

Leesa watched his face.

"This is all too much right now," he said, trying to explain something his own brain couldn't process. He wanted what he knew; weapons, hard work, even fighting. Fighting creatures he recognized, in a world where the ground was down and the sky was up. Where the sun rose and set at the same horizon. Where he knew the rules.

Leesa was still for a time, then she jutted her hand toward the trees, offering him an exit through the jungle of greenery. Then she offered him the rope, instead, and indicated her hand upward.

Some choice. Jastin hadn't done well in his fight with the forest, but then, he hadn't seen it coming, either. But now he couldn't even put full weight on his wounded leg, so what kind of combat was he good for, let alone walking?

He took the rope.

"For now," he said. It was starting to become a familiar phrase.

CHAPTER NINE

Fane Whitetail waited at the huge boulder in the bend of the path that led from Riddess Castle, through the maple grove, and down toward the only patch of grassland that hadn't been overtaken by villagers and farmers. No one knew how old the boulder was, or how large it might originally have been, because time had sculpted it into an elongated wave, like a seashore splash frozen in time.

He dragged his claws along carved rivulets in the stone, wondering at what kind of wind had the strength to leave its mark on the hard surface. Then he turned to meet Jia Greenscale as she descended gracefully beside him.

Her eyes were on the boulder, too, where starshine brightened the sharp surfaces, and darkened the shadows between them. "Maybe it is not the strength of the wind that changes the stone, but the persistence," Jia said.

"I wondered if you might change your mind about

meeting me," said Fane.

"Why would I do that?"

"After talking with Blackclaw," said Fane. "He is a filling presence. He often leaves no appetite for more conversation."

"Not terms I would personally use to describe the dragon," said Jia.

"Not many would, I suppose. I do not fool myself out of realizing those who serve him do so out of fear, or a hope to borrow his strength. Few join him out of loyalty."

"Such as you?"

Fane circled behind the boulder to peer at her across its pocked surface. "You dislike him, yet you have joined him."

"I dislike him intensely; I will not lie about that."

"I ask again, then. Why are you here?"

Jia eased around the edge of the boulder to join him, but rather than inspect the rock, she turned her yellow gaze to the starlit sky. "When you lived on Mount Gore, in the days of Blackclaw's leadership, I was barely a fledgling. I am sure you do not remember me." She lowered her gaze to his face. "But you must remember my father, Min Greenscale."

"I do," he said.

"A dragon as entrenched in the old ways as any. Blinded to changes all around him, deaf to the messages the land has been trying to send us."

"Messages?"

Now Jia touched the boulder, and dragged her

delicate digits down the ripples. "If rock cannot resist time, how will dragons survive it? Not by serving humans. Not by giving away our very strength. Our complacency has brought us to this place, Fane. Our land will bury us as long as we do nothing."

"So you do have something in common with Blackclaw, after all."

"I believe we must evolve, or die. I do not share Fordon Blackclaw's ideals entirely. But we have the same goals."

"Admirable," said Fane. He'd never really developed any firm ideals of his own, save those involving self-preservation. It was so much easier to let others take the responsibility of leading, breaking wind resistance, so he could follow along with less effort. "Not that I couldn't lead, if I so chose. I have a mind for manipulating circumstances."

"And the constitution for it."

He sat back at that. Curled his tail around his legs, and relaxed his wings. "What do you mean?"

"It is one thing to have the foresight for manipulation, but it is another strength altogether to see it through," said Jia. "Do you not see it as commendable, that you can use your talents without the heavy burden of a guilt-ridden conscience?"

Fane felt himself smile. He tried to read sarcasm in her voice, in her mannerisms, but she openly met his gaze. Honestly. Until she noticed his smile, and her eyes lowered to his mouth. She smiled, then, too.

"I suppose that does come across as humorous," she

said.

"Not at all," said Fane. "I do find it commendable. It is rare to discover someone else who agrees with me."

"Blackclaw agrees. Certainly. He is not creative enough to think the way you do, but he is intelligent enough to appreciate the results."

"Is he?" Fordon could give orders. He could rant and roar, and could frighten. But he couldn't finesse, that much was true. He'd always relied on Fane for that. But had Blackclaw ever, truly appreciated how much of his success rested solely on Fane's follow-through?

"You think he is not?" she asked.

Fane mulled it silently.

"Then at least," Jia continued, "He must value your other traits. Your loyalty, for instance. Your obedience."

"Yes, he despises when I think for myself," Fane said. "But at the same time, he thinks me incapable of it, and he resents that about me."

Jia tipped her head. "You really believe he thinks you incapable of your own ideas?"

"A failure at my own thoughts. I have sensed it often in his mind."

"Then, Fane, why…" She clenched her mouth shut. Looked at her feet.

"I know what you wish to ask," he said.

"It is not for me to question.

"No," said Fane.

"It is even more difficult to respect Blackclaw's leadership, discovering he is far more dim-witted than I suspected." Jia eased back, and created enough space between them for her to stretch her wings, and billow them in a light breeze. "I will fly, and think."

"You are angry," said Fane.

"I am conflicted," she said. "I gave up much to serve a fool."

Fane pushed off to walk closer, and eyed her jeweled paw against the dry grass. The moon reflected faintly against her green scales. His own milky paw, in contrast, luminesced like a white torch. He shouldn't have been considering touching her, with his shamefully colorless digits. But he was.

"It seems as though you are offended on my behalf," he said, unable to lift his head to see if she was watching him.

"He does not deserve to lead," Jia said.

"I should defend him," said Fane. "I should make you understand him from my perspective."

It was Jia who touched him. She laid her emerald paw onto his claws, and lowered her head to find his eyes as she spoke. "Then allow me to ask, although you owe me no explanation."

He regarded her eyes. Then he looked at their paws. He traced one white, arching claw over her knuckle.

She didn't withdraw.

"First tell me something," Fane said. "Answer honestly. I will know if you lie."

"I will be honest," she said quietly.

"How do you know so much about me? And why did you really meet me here tonight?"

She was silent for a long time. She searched his

eyes, silent.

He stiffened, uncomfortable by the long gaze, and unaccustomed to the intimacy of a shared, unspoken moment.

"You do not remember me from your days in Leland. But I remember you, Fane Whitetail." She turned her paw so their palms touched. The pads of their digits connected. As her mouth spoke the words, her emotions surged through the contact, rocking him back. "I knew, even then, that one day you would see me, would know me. And I would be given the chance to touch you in a way you would never forget."

Her words were true, her emotions too powerful to be deceptive. They blindsided him, filled him too much. He was a receptacle too vacant and desiccated to know how to process feelings, real feelings. He pulled back his paw. Retreated a step, so he could breathe again.

"Why me?" he asked through his confusion.

"I can only tell you my heart made the choice for me."

"Your heart," he said, feeling the comfortable numbness return to his insides. "I know little of that sort of thing."

"I believe you."

"But I enjoy this," Fane said. "This talking together."

She smiled. "I am happy to speak with you whenever you wish." Then her smile faded, and her brow wrinkled. "Oh, but, you will be leaving in the morning. For Murk Forest."

"Will I?" He looked down at his paw, where

she'd touched him. "You may ask me now. What you have been wishing to ask me since we first spoke this morning."

She lifted her head. "Why do you serve him, Fane?"

He owed her an honest answer, like the one she'd given him. He battled himself over it, though. He tried to resist the spell she'd begun to work on him. As a master manipulator, he recognized her overtures. Her maneuvers. Trouble was, he couldn't ascertain her motives. Until he could figure out exactly what she was up to, he would have to play along.

Play along. He could tell himself for hours he was only in this for the game, but he knew better. The female was getting to him. In here, somewhere, deep. He wasn't sure how far he could go before the game became real, but he wasn't ready to quit, yet. All he needed was a reason, a strong, compelling reason to keep playing the music, so he could continue their dance.

So he told her the truth. "I serve Fordon Blackclaw because no one else would have me." The unfortunate side effect of that statement was feeling suddenly like a foundling. Afraid. Vulnerable.

She regarded him with a soft face, and it helped chase the fear into the back of his mind, where he could control it. He appreciated that.

"I would have you, Fane."

He blinked. His lungs went cold, both because he wasn't expecting her to say that, and because he was glad she did.

"As a leader," she quickly added. She laughed, and

her emerald cheekbones saturated with color. She shook her head. "That is what I mean to say. As a leader."

Which was flattering, to say the least. And yet… "There could be no other way?"

Jia's smile deepened. She drew in a breath. Then she thrust out her wings, and lofted, just a few feet, and hovered. The tip of her tail rested on the buffeted edge of the bend's boulder. "Take care in the forest, Fane. What we understand of magic can't be contained there."

She swept upward. He lost sight of her, her green scales enveloped by the night sky. He listened, though, to the rush of her beating wings, and to the sharp percussion of his heart against his ribs.

She hadn't spoken it, but she'd given her answer. In a glimpse. A shared understanding of her smile.

She'd given him something else, too. His reason to keep dancing. The prize? Something Blackclaw wanted, but that he, Fane Whitetail, could claim, instead.

And, oh, at the thought of that, his numbed insides gave way to a warm and surprising, but enthralling, sense of purpose.

CHAPTER TEN

Sela flew Orman toward a spot of morning sun, low in the sky. Behind her followed Drell, with Layce Phelcher. She glanced back, then shifted her balance, extending her wings for a smooth landing.

Sela touched down on Mount Krag, the sheared-off peak that had been Orman Thistleby's home in the years before her father became Herald of the Reds. She'd never before seen it, not even in the few visits she'd had to the mountains, but she remembered seeing it through the trees of Wren Meadow, and had hoped, even then, for the chance to visit.

Now she understood why Orman missed it so much; from the vantage point, she could see fully across the Leland peaks. The stippled gray-brown spires rounded up through the land as though the ground was smooth water, and the mountains, the arched spine of a sea serpent winding its silent way. Pine trees gave the mountains depth and mystery. She loved staring down at the mountains as she flew, seeing them as hidden treasures. She could do the same thing here on Orman's mountain.

Plus, the stream! Ares River flowed through the Leland Mountains, carrying magic out and around toward Wren Meadow. Just over the edge of Krag, a bright stripe of Ares water splashed from a high boulder, collected in a limestone basin near her feet, and then bounced down the mountainside as a waterfall.

"But where do you live?" she asked Orman.

He swung spindly legs from around her neck, and slid to the ground. He tugged his overly large trousers up to his waist, and then passed his hand down his long, unruly whiskers, before he pointed. "My house."

All Sela could spot was a few, scattered shards of crystal beneath a broken wooden table, and a mound of moss-covered timbers. Had he figured out how to make his house invisible?

"Invisible?" Orman snorted. "Only charlatans and swamp-water salesmen sell that lie." He stomped to the timber mound, and rested a foot on it. "It stood once. And it would have lasted a hundred years more, if those dang-blasted traitors hadn't breathed their poison all over everything, and weakened my spells."

Drell floated into a landing beside her, and Layce peered over his horns at Orman. "It'll stand again," she said.

Orman squatted beside the rubble. "All my books. My shards. My equipment." He poked at a rotten log, and the wood came away in soggy dust. "Haven't been the same since I lost them."

"We'll replace them," said Layce.

Sela looked toward Layce, but found Drell's gaze, instead. He was regarding her. She was going to smile, but he looked away. Too fast. He'd hardly spoken two words to her since they'd visited Wren Meadow. Or... maybe it had been longer than that. She tried to remember back to when he'd started avoiding eye contact. She wasn't sure what to make of it. She considered him a friend, but she'd either done something to upset him, somehow, or he didn't share the sentiment.

Layce dropped from Drell's shoulders. As she walked around the dragon to meet Orman, she pulled a long, entangled necklace of multi-colored crystals over her head. "We'll start with this. One of every color I've gotten my hands on over the years."

Orman stood, and gaped at the necklace. "You've been wearing that this whole time?"

"Not the whole time."

"No wonder you can't tell a talisman from a tadpole. You've got white, gray, brown... what is that one, turquoise?"

Layce pulled the crystals just out of his reach, and lifted her chin. "I can control them just fine! Do we have to go through this argument again?"

"Bah. You're hopeless."

"You're jealous. You wouldn't be able to wear all these crystals and walk a straight line."

"I wouldn't wear all those crystals to begin with! If you had any idea what kind of cockamamie storm they could stir up on my mountain—"

"*Your* mountain?"

Orman stomped to the remnants of his overturned table, and knelt to dig around in the dirt. "Why I let you come with me," he muttered. "Blasted females and their ways. No use to me! No use at all!"

Layce deliberately placed the necklace back over her head. "No use at all, hm?" She turned to Drell. "I'll need a ride back, now, Drell, if you don't mind."

"I don't mind," said Drell.

Sela watched his dark profile. His eyes were intense, focused. He was trying to keep Sela from sensing something again. Why did he keep doing that? Didn't he know she could tell he was doing it, and that it only made her more curious? And confused.

"Is it because you first met me as a human, and now I'm a dragon?" she blurted.

Drell swung his head toward her. "What?"

"Now, wait, Layce," called Orman, holding up a clear crystal shard. "Wait a minute."

"I don't stay where I'm not wanted." Layce gripped Drell's leg to climb on.

"Yes, you do," said Orman. "All the time."

"You've been ill at ease around me for a while now," Sela said to Drell. "And especially since Wren Meadow."

"I have?" Drell winced at Layce's tugging on his neck.

"You know you have. And you know I know you have."

"Layce," said Orman, his voice turning sharp. "I want to see your crystals."

"I don't want to show them to you." She lost her grip, and slid back to the ground. She faced Orman. Crossed her arms. "You're a rude, ungrateful old dope, and I don't even know why I bother."

"Ungrateful?!"

"Are you angry because I didn't tell you about me? And my tribe?" asked Sela.

Drell rubbed his paw at his neck, where Layce had been dangling. "Of course not."

"Then what is it?"

"Do we have to talk about this right now?" he asked.

"Yes, ungrateful," asked Layce. "After all I've done to help you. And Sela."

"What?" Orman's face turned blotchy. "Your meddling is what got me and Sela into all that trouble to begin with!"

"Yes," Layce sniffed. "And then I helped you get out of it."

Orman pressed his wrinkled hands to his face, and released a kind of growl she'd only ever heard her father make.

"I made a mistake," said Layce. "But then I tried to make it right. But you can't let it go. Looping it round and round like a spinning memory crystal, right in my face."

"I'm just wondering if I've done something," said Sela.

"What do you mean?" asked Drell.

"Something to make you angry."

"I told you, I'm not angry."

"But there is something."

"Yes," said Drell, with a snort. "Yes, all right?"

"But *you've* never made a mistake," said Layce. She crossed her arms again. "So I guess you have every right to judge."

Orman lowered his hands. He clenched his teeth.

"I know you don't need my help," said Layce. "You don't need anyone."

"Fine," said Orman, releasing a long, airy breath. "Yes, if it will get you to stop bellyaching."

"Yes, what?"

"Yes, I'd like your help. I want to look at those crystals."

"I know you do." Layce pinched the necklace with two fingers, lifted it away from her chest, and waggled it. "But there is a magic word for that."

Orman ground his teeth together. "Please."

"Wrong."

A wrinkle on his forehead swelled into a throbbing vein. "I'm sorry?"

Layce smiled. "For what?"

"For... saying you're not a wizard, and—"

"Actually," said Layce, moving smoothly toward Orman. "You didn't say that this time." She began to lift the necklace over her head again.

Sela eased closer to Drell. "I wish you would tell me what I've done so *I* can apologize."

"You don't need to apologize," said Drell. "You've done nothing."

"You said I did something," said Sela.

"I said there *is* something," said Drell. "Something that has changed the way I... the way we..."

"The way we what?" Sela asked.

"You're too beautiful!" Layce shouted, twirling to face Sela. "I liked you as a friend when you were human, but now you're a dragon, and you're too beautiful."

Silence, except for the falling of the water down the mountainside.

Layce put her hand to her forehead. "No, that's Drell. Sorry about that. I had too many voices in my head, I lost track of which was mine."

Drell looked from Layce, to Sela, his golden eyes wide. Sparks crackled from his snout. Then he blustered upward into a flurry of wings, and smoke, and scales, and shot out into the sky.

Layce winced. She turned to Orman.

"I suppose that's somehow my fault, too?" he said.

Sela shifted her weight, wanting to follow Drell, but that would strand Layce and Orman on Krag. She clutched at the ground, resisting the urge to fly.

"Go on," said Orman. "Talk to the boy. Just don't forget to come back for us."

Sela pushed off, and soared after him.

She spotted a dark shadow against a distant cloud. She strained to pull the shadow into focus. How had he gotten so far, so fast? She had to lengthen her wing strokes, and pump hard to catch up.

Within shouting distance, she called, "Drell! Wait!"

He didn't wait. He sped up.

She tried again. "Please! I want to talk!"

After a moment, he let his wings coast, and he slowed. Sela managed to dip alongside him, and they beat their wings in matching rhythm.

"You think I'm beautiful?" she asked.

"It was not the wizard's place to speak of that." He switched to the formal, elongated language of dragonspeak, but she couldn't tell if it was because he was more, or less, comfortable.

"But you were going to tell me, eventually."

"I was not." He rose up on a wind draft, and looked downward, at her face. "Is that all you wanted to ask me? Because I would like to fly alone."

She shifted to catch the draft, and let it loft her even higher than he was. "I am wondering if we will continue being friends."

"I am wondering the same thing," said Drell.

She felt lonely, then, somehow. Even surrounded by family, and the trees and mountains she loved; still his words poked an empty place into her heart. "I find you attractive to look at, too," she said. "The way your scales absorb the sun, and turn the edges into blades of midnight. But it does not make me want to end our friendship."

His wings stumbled. "You do not look at me and see my father?"

"Do you look at me and see mine?" she asked.

He smiled, then. He pulled up, and languidly stroked his wings to tread air. "Definitely not."

She used her momentum to circle him, and then

swooped into place before him, meeting his gaze. She wanted to smile, too, but she only felt mysteriously sad.

He regarded her for a time, legs pulled in, and leathery wings drawing back and forth like a butterfly. Then he spoke. "I have promised someone a meeting with you. I have been slow to keep that promise. I think because, for a time, I have wanted you to myself."

"I do not understand."

"I know," he said. "But you will." He spread out, and began a descent. "Follow me."

He led her around Mount Gore, toward the pebbled path of outcroppings and shadows, toward the dragon village. But just as they reached the hem of fir trees along the trail, he veered west and shot toward a knuckle of mountainside bulging from a short peak. A tall sycamore sprouted from the marbled boulder, and its root system all but obscured a slim chasm down the face of the rock. Perched on one root was a golden eagle. *The* golden eagle. Head cocked. Eyes riveted on their approach.

"Do I know that bird?" Sela asked.

"You do." Drell drenched the boulder, and the bird, with his shadow as he landed on the ground.

Sela hovered a moment, trying to make sense of this 'meeting'. Then she, too, landed, and pulled in her wings to her back.

The eagle hopped sideways on the sycamore root, and then dropped, hidden, into a wild patch of tall wheatgrass. Drell drew out a cloth bundle from inside the boulder chasm, and tossed it into the grass.

Rustling. And then Bannon Raley stood up, wheatgrass to his waist, and pulled a long, linen tunic over his head.

Sela's insides bubbled over with joy, and spilled out into his name. "Bannon?"

He straightened the tunic across his shoulders, and smiled.

"I knew I knew you. Somehow." Her memories flooded in of his sudden departure from Riddess Castle, and the sight of a golden eagle in the sky moments after. Of the bird saving her in the castle battle, and following them all to Leland. Watching her from the trees. "All this time? All this time, and you never said anything?"

"Things have been hectic," he said. "Blackclaw starting a war, wounded refugees from Esra..." He swished through the grass to draw near, wearing wrinkled trousers and his tunic. "...dragon council meetings." He shook his head, and, his smile widening, he touched his hand to her scaled collarbone. "Dragon council meetings, Sela. I'm so honored to observe it all."

Her scales quivered beneath his hand, as though a fly landed. She looked at Drell, who was watching a burly kutterbug work its way across the sycamore root. Too intently.

He was right. Now she understood.

"I wondered if I'd see you again, Bannon," she said.

"I've been seeing you," he said. "Wanting to talk to you. Wanting to explain."

She lowered to her haunches, and drew in her tail around her legs. She tipped her head, and passed her snout over his hair, which smelled of sunlight and grass, and deep soil. Then she moved her mouth close to his ear, and whispered, "Is it difficult to see me in this form?"

He drew his hand along her muzzle, and met her gaze with his hazel eyes. "No," he said. "I see who you are in either form. You're one of us. You're a shifter."

"One of whom?" she asked, looking from Bannon to Drell.

"He thinks you're a Murken," said Drell. "The healer of their land."

"A Murken?" Sela rose to her feet. "You mean, from the forest?"

Bannon nodded.

Sela eased a step back, her scales prickling. "That's where you're from?"

Bannon frowned. "Why do you move away from me?"

She hadn't meant to, exactly. "Because you're a... you're a..."

"A what?"

She looked at Drell, and then back to Bannon.

"What, exactly, does your Kind believe about Murkens?" asked Bannon.

To answer that was tricky. Her Kind rarely talked about Murk Forest, and when they did, it was with the hushed tones of awe and respect. Fear. "We only know to never go there. To never fly over the trees or breathe the air the forest exhales."

"Whenever I would visit my mother here," said

Drell, stumbling faintly over the word 'mother', "she warned me of the forest, too." He looked at Sela. "She would let me risk flying too close to Wing Valley, but never, ever, did we get near to Murk Forest."

"But you're not afraid of me, Drell," said Bannon. "And you even agreed to come to the forest with me."

"You've been to the forest?" asked Sela.

Drell shook his head. "No. Not yet. And I think I won't, now."

"Because you're afraid?" asked Sela.

"No. Because I'm not the one the Murkens have been searching for."

Sela sat again, and rubbed her left paw against her eyes. "You are both confusing me. I think you've had a conversation and forgotten I wasn't there."

"We did have a conversation. Back in Esra. When Leesa first brought Drell to me, that day at the castle when I had to leave. You remember?"

He'd given her his sword, which she lost track of, in the confusion. And a goodbye kiss. "I remember," she said.

"You weren't afraid of me then."

She met his eyes. She wasn't afraid of him now. Not really. "It's just that the forest has magic even dragons don't provoke."

"But you're no ordinary dragon, are you?" Bannon stepped in, closing the distance between them. "Will you shift for me? Back into human?"

"I don't have clothing."

Bannon tugged his tunic over his head, and offered

it out.

She regarded the tunic. Glanced at Drell.

"Would you like me to leave?" Drell asked.

"No," said Sela, grasping the fabric with her teeth. She loped into the wheatgrass. "I want to hear from both of you about this conversation," she said around the fabric. "And I want it to make sense."

Then she hunkered tightly, hoping the grass would obscure all her important human bits. And she thought small thoughts. Small, and a little scary.

CHAPTER ELEVEN

Fordon Blackclaw didn't sleep well. He hated when he didn't sleep, because he was a ponderous form with important thoughts, and deserved the rest a night could give in order to be at his best. Besides, it made him cranky. He didn't think as well when he was cranky.

Not that he would confess to that.

So when he stumbled out of his quarters in the charred Riddess Castle, and found Fane Whitetail holding his brined squirrel platter, he considered clobbering his advisor over the head with it.

Too much of a waste of his favorite breakfast. He just growled, instead.

"Aren't you supposed to be doing something this morning, Whitetail?"

"Yes, Leader Blackclaw."

Blackclaw scowled. Whitetail hadn't called him Leader Blackclaw in ages. Excess groveling, as well as a breakfast tray? What was the scrawny dragon up to now?

Blackclaw pointed to the crackled wooden floor

beams. Whitetail obliging laid down the tray. Blackclaw stirred one digit through the mass of shredded meat, testing the temperature. Warm, but not hot. Perfect. "The humans learn dragon fare quickly."

"Amazing what can be accomplished with the right motivation," said Whitetail.

Cook well or die. Blackclaw smiled briefly. "I am never sure what to do with the others, though. I would just as soon be rid of them, for the care and maintenance they require."

"They will soon serve their purpose, as bargaining tools in the weeks to come."

"I suppose." Blackclaw lapped at the brine on his foredigit. "Jia Greenscale has said as much. She has a brain accustomed to thinking several moves ahead." He scooped a mouthful of meat onto his tongue. He regarded Whitetail as he chewed.

The White bowed his head. "Agreed, venerable ruler. It is exactly this point I would like to address."

"I wondered when we would get to the part of you weaseling out of your assigned task."

"I think only of you, and your ultimate success, Leader Blackclaw."

"Just tell me what you came here to say."

Whitetail lowered his head until his snout brushed the floor planks. A speck of sunlight pierced through a hole in the castle's burnt ceiling slats, and reflected so brightly off Whitetail's cheekbone, Blackclaw had to squint. "And be quick about it."

"As you say, Jia Greenscale has a mind for strategic

matters. Soldier-like, in her abilities."

"Yes, yes."

"Where my skills are more to the subtle side of warfare," said Whitetail. He tipped his head, and peeked one eye. "Which may not be in best service to my assigned task at hand."

"Hmm." Blackclaw scooped another clawful of meat into his mouth, and swallowed. "You occasionally surprise me with your insight, Whitetail."

"I'm more than willing to go to Murk Forest, you understand." Whitetail straightened his neck. "But I believe I would benefit from Greenscale's company. Her guidance, perhaps."

Blackclaw rolled back against a stone wall, and scratched at his belly. "Since when have you ever been open to anyone's guidance but mine?" Blackclaw smiled again, watching the White stiffen. "Taken a fancy to the green beauty, have we, Fane?"

Whitetail was quiet for a time. Too long. Blackclaw sniffed at him. Narrowed his eyes to study him. Was the White having a difficult time forming his words, or about to retch?

"Have you ever known me to take a fancy to anyone, Leader Blackclaw?" he finally asked.

"Well, there is a first time for everything." Blackclaw rolled forward onto his feet, and took a heavy step toward Whitetail. The floor planks shuddered, which suited Blackclaw. "Speaking of 'first times', and the green beauty," he said, slipping in a low growl beneath his words, "That honor will go to me. Are we clear on that?"

Whiteclaw's pale eyes focused on the floor. "I daresay the female would find little interest in me, in comparison to your great presence."

Blackclaw snorted a puff of steam across Whitetail's horns. "Well-spoken insight yet again." Then he sat back onto his haunches. "I have been helping her plan a fresh attack, this time on Shornmar Castle in Leland. We are still collecting dragons from their assaults on South Morlan, Meedes, and Blaisvil. Once they have all re-gathered, we will be ready. I will need her back here by then."

"Understood." Whitetail eased back one step.

"And Whitetail."

The White regarded him, expression empty. It set Blackclaw on edge. Whitetail was his usual choice for discerning others' loyalties, but who did he have to watch Whitetail? "Send Greenscale to me before you go."

"Understood," said Whitetail again. Then the White billowed his wings, and like a gaunt flying mouse, set off through the broken castle ceiling.

§

Sela knelt in the tall wheatgrass, feeling the sun on her skin, and running her hands across the dirt. She hadn't been a human in over a week, and had just been adjusting to the sensory bombardment in her dragon form. Now she reacquainted herself with the mountains in the skin she'd worn for her entire youth. And she liked it. In a different way than she enjoyed as a dragon, but nevertheless, she liked it.

"Thank you, Drell," she heard Bannon say.

"For what?" asked Drell.

"Keeping your promise."

Sela tugged the linen over her head and pulled it as far as it would reach down her thighs, almost to her knees. Then she stood, and parted the wheatgrass blades to step through them.

Drell cocked his head, his amber eyes steady on her as she emerged. And Bannon's shoulders lifted with breath. He met her, drew his hand down her dark hair, and smoothed it back behind her shoulder. "You look older," he said.

"I do?"

"Yes," said Drell. "A little."

"Maybe because I was a dragon longer this time. Orman always suspected the age shifts wouldn't translate well."

"It has translated well," said Bannon. He smiled. For a flickering instant, she heard a thought behind his smile. He wanted to kiss her. She wondered if he knew she wanted to kiss him right back.

He knew. Before she had the chance to fully form the mental question, she already had the answer. Even as a human, their thoughts traveled between them as easily as any magical beasts.

"Because you are one of us," said Bannon.

"But that's not possible. I was born, right here. In these mountains. By my dragon mother and father."

"But your mother hasn't always been a dragon," said

Drell. "I heard the wizards talking."

Bannon turned to Drell. "What's this you say?"

"It's true, Bannon," said Sela, smiling. "It's an unbelievable story, but when my mother and father first met, she was a human." She turned to Drell, also. "But she changed because of magic. Because of a circlet that could grant wishes. It's not the same thing as how I do it." She turned, then to Bannon. "And she was born miles away, on the other side of the mountains. In Cresvell. She's never been to Murk Forest, either."

"One way or another, Sela Redheart, you were born with the ability to shift, and the only ones I know of who can do that are Murkens." Bannon took her hand. "Come sit. I have so much I want to talk to you about."

She let him lead her to a smooth rock, and she sat. He crouched beside her, elbows on his thighs. She tried not to stare at his broad shoulders, his bare chest. At the curl of blonde hair dangling in his eyes.

"Are you sure you wouldn't rather I leave?" Drell asked, still near the sycamore root. He hadn't moved from the spot since he first landed.

"No. No, please stay. I'm sorry." Her thoughts must have been pummeling them both. How embarrassing. She closed her eyes to shut out the distractions. "Tell me about how you and Bannon know each other. And what Leesa has to do with all this."

"Leesa took me to meet Bannon at the edge of the desert, after I escaped Whitetail during the dragonhunt."

"I always wondered what happened to you after that."

"The reason being, she thought I was the dragon of the Murken myth; the one that can heal their dying forest."

Sela's eyes opened. "So that's how you know about the prophesy," she said. She touched Bannon's arm. "The council is discussing it even now. It's been told in one of our scrolls how the desert is overtaking Esra because her magic is out of balance."

"The way you've explained the forest is dying. With the heart of it drying up," said Drell.

"Yes," said Bannon. "Drying up. Or poisoned. We don't know exactly. Generations of us have been searching for the wellspring of the forest, for the water that delivers her magic. We've only ever gotten as far as the swamp caves."

"Swamp caves?"

"I've never seen them. But our shepherdess has."

"What's a shepherdess?" asked Sela.

"Our leader. She's our eldest. Our wisest." Bannon shook his head. "But our leader isn't as old as elders in the past. As the forest dies, it fights us harder than ever. It's as though it's hoarding whatever magic is left, and so as it dies, our people die, too."

"I'm sorry," said Sela.

Bannon nodded. He laid his hand over her fingers, where they rested on his arm.

"It does sound like what the Gold described to me, as it happened in Esra. At the garden where dragons were first created."

"You met the Gold?" asked Bannon, his eyes

glittering. "He still lives?"

Sela smiled. "My father and mother have met him. Even Orman, I think."

"I wish he would visit us in Murk," Bannon said. "We could all use some hope."

"He told me he's drawn to magic, and to the places of belief," Sela said. "Maybe if you had more hope, he would be drawn to visit."

Drell pushed off from where he sat, and lumbered closer to them both. "Tell her why you've been searching for a certain dragon."

"Right." Bannon cleared his throat. "The myth from the caves say only a certain dragon can find the wellspring of the forest."

"But dragons know better than to venture into Murk," said Sela.

"Which is why some of us have gone out looking," said Bannon. "It's how Leesa and I ended up in Esra."

"You didn't belong there any more than I did," said Sela.

Drell nudged Bannon's shoulder with his snout. "Tell her about the dragon," he said again.

Bannon nodded. "Yes, I'm getting there." He pushed up to stand. "He's described as hidden from his Kind. He's a leader of his Kind, but taken from them and kept secret."

Sela stood, too. "The way Drell has been kept in the desert, away from Leland."

"And the way you have been taken from Leland, Sela," said Drell. "Hidden as a human, away from her

Kind."

"Me?" She looked from Drell, who nodded, to Bannon, whose face filled in with realization.

"I agreed to go with Bannon into Murk," said Drell. "I let him and Leesa convince me the myth dragon might be me. But now, I'm sure it's you, Sela." He inched forward, and tilted his head. He laid his paw on her shoulder. "I think you're the dragon from the Murken myth, and the one who should go."

Sela looked between them again, her throat tight. "But I just got here. I've spent my whole life trying to get home, back to these mountains."

"And the mountains need you. Heal the forest, heal the land," said Drell.

"So now you know what the mountains need? You've been here a week." Sela turned to stomp back into the wheatgrass.

Bannon took her arm. "Sela, wait."

She yanked her arm from his grasp, but she waited, frowning.

"I've spent my whole life trying to get home, too," Bannon said. "Back to Murk, to stay. Back to a forest magic that protects us instead of attacking us." He gripped her shoulders, and set his gaze on hers. "You're not the only one who's been homesick. And lonely."

"That is true," said Drell. He breathed out a long, steamy breath, and turned his head to gaze off to the distance. Toward the west, and the Rage desert.

"But you don't even know if it's really me," said Sela. "Shouldn't I think it's me, somehow? Wouldn't I know?"

"Maybe you do know, but you don't want to see it," said Bannon.

"And maybe you want to see it too much," said Sela. She shook her head. "I'm sorry. I can't."

She continued into the wheatgrass, and crouched. This time, she didn't wait for anyone to speak again. She closed her eyes, tried to think red and daring thoughts; large and exciting...

Except she couldn't.

All she could think was how much she wanted to stay, right here. And how large and exciting seemed just a little too risky. Red and daring could make her lose her home again. Couldn't it?

"Sela?" called Bannon. His hands reached into the wheatgrass and parted the blades. He peered in. "Are you all right?"

She looked up from where she hunkered. "Fine," she said.

Drell arched his neck and lowered his face down into the grass, too. "You don't seem fine."

She pushed to stand, yanked her tunic straight, and glared at them both. "Personal space?"

Bannon and Drell exchanged a look.

"I'm too distracted right now."

"Were you trying to shift?" asked Bannon.

"I'll do it later, when I don't have others staring right at me," she snapped. She pushed through the grass, and reached up to Drell's shoulder. "Take me to the manor?"

Drell bent his front leg to offer her a step up. She

hoisted, and swung her leg, and settled onto Drell's neck.

"Shall I take you both?" Drell asked in dragonspeak.

Sela looked down at Bannon, in his too-short trousers, and dirtied, bare feet. With his confused concern, and his steady hazel eyes. So different from the soldier she'd met him as. And yet, so very much the same.

"Both of us," she finally said, and offered down her hand to Bannon. "You need to talk to my father."

§

"He asked me to spy on you," said Jia Greenscale.

Fane sat at Boulder Bend, and watched her lower her feet to the dirt so gently she barely stirred a pebble. Then her wings contracted, and she tipped her head. "He suspects you are up to something."

"It is his nature," said Fane, with a shrug of one shoulder. "He trusts no one, and suspects everyone."

"You would know his nature better than most," said Jia.

"True."

"You, however, are quite the mystery."

"Me?"

"How did you get Blackclaw to agree to have me join you? And why do you need my help in the forest?"

"Your first question has an easy answer. I can get Blackclaw to agree to anything." Fane inspected his pearly claws. "It is a simple matter of playing to his weakness."

"Which is?"

"His overgrown ego."

Jia smiled. "Once, a long time ago, a friend and I snuck close enough to a human village to see a traveling show. Have you ever seen one?"

Fane shook his head.

"Dancing women and men, and instruments with strings and reeds. Such tiny little instruments, it is hard for me to fathom how humans manage to create such loud sound." Jia held out her paws, and wiggled her digits. "I play the funnelchord. It was my mother's."

A large, cornucopia-shaped instrument, carved from the wood of a Dandria tree, with wound wires of bronze or brass looped over the mouth. Fane had only seen one in his lifetime. "I should like to hear that," he said.

"Then I will play for you," she said. Then she lowered her forepaws to the ground. "But, anyway. One thing that really caught my attention was the rag doll puppets, made with cloth and straw, and bits and bobs, to look like even smaller versions of humans."

"Puppets?"

"Yes, they danced to the music, too, with knots for knees, and fingers, and toes. At first glance, the puppets seemed to move on their own, telling a story with their little button faces. But, when I looked closer at the puppets, I saw their strings. And then, when the show was over, I stayed long enough to see a man come out from behind his homemade stage, with the puppets dangling from his hands. Which is when I realized."

"Realized what?" asked Fane.

"I realized the puppets only danced because the man made it so. He was hidden, behind his stage. But he was the one making all the decisions. His puppets merely played them out."

Fane smiled, a little. He laid his white paw over her green one, and she didn't withdraw. "Few realize the power behind the stage," he said. "It is a strange comfort to have someone understand." But maybe that was too much to have said. He regarded her eyes.

She didn't seem to mind.

"But," he continued. "Blackclaw is more than a puppet. He makes decisions; I merely see they come to pass."

"You told me yourself you can get him to agree with anything."

Fane smiled again. That much was true. He often lived out his life beneath the nose of Blackclaw, and the overstuffed black dragon himself couldn't tell if Fane was coming or going, leading or following. Trouble was, Fane often couldn't tell the difference, either.

But was it trouble? Fane had never really wanted anything for himself enough that Blackclaw got in the way of it. Not really.

"Not ever?" asked Jia. "Have you always let others define what you should want for yourself?"

"I have gotten what I wanted," said Fane, his shoulders stiffening. "Perhaps behind the stage is exactly where I wish to be. Out front, dancing to music, that is the ridiculous part."

"Ridiculous? To be noticed?"

"Yes. Dangerous."

Jia stepped closer, dislodging his paw. The movement startled him, broke the spell of their discussion. "Dangerous," she said. "How?"

But he was through with talking. Angry, somehow. He eased back to make room between them, and thrust out his wings. He leapt onto the road's boulder, and, from there, shot up into the sky. "Come with me, or do not."

"I will come, Fane." She pushed off to join him. Her wing tips brushed his; her wingspan was half again the length of his. He tried not to notice.

"But you have not told me why you need me with you in Murk Forest."

"I am not going to Murk Forest," he said, curling around to find her face.

She smiled, if a bit confused. "Then where are we going?"

Fane didn't answer. He returned her smile, and then plunged upward, leading the way.

CHAPTER TWELVE

"You haven't really said anything about how you feel in all this," said Riza.

She reclined back against the bed mat in their quarters in Mount Gore Manor. Kallon realized it was the first time they'd had in privacy for weeks.

He hadn't talked about his thoughts because he'd been guarding them; it wouldn't do for the Dragon Council to know how deeply afraid he was. "I don't think I'm suited for this, Riza," he said. "I've only just gotten my family back, and now to have to make wartime decisions? I'm seriously thinking about giving the leadership to Brownwing. He's so much more experienced than I am."

"With wartime decisions? Has he been leader during conflict?"

"Well, no." Kallon settled onto his belly, and laid his chin onto her foot. "But he's lived through them. Seen them up close."

She stroked his horns with her paw. "So, your

hesitation has nothing to do with Fordon Blackclaw?"

He jerked up his head. "What do you mean?"

"He is the looming shadow of your youth. Your monster under your bed."

Kallon regarded the sleeping mat beneath Riza.

"It's a metaphor. Look," she said, and twisted around to lay out on her belly, too, looking straight into his face. "This is a unique situation, Kallon. Brownwing has never seen it. Your father had never seen it. Blackclaw isn't just fighting a territory skirmish, he's laying claim to all of Leland. Human stronghold, dragon stronghold, he plans to destroy them all."

"I understand that."

"He's a monster. The one you never quite vanquished."

"I understand that, too."

She tipped her head. "That's my point."

Kallon narrowed his eyes, trying to find a joke in her words. He didn't find one. "Well, I missed it somewhere."

She breathed out quietly, fanning cinnamon warmth across his face. "It's how you see him, Kallon. A monster. But what is he really?" She shook her head, her green eyes soft. "He's a dragon, like any other. He's cruel and egomaniacal. Greedy. But he's just a dragon. You fought him once, and he got away. That's all."

"He's stronger than I am."

"And as long as you believe that, he always will be."

Now Kallon shook his head. "I don't know how to un-believe something, Riza. Something that in my heart feels true."

She leaned in to press her paw against his chest. "You let your heart see things from a different place. Try seeing yourself through my eyes."

Kallon couldn't even meet her gaze. "I've done that, but I don't like it."

Her paw slid to floor. "You don't like how I see you? You think I don't see your strength, your love for your family, your devotion to your father's memory?"

"Do you?" he asked.

"Look at me."

He lifted his chin, managed to meet her gaze.

"What do you see now?" she asked.

"Disappointment," he said.

"In what?"

"In the fact that I'll never be enough for you."

Riza's eyes welled with tears. Steam leaked from her snout, and trailed fog against his throat. "What you really see is disappointment that you'll never really feel how much I love you, because you'll never really feel as though you deserve it."

His gaze faltered. He turned his head. "Not as long as Blackclaw lives," he said.

"Even after that. Even if he dies, even if you kill him yourself." She moved past him, toward the doorway. "Because, in your mind, you're not fighting a real dragon. You're fighting his shadow."

She put her paw on the carved, arch door.

"Riza," Kallon called quietly, although he didn't know what he wanted to say. He only knew he didn't want her to leave. Not like this. Again.

But the door swung open, against her paw, and startled her.

Shera Yellowfang called through, "Leader Redheart?" She poked in her face. "Apologies. Your daughter is asking for you." She glanced to Riza, too. "And you. All the council."

"We'll be right there," said Riza.

Yellowfang nodded, and disappeared. Kallon heard her scuffling feet traipse toward the Great Hall.

He moved toward Riza, but she didn't exit, she hesitated. "I just wish I knew how to help you see," she said.

Kallon nuzzled his nose against hers. They met gazes. And then, side by side, they stepped into the hall.

As they made their way toward the Great Hall, Kallon heard voices talking over voices; dragon and human. And, of course, Orman Thistleby, who was loudest of all. Something had the old wizard all wound up, and he guessed it was that woman, Layce Phelcher, who'd come as a refugee from Riddess Castle. All Kallon knew of her was that she'd been Vorham Riddess's wizard for years, and had been involved in helping Sela escape the castle. Kallon knew there was more to it, though, because Orman was so closed to talking about Layce.

Even with Layce, herself. Orman was either angry at the woman, or ignoring her, it seemed. Kallon suspected what that meant; that the old geezer had developed feelings for Layce, as unbelievable as it might be. The situation might have otherwise made Kallon laugh, if it wasn't so deeply embedded into other, more serious issues of the day.

But this time, Orman's energetic rant wasn't directed at Layce. Kallon loped into the Great Hall to find Sela, dressed in a long blouse and short pants, barefoot, and as human-looking as he remembered her. Startling. He'd grown so used to seeing her as a dragon he'd actually wondered if she would ever change back; or even if she could. He'd sort of hoped she couldn't.

Orman gesticulated at Sela, his voice high. Layce stood with her arms crossed, looking up at Drell, the other tag-along of the group. How Drell was mixed up in all this, Kallon still hadn't fully understood, but he seemed sincere enough, and gentle, and nothing like his father, which was a huge relief. Kallon had even noticed how Drell had been looking at Sela whenever his daughter wasn't looking back. He wasn't sure how he felt about that, but as long as Drell continued to show himself as a Leland dragon loyalist, he'd try to be open-minded.

Other council members talked among themselves, and occasionally tried to interrupt Orman, but the wizard was hot onto an argument, and wouldn't be deterred. Sela, for her part, was quiet, and regarding Orman with a sort of determined patience she must have developed over the years, living with him.

Beside Sela, there stood a man Kallon didn't know. He was pulling a tunic over his head, and talking through the fabric at Orman. Kallon's scales bristled. Another human? Here? He didn't like the timing.

"Orman," said the man. "If you would just let us explain."

"Don't think I don't remember you," said Orman, switching his attention, and his wagging finger, to the man. "Don't think I don't recognize you, you soldier. You kidnapper!"

"Kidnapper?" asked Riza, who immediately moved toward Sela, and glared suspiciously at the man.

"He didn't kidnap me, mother. I went on purpose."

"Went where?"

"To hell and back, that's where," said Orman. "What she's doing here with that hooligan, she hasn't explained—"

"I've been trying," said Sela.

"...but he needs to be thrown off the nearest mountain and done with!" Orman stamped a foot.

But, apparently, he'd said his full, because Kallon managed a word. "Who are you?" he asked the man.

"He's Bannon Raley, father. And yes, he's from Esra, but—"

"I believe the man can speak for himself," said Kallon.

"Yes, sir," said the man. He turned to Kallon. "Bannon Raley, as your daughter said." Then he turned to the other dragons. "I came with the rest of the group from Esra, and I promise I mean no harm. I want to help."

"Help whom?" asked Kallon.

"You, sir," said Bannon. "And Leland. I only worked in Esra as a soldier—"

"A kidnapper," said Orman, scowling.

"That's a long story," Bannon said to Orman.

"And he didn't kidnap me." Sela took Bannon's hand.

At that, Bannon startled, and smiled at Sela. She smiled back.

Oh, great. As though all of this wasn't convoluted enough, Sela had to go and fall for a human...

Kallon felt eyes on him. Heat, in his mind. And he found Riza staring hard at him.

He'd just been hoping for a normal, dragon continuation of the tribe, is all. That his daughter had managed to fall for a human being, of all things...

Riza's stare became searing hot. And Kallon felt himself gulp. Not in his mind, of course. But he did stop thinking.

"I only worked in Esra," the man continued. "But I'm from Leland." Bannon hesitated then, and Kallon arched his brow ridges.

"From Murk Forest," said Bannon.

The other dragons gave gasps, or grumbles, or silently stared. Even Orman stiffened, a little afraid. Kallon laughed. "Do you expect me to believe that?"

"It's true," said Bannon. "I've come a long way on a search, and I think I may have found who I'm looking for."

"Oh? And who is that?"

Bannon looked at Sela again. "Your daughter."

"You already kidnapped her once, you big bully," said Orman. "What more could you want?"

"It will take some explaining," said Bannon.

Kallon settled onto his haunches. "Then you'd better get started."

CHAPTER THIRTEEN

Jastin awoke, groggy. His eyes burned, and the back of his throat felt like sandpaper. He rolled to his side, and felt the whole room shift beneath his weight as though it wasn't attached to anything. And then he remembered. The forest. The trees. The woven nests among the branches.

He sat up, instantly alert.

A hand touched his shoulder. Leesa.

"Relax," said a voice.

Jastin didn't at first recognize it. He studied the room around him, and the way the low evening light suffused through stick-woven walls; how the branches beneath held his weight. The braided base cushioned as soft as pine needles. The scent of the room was wilderness, with a hint of beeswax. Must have been the candles wedged into the walls.

Then he spotted Farin in the low doorway, hunched where he peered inside. "Relax," the man said again. "You're safe. Leesa has been tending to your leg while you slept."

"How long was I out?"

"A few hours. Leesa says the two of you had quite a journey getting here. We wanted to give you a chance to recover, before you meet the Shepherdess."

Jastin shifted to put weight on his torn leg, but pain screamed down toward his foot. He clenched, and dropped back. "Looks bad," he said, poking at the gash from outer thigh, down to his calf. Reddened, and not just from dried blood.

"That's the poultice," said Faren. "Not infection. Leesa crushed pithberries that closed the skin. The juice will turn black and eventually fade, but that red, there, that's a good sign."

Jastin nodded, and poked once more. No blood oozed. And then, he realized he'd been staring at his bare leg. His other leg, also bare. And his upper body. He was wearing a loin cloth, like Farin.

Which was a lot more naked than he liked. "Where are my clothes?"

"Torn, bloodied. And here in the forest, those leathers will suffocate you."

He finally focused on Leesa, who sat cross-legged beside him. A wooden bowl of purple juice rested beside her, with a cloth dangling over the side. She wore what looked like a grass-woven cloth wound around her hips and through her legs, and then wrapped over each shoulder and around her chest. Her black hair was oiled back behind her ears, and a small, white handprint was pressed at her collarbone.

He touched the handprint, and traced a finger over the bumps in the paint.

Leesa touched his collarbone, too, and he looked down to find he carried his own handprint, pressed and matted into the dark hair on his chest.

"Leesa feels there will be fewer questions if everyone understands you're together," said Farin. "Especially where the Shepherdess is concerned. She's beside herself someone brought an outsider." Farin shook his head at Leesa, but she just glared back.

"How do you know all of this about her?" asked Jastin. "Leesa, I mean. It's as if she talks to you."

"She does," said Farin.

Jastin lowered his chin to find Leesa's eyes. "Then why doesn't she talk to me?"

Farin chuckled. "She does."

Jastin looked from Farin, back to Leesa, who sat motionless, although her steely gaze was intense. "What, exactly, does 'together' mean to your people?" he asked, grazing his handprint with his fingers.

Her olive skin tinged red, deep in her cheeks, and she looked at her hands in her lap.

Jastin didn't need her words to understand exactly what she was saying, then.

In the distance, a horn bleated. Jastin felt the vibration of hurried feet through the treetops. Leesa sucked in a breath, and then studied Jastin; she smoothed his hair, and brushed her fingers over his beard, which must have needed a trim by now.

"Here she is," said Farin, and moved away from the

door.

Jastin actually felt a stab of nervousness in his belly.

Then the Shepherdess swept inside the room-like nest, ducking through the doorway. When she reached the space at the end of Jastin's outstretched legs, she pulled herself straight, and regarded him.

She wore the same twisted, woven material around her hips and thighs as Leesa, but a sheared-off tunic covered her torso. Vines enwrapped her arms from shoulder to wrist, and more vines entwined her graying hair, in braids, piled up and around her head. She shared the same olive-toned skin as the others, although it was soft with wrinkles in all the pleasant places on her face.

Whatever Jastin had been expecting from her next, it wasn't this: she smiled. "And here you are." She crouched, and probed Jastin's wound. "Made it all the way into our humble little village, and this is all you have to show for your troubles? Not bad." She straightened again, and studied him. Her eyes lingered on the gold scale on the leather around his neck, and he touched it. Then she examined his face, his shoulders, his legs. "Mm-hmm. I see what she sees in you. You're strong, in here." She jabbed a finger against his chest. Then she leaned close enough to whisper in his ear, "Are you two really together, or did she just handprint you to keep you all to herself?"

She laughed. A rich, rumble of laugh. She elbowed his arm, and winked. "Don't worry, I'm just teasing. You couldn't handle me." She laughed again, and turned. "What's an old lady have to do to get a seat in here?"

Farin appeared instantly by her side, and set down a toadstool-shaped sack behind her legs.

The Shepherdess lowered herself slowly, and then rested her arms across her knees. "So, mysterious outsider. What can we do for you?"

Jastin looked from Farin, to Leesa, to the woman. Leesa nudged him.

"I, uh," Jastin said.

The Shepherdess arched her brows, but patiently waited for a more coherent answer.

He tried again. "I don't mean to ask for anything. Time to heal, I guess." Which he wouldn't even need, if he hadn't been dragged here in the first place.

"I see," said the Shepherdess. "Tell me how you came to find us, then."

Jastin looked at Leesa. "Leesa brought me. We were being chased down by dragons—"

"Dragons were chasing you?" The Shepherdess frowned. "Why?"

"It's a long story."

"It usually is."

"Well," he began, and cleared his throat. He shifted his hips to find a more comfortable position. "Shepherdess," he said.

"Call me Jade." The woman pointed at her eyes.

In the low, filtered light inside this room, he couldn't see the color of her eyes, so he took her at her word.

"All right, Jade. In Esra, the dragon Blackclaw came out of hiding to declare war on Riddess Castle."

"Fordon Blackclaw?" she asked.

Jastin nodded. "With the help of Whitetail. And plenty of other dragons, from what I could see. I was with a group, at the time, and we fought back. But we were outnumbered. The others headed for Leland, and Leesa and I were trying to get to South Morlan, but dragons pursued, and didn't let up, all the way east until we crossed into the forest."

"Who are you to Blackclaw?

"What do you mean?"

"Why would he pursue you, if he's busy starting a war?"

Jastin shook his head. "I have no idea."

"What's that, then?" She pointed to his golden scale.

Jastin touched it again. "A gift."

Jade stood. The pleasantness drained from her face, and hardness tightened around her mouth. "I'm supposed to believe that the Gold handed you over a key to the boundary, just like that? He gave it to you? You, a hunter who kills dragons for money?"

Jastin felt as though someone had dumped a bucket of cold water from above him. "How did you..."

"Oh, you don't say much with your mouth, but your head is chock full of interesting things," said Jade. "Trouble is, you have too many thoughts all jumbled up together in there, all coming from the same place." She stepped toward him, and he saw the green of her eyes, now. Fierce and snapping. "You don't see anything except through fighting."

"That's not true," he said, but he knew it was.

Even before hunting dragons, before he lost his wife, before becoming a soldier. As a boy, he learned his fists were faster than words, and how to give a bloody nose before he received one. No, it was more than learned. It was natural. "But, so what?" he asked. "This world is a place of violence. Even your people had to fight your own forest to make a home here. Fighting is survival. Fighting is never giving up."

Jade's eyes narrowed, accusing. "Unless violence *is* giving up."

"How does that make any sense? How am I supposed to tell the difference?"

Now Jade's face calmed, and she gripped his chin with her sun-darkened hand. Her gaze searched him, as though she might find the answer just beneath his skin, or behind his eyes. "You tell me," she said.

Jastin felt her eyes like heat, and he wanted to push her hand, make her give him some space. But he clenched against the urge, and let her stare. "I don't know," he said.

"In that case," she said, releasing him. She patted him on the head. "There's hope for you, yet."

She turned to Leesa and Farin. "He can stay as long as he needs to heal, but be on guard. This forest will sniff out his weakness, eventually."

Leesa nodded.

"No word from Bannon?" Jade asked Leesa.

Leesa frowned.

"No, me either." The woman put her hands on her hips, and eyed Farin. "Maybe it's time to send you out to search."

Jastin realized he must have passed some sort of test. And, regarding Jade's profile, and her worried expression as she spoke to her Farin and Leesa, he began to understand the meaning of the word Shepherdess. The wise one was less of an inquisitor now, and more of a mother hen, really.

The name Bannon seemed familiar to him, somehow, but he couldn't place it.

"You're probably right," Jade said to Leesa. "I'll give it some time." Jade moved to duck through the nest opening.

Jastin wrestled himself onto one hip, and tried to push up onto one knee, leaving his wounded leg outstretched. "Wait," he called.

The woman paused, turned.

He lifted the dragon scale of his necklace toward her. "What did you call this?"

"It's a key," she said.

"A key? To what?"

"To the boundary."

Jastin released the scale and struggled to stand. "What's the boundary?" he grunted. And, the moment he touched his wounded leg to the floor to put weight on it, hot pain shot through it.

Leesa wedged herself against his side, and helped steady him.

"You're going to take twice as long to heal if you keep moving around," said Jade.

"What's the boundary?" he asked through his teeth,

gritted in pain.

Jade shook her head. One thin, graying braid fell loose from her hair bundle, and traced down her face. "There's the rub. You got that thing around your neck, you shouldn't even have to ask." Jade stepped forward, and searched his face again. "I hope the Gold knows what he's doing."

Jastin hopped, found his balance. Leesa adjusted his arm around her shoulders. "Well, I have a lot of questions, but all I seem to get are riddles and more 'you should know already'. But I don't know, all right? It's why I'm asking."

Jade smiled, indulgently, and he didn't like it. "I don't suppose you can be bothered to explain anything, either."

"Oh, I can be bothered," said Jade. "I'll tell you anything you want to know." She held up one finger. "But first, since you're up, Leesa can walk you to our latrine. I'll have Farin wrangle up some fig stew. Once you're comfortably resettled, I'll come back, and see what I can do about filling in some of your blanks, hm?"

Well. Since he was up. He nodded.

Jade nodded, too. Then she turned, ducked through the opening, and he heard her bare feet, in measured steps, work their way up higher.

For a moment, he drank in the silence. Or, at least, the lack of conversation. Bird call zig-zagged from one angle to another, the wind rustled leaves throughout the treetops and whispered in through the woven walls of this nest to brush through his hair, and down his bare back. An insect sort of buzz hummed on and off from below. But for now, there were no words, and it gave his mind a chance to rest.

He looked down at Leesa, at his side, and considered her silence, too. He wondered what her voice would sound like, if she had one.

She used to have one. So he wondered what it sounded like, then. Before he knew her.

It took him a moment to realize she was smiling at him, in a way he didn't recognize. A grin of expectation, as though she was waiting for him to say...

"Wait. How did I know you used to have a voice?"

Her shoulders lifted, and she gave that short burst of movement across her chest that should have been a laugh.

He would have liked to hear her laugh.

But he wasn't sure what had just happened, or why it was funny, even though he was smiling a little, too. He felt as though a joke had been played on him, but he didn't mind, he just didn't understand.

Leesa nodded her head toward the outside, and, still grinning, began to lead him across the braided floor. He hobbled slowly, his good leg trembling to hold him up every time he swung his wounded leg to limp onward. He was tired, everywhere. Even his bones felt like maple syrup.

"I've never, all my life, needed so much help," he said. He paused to collect his strength. "This is all you've ever seen of me." She kept taking care of him, even though she hardly knew him. Maybe because she hardly knew him. Maybe, if she'd met him months, or years, ago, and had seen what he was capable of, she'd have left him there in the Esra wood, poisoned, betrayed, half dead, and lying in his own vomit.

He was glad she didn't. He only hoped she'd give him a chance to repay the kindness, and let him take care of her, some day.

Leesa looked sharply at him, then. Surprised.

And then it made sense.

"You can hear me, can't you? In my head?"

She hesitated, then nodded.

"Like a wizard. With magic." He frowned. He burned inside. He hated magic. It was unnatural, and confusing, and made people see things, do things, they wouldn't otherwise do. And using it to listen in on someone's own thoughts? "A man needs a place to be alone, you know. I ought to be able to think in privacy."

Her face tightened as though she felt pain. She urged him gently on, without looking at him.

They stepped through the doorway onto a rough plank of wood. More planks extended outward into a platform, with branches as thick as his wrist bound end to end along both sides as a railing. To his right, wooden ramps continued up and around, higher and higher, dotted with woven huts that blended so deeply into the gray-green treetops he lost track of how high they went. To his left, the ramps circled downward a few feet, with just a few huts that ended where the tree trunks turned mottled brown and leafless.

Ropes dangled from the drop off. More ropes were

twisted and strung across gaps as bridges to neighboring treetops and the microvillages of more huts.

Leesa guided him to the edge of the platform. He gazed down at the ground, some thirty feet below him. Wind cut through branches to rustle his hair, and tickle across his bare chest and arms, and his legs. The sensation of it on skin he rarely exposed was unsettling. Made him feel vulnerable. And yet, content, somehow.

"This must be what it feels like to fly," he said.

Leesa inhaled deeply, and closed her eyes.

He regarded her profile, then, and the blue-black strand of hair caught across her nose. He impulsively reached a finger to tuck it behind her ear.

She opened her eyes and turned her smile to him.

It had been a long time since a woman had looked at him like that. With an open face, a soft expression. As though she trusted him, liked him. Even his wife Rimin had never really looked at him that way. Sure, she'd often said she loved him, but he was never sure if she'd ever liked him.

He was never sure he liked her, much, either.

But he liked Leesa. Her strength, her will, and the way she was always thinking, despite her silence. And the way she was watching him now, with her face upturned, and her eyes intense, he knew she was probably listening in, too. So before his mind could wander any further into his feelings, and before he explored what any of this meant, he spoke.

"Jade said something about showing me the outhouse?"

Leesa nodded over the side of the platform.

"Uh." Jastin blinked. Looked around. "Right here? I just go over the side?"

Leesa disentangled her arms from around his waist and propped him against the rail. She stepped away, and turned her back.

Well, if this wasn't the most awkward thing. Still, his bladder was banging against his spine, and so if that's how the tree people did things around here, who was he to argue?

But he was glad no one happened to wander by, out on a stroll through the treetops.

Or below.

Finished, and feeling better for it, he tried to step back without help. His wounded leg crumpled. The stick railing bent under his weight. He heard a snap.

Leesa was there, bracing him, and he clutched at her. He felt many things at once: panic, from feeling his weight too close to the edge; relief, from Leesa's steady hands; anger, from shame and helplessness. "I hate this," he seethed through clenched teeth.

It was only as he limped away from the edge that he realized his grip around her shoulders was making her wince in pain. He relaxed a bit.

When they finally reached the grass mat inside the woven hut, he was panting from the effort of walking. Perspiration trailed down his back, his hamstrings. He tried to sit, but dropped too hard, and landed awkwardly on his hip. He shifted, his legs outstretched, and finally found a position that helped his wound dull to a mere throb.

Leesa drew a cool cloth down his back.

Farin stepped in, carrying a clay pot. Steam rippled from the top. Clay bowls clattered where they hung from hooks on a belt around his waist. He crouched, set the pot on the floor, and began stacking the bowls. "You're going to love this," he said. "Nobody makes fig stew like Maina."

"Maina," said Jastin. "Is that your wife?"

"One day soon, I hope," said Farin. He winked.

"She lives here, then? Does she change shape, like you?"

Farin scooped stew with one bowl, and poured it into a second. "We all do. It's our secret; how we survive in a forest meant for no man."

Jastin turned to Leesa, who took a bowl of stew without making eye contact. "So you can become an animal."

"Not anymore," said Farin. He offered Jastin a bowl. "She can't shift, she can't speak. She lost both abilities at the same time."

Jastin enwrapped his hands around the bowl, warmed from the stew. Cinnamon spice tickled up into his nostrils, along with the syrupy scent of boiled figs. White chunks bobbled against the fruit, and strings of something that might have been meat, or mushroom. His mouth watered. "What happened to her?" he asked.

"We don't choose our forms," said Farin. "The forest breathes them into us. Families tend toward the same alters. Leesa and I are cousins, and we're both ground walkers. Jaguars." Farin stabbed at a fig with a pointed stick and put it in his mouth, and chewed. "Well, she *was.*

"But some of us are birds. Air travelers. Some of us are monkeys. Tree climbers. We don't know until our first shift, as infants. Some of us spend more time as our alters than we do in our human form."

"But you are humans," said Jastin. "Humans who shift, not animals who can look human."

Farin smiled. "We mate as humans. Give birth to human babies. Does that make you feel better?"

Jastin sat back. "It isn't what I—"

"Isn't it?" Farin ate another fig. "Or would it be easier to hate and distrust us knowing we're human-shaped, mindless beasts?"

"I don't hate you," said Jastin. "And my distrust isn't personal."

"You don't trust anyone."

"You got it."

After a moment, Farin smiled again. So did Jastin.

He put a fig into his mouth. It burst with sweetness. "You're right, this is delicious." Like nothing he'd ever eaten before. He enjoyed the taste and the texture, trying to place the other flavors in the juices. Nutmeg, maybe. Then he lifted the bowl to his lips for a long, satisfying drink.

When he lowered the bowl, he regarded Leesa. "You still haven't told me how you lost your voice."

"She tried to choose her shape," said Jade's voice from the doorway. The elder loomed there, silhouetted against evening light, one hand on her hip.

"Which isn't possible," said Farin. "Some of us believe she was foolish."

"Some of us believe she was brave," said Jade. She pushed into the room, and stroked Leesa's hair. "She knew the danger, but she tried, anyway. For all of us."

"Why did she try?" asked Jastin.

Jade stepped across the edge of Jastin's grass mat, and crouched beside Farin. She served herself a bowl of stew, and lifted it to her nose, drawing in a deep breath of the scent. "Once we were many. Now we are few."

It seemed to be the same refrain he'd heard throughout Leland over so many years. As much from dragons, as others. Guilt stabbed him. He'd killed so many dragons in his quest to destroy them all.

"Our magic is dying," said Jade. "We don't know if it's because the land is drying up and taking the magic with it, or the other way around. But the forest knows its lifeblood is being drained, and it's become more desperate, more violent against even us."

"And we are a people of the forest's lifeblood," said Farin. "We survive as much on the magic that breathes us, as we do on fig stew."

"As the forest starves, so do we," said Jade. "And we only know one way to restore it. We have to find out what's happened to the eternal spring."

Jastin's stew bowl was empty, and his belly satiated, so he set the thing beside the pot, and waited for Jade to continue. When she didn't, he prompted her. "Eternal spring?"

Instead of answering, she asked another question. "What do you know about the Leland Mountains?"

Jastin shifted. He cleared his throat. "They're full of dragons."

"And crystals," said Farin.

Jastin nodded. He did know that.

"There's a reason for both," said Jade. "They are the same thing."

Jastin took a moment to process that. "Are you saying dragons and crystals are the same thing?"

"Made from the same thing," said Jade. "In the same way. Slabs of colored magic; reds, blues, grays, greens, browns. Magic and time compressed." Jade set down her bowl, too, and looked deep into Jastin's eyes. "Water moves silently, mysteriously, feeding and pulsing, throughout all the land. Underground, where magic concentrates, and becomes trapped in layers of rock and soil, it waits. Changes under pressure. We dig that up, and we call it crystal.

"But before all the rivers and streams we have now, before so much water reached so much surface and spilled its magic into grass and growing things, there was the first time. The first place. And then a second. And a third. Water found the earth's crust, and burst through it, spraying its magic into the sky. Released, it grew wings and flew. These, we call dragons."

It sounded more a story for children at bedtime than something Jastin could put any faith into. But he'd asked for answers, and so he politely let Jade continue.

"We know the three places where water first

touched air. One is in Esra, in the place now called Rage Desert. One is in the mountains. And the other is here, in this very forest."

"So you're saying there's something wrong with your water, and so there's something wrong with your magic," said Jastin.

Jade sat back, and pulled into a cross-legged position. "You don't like magic. You don't like talking about it, thinking about it."

"That's true," said Jastin.

"That's how weak our land has become," said Jade. "You've lived so long without magic, you don't even know you once survived on it. Thrived on it."

"I do just fine, thanks," said Jastin.

"Yes," said Jade, but her voice was heavy with grief. "And maybe that's the fate of the Murkens, too. Maybe we will wean away from our own land and become as dry and hollow a human as you."

Jastin stiffened. "I wouldn't say I'm hollow."

"You wouldn't say it because you don't see it." Then Jade reached out a finger, and touched the golden dragon scale against his collarbone. "But, then again, you are different now. Something about you. He recognizes it in you, or he wouldn't have given you this."

"You called it a key," said Jastin. "To the boundary."

"Yes, the boundary." Jade lowered her hand, and let it rest on Jastin's knee. "The invisible place, high in the sky. No living thing can pass through it, and so no living thing knows what's on the other side. But," said Jade, lifting her hand again, and pointing a finger. "When a body dies, the soul inside must go somewhere. It's made of magic, after all."

"So what does a key do?"

Jade shrugged. "That, I can't tell you. I only know what it is, I don't know what it does."

"The Gold must know."

"Of course he does. He knows everything. He was the first."

"The first dragon?"

"The very one. Burst from the ground into the sky."

Jastin clasped his hand around the scale. "All these years, though. No dragon lives that long."

"He is the first," Jade said again, as though that was the simple answer to explain the unexplainable.

"You really believe all this," Jastin said. He looked from Jade, to Farin, to Leesa. "All of you believe this?"

"What's not to believe?" asked Farin.

Jastin gave an empty laugh. He shook his head. Then, eyes still on Leesa, he said, "What about Leesa? What happened to her?"

Jade moved her hand from Jastin's knee, to Leesa's. "There is a long, deep cave leading to the forest spring. We've walked it, but can get only as far as a... a sort of blackness. We can hear the water as it falls over the edge of something, and we can even feel the mist on our faces. But we can't reach it. We can't get *through* to it."

"It's an ancient barrier," said Farin. "Made by dragons. For dragons. A prophecy is scrawled throughout the cave of a special dragon, hidden from his kind. Only this dragon can reach the water to heal it." He scowled at Leesa.

"But Leesa tried," said Jade. "She shifted, and she tried to choose a dragon alter. Right there in the cave." Jade stroked Leesa's knee, like a mother soothes her child. "She broke into fever, and got very sick. We thought she wouldn't survive. But she's strong."

"Yes," said Jastin, and found himself touching Leesa's knee, too.

"But when she recovered, her voice was gone. And she hasn't been able to shift since."

Jastin tried to picture her as a jungle cat, on all fours, and covered in dense, brunette fur. Then he saw her in his mind sprouting scales, and wings, and long, predatory claws. He imagined a musty, ancient smell rippling off her in waves, and the hot, stinging breath of... Riza Redheart. The woman-turned-beast.

His heart clenched. He pulled his hand from Leesa's knee.

"I've heard enough," he said. "I don't think I can handle any more answers."

"Just as well," said Jade. She studied him, he could feel it. But then she pushed to her feet, and rearranged the twisted cloth around her waist and hips. "I don't have any more answers to give." She waved for Farin to follow, and paused in the doorway. "Bring the stew."

She disappeared, followed by Farin, and he listened to the quiet groan of wooden planks as they made their way higher along the tree path.

He was alone with Leesa. It had been just the two of them before, in the woods. On the path. Watching his burning home. But before, she'd been a woman of flesh and bone. Now, he could only see her as a changeling creature, as an animal wearing human skin.

She reached toward him, and he flinched. She noticed, paused, and then continued. She pointedly set her empty stew bowl on the floor, and then held out her hands. She scooted against the wall of the hut, pulled her knees to her chest, and wrapped her arms around them.

"I knew someone once," he started to say. But then he couldn't figure out how to explain something he didn't like to talk about, or think about. Magic. Feelings. Betrayal.

"I probably don't need to explain it to you, anyway. You're in here," he said, tapping his temple, "hearing it all for yourself."

She shook her head.

"You're not in here?"

She shook her head again. She clenched her eyes closed, and put her fingers in her ears.

Well, he had that, then. A quiet place in his mind for a little privacy. Trouble was, now that he had it, he didn't know what to do with it. He didn't feel like thinking anymore, anyway. His leg stung, his belly was full, and he was tired.

He laid back, and stared up at the hut ceiling, where it pulled away into a point on top. From inside, it looked like a funnel. Then he gazed down at himself. Moonlight speared through the woven walls to carve beams across his chest and legs, and waving treetops danced shadows through the light. Crickets sang somewhere, far off. For the moment, he felt peaceful, cradled in nature's arms, sheltered from the night while somehow being fully a part of it.

Peaceful, yes. Comfortable.

He hadn't realized he'd fallen asleep, until Leesa stirred beside him. It jarred him suddenly awake. She dozed beside him, her ribs against his arm, touching him with her beast skin, breathing her animal breath near his ear. He tensed.

And then she rolled over, and rested her cheek on his bicep. Her hand settled onto his chest.

The moonlight found her eyelashes, and glittered them, reminding him they belonged to a woman who regarded him with kindness. Her hand on his chest was soft; the hand that had been bracing him in his weakness. Her breath tickled his skin; from lungs that expelled air, not sparks. She wasn't an animal, not really. She was just a human with the potential to become a beast.

In the end, wasn't that his own story? Except he didn't have the fur, and claws, and teeth as an excuse.

He relaxed beneath her touch. Nuzzled into it, a little. And he spotted how her fingers just grazed the glowing white handprint on his chest. He reached to her hand, and slid her fingers into place, aligning them with the shape. Then he held it there, and watched her in the moonlight, until his eyes grew heavy, and his own breathing turned deep.

Peaceful. And comfortable.

CHAPTER FOURTEEN

Fane Whitetail flew south, without speaking, over the smoking ruins of South Morlan. Over scorched patches of maple trees, and rubble piles that were once houses. Dragon attacks on Esra's people had hit their mark well, and although Fane didn't have direct knowledge of the fate of the humans below, he could guess. Mingled with the scent of burned wood and stone was the stench of singed flesh.

Jia smelled it, too. Her nose wrinkled, and she gazed down at the wrecked village with heartbreak in her eyes. He watched her, as their wing tips nudged against each other, and she didn't notice it. She just stared downward, her face tight. Beautiful, in its suffering.

Fane had been expecting it, of course. Still, he felt a pang of disappointment.

He swerved southeast, away from the damage. She dutifully followed, and when he drew up to slow his speed, she caught up beside him with tears in her eyes.

He didn't watch her after that.

He spiraled down toward a crevice that split South Morlan's sandy crust like a slice of meat pie. No trees, except a few withered saplings that never had a chance. No water, no colorful layers of sediment. Just a crack in the tawny land, surrounded by dust and dry wind. He landed at the edge.

Jia descended beside him, soundless. She regarded him, but her thoughts were far away; he could feel them lingering back at the village.

"You betray yourself," said Fane.

"Yes. My father often says he doesn't need to hear my thoughts to know me, he sees them on my face."

"A disadvantage for a soldier."

Jia shook her head. "I have never claimed to be a soldier."

"What, exactly, do you claim to be, Jia?"

She peered over the edge of the crevice. "I have reasons for everything I do, Fane, like you." She turned her eyes to his face again. "But I have my doubts, sometimes. I wonder if I want the right thing, and if it is worth doing what I must to get it."

"What is it you want?"

He saw the search in her eyes for the right word. "Change," she finally said.

"Strange," said Fane, sitting back. "Seems I have always fought to keep things just the way they are."

"We do not have to share the same reasons to be in the same fight."

Across the crack, against the horizon, the sun began to nestle against wind-scarred dunes. Orange, filtered beams crawled across the sandy plain and dropped over the fracture's edge, lighting it with a fire-like glow. Inside the crack, where white, bleached bones wedged deep into craggy rocks, the sunset turned them peachy red.

Jia saw the bones when Fane did. She craned her neck, and squinted. "Is that a skeleton?" she asked. "A dragon skeleton?"

"More than one," Fane answered.

"A graveyard?"

"You could say that."

"I don't understand."

"They are the bones of my parents," said Fane, quietly. Steadily.

"Oh. I—"

"Plus one female. Blackclaw wanted her disposed of, but that was so long ago, I do not even remember why anymore."

Her face tightened again. Not alarm, though, surprisingly. "In other words," she said, "You are not here to grieve."

"Not in the least."

"You are here to gloat."

Fane raised one shoulder in a shrug. "If I were the gloating type."

She crossed her forelegs. Pierced him with her yellow gaze. "Why did you bring me here?"

"To show you," he said. "What do you think you are playing at, Jia? Who do you think you are fooling, with your shimmying up to Blackclaw, worming your way into his confidence? Pushing me out, and at the same time, enticing me into thinking it is for my own good?" Fane lunged at her, gripped her foreleg, hard. She winced. "But look down there with your own two eyes, and see just what I do in order to *keep* things exactly the way they are."

She wrenched out of his grasp. Her wings stabbed air, and she lofted just enough to put space between them. "This is not about me," she snarled. "You brought me here to remind yourself."

He swiped his paw to grab her again, but she dodged back, just out of range.

"You have feelings for me, Fane! At least, you entertain the idea." She dropped to her feet, and stuck her snout in his face. "You know I am right. For some, brief moment in time, you actually felt yourself think about someone else, about having someone else. And you cannot stand it!"

She pushed at his chest. "What was I supposed to do? Be frightened? Surprised? You think I do not know who you are, and what you are capable of?"

Yes, frightened. A little surprised, at least. Fane had meant to scare her, to dominate. Threaten. To make her see that if she didn't retreat, he would do whatever he needed to get her out of the way.

Her eyes narrowed. "Out of the way. Me, out of your way." She eased back, her jaw clenched. "Like the others. Your parents. Blackclaw's female problem. I see." She swept her foreleg out over the crevice. "In my frightened, terrified confusion, you were going to throw me over the edge. Or, was I supposed to politely throw myself, to save you the trouble?"

"I had hoped it would not come to that," Fane said.

She laughed, bitterly. "Well. Thank you."

"Jia—"

She held up a paw. "From the depths of your mercy, you have spared me my death sentence for the unforgivable crime of trying to be your friend." Her wings billowed. She lifted into the air. She pushed up and away, a dark emerald shape against the failing light.

He jumped, opened his wings, and pursued. "Jia!"

To his surprise, she slowed to let him come beside her. Then she spoke again, without looking at him. "You have done me a favor, Fane."

He didn't reply, he only watched her profile, and silently coasted.

"I *was* having doubts about whether I am doing the right thing for the right reasons. You have renewed my purpose."

"Me?"

"You have reminded me why I am here, and why I must be true to the promise I made."

"Promise to whom? Blackclaw?"

She curled her wings into leathery crescents, slowing herself, and turned to look him fully in the face. "To myself, Fane. A long time ago."

He pedaled his feet against the air, and shifted to meet her position. "And what promise is that?"

She only regarded him for a long, quiet moment. He could hear the whisper of wind against her wings as she treaded them back and forth, and he could smell the churning of heat from her rushing heartbeat, stirring the sulfur in her lungs. "You brought me here to frighten me off, because you do not have the courage to tell me to stay away." She shook her head. "But nothing here surprises me. I am not afraid of you."

Her words stung. She was right, of course. As time wore on, he knew he was growing dangerously close to trusting her. And yet, as he regarded her eyes, dull and intense against her softly glittering face, he sensed she might have just told him her first lie.

"At least," she said, blinking away shadows. "I am not afraid to die."

That, he believed. Most of his life, he'd carried that strange sensation within himself, unable to fully grasp what made others so determined to live, so heroically stubborn to fight. His lack of fear gave him the advantage over everyone else. He played with their lives, without the annoying concern for his own. He had never understood, even in a small way, what gave someone, anyone, a reason to live.

Until her.

It infuriated him.

"You have some deciding to do," she said. "In the meantime, I am going home."

She peeled upward, circled round, and barrel-rolled toward the trees. Then she flattened out, and flew toward the moon.

§

Jia Greenscale trembled. From her nose to her tail tip, she shook with such tremor she missed her landing. She flew toward the gaping mouth of her Esra home-away-from-home, a circle of enormous boulders she'd covered over with thatch. The closest thing to a cave this side of the desert sandstones.

But she misjudged, and her twitching legs scraped earth, and then collapsed. She tumbled, and rolled, and, finally came to a heap against one boulder.

She knew she should feel pain, but all she could feel was her trembling, her heartache, and the tears turned muddy on her face.

What was she doing? What made her ever think she could play a game in which she didn't know the rules, and had to compete with a dragon like Fane Whitetail, who invented them? She was no political cut-throat, no seductress.

She was just a lovesick dragon whose grief made her vow to herself that one day he would pay. Fane Whitetail would pay.

But she couldn't even do that right.

She struggled to her feet, so overwhelmingly tired from it all she could barely stand. From the fight to hide her memories from him, from the disappointment in finding the creature has no heart to break. She did manage to drag a threat from him. To throw her over a cliff. She'd touched a nerve somewhere.

Not enough. She wanted him to love, and to lose, and then, to die.

But he would never love her. Never want her. He

wasn't capable of that sort of thing.

He was a monster.

Is this what she left her home for? Turned her back on her tribe, and her Leland dragonkind and betrayed them all to fight on Blackclaw's brutal side? As far as they knew, she was a traitor. She had little hope of ever returning to Leland as anything but a pariah, and, when she left, she thought the sacrifice would be worth it. But not now. Not if it came to nothing.

A drop of something tapped her on the forehead, and she looked up to find a blotch of a raincloud pass across the stars. Another drop, and then another. The sky gently showered her, washed the muddy tears from her face.

And then she heard a squeak, from inside her makeshift cave. She trudged into the boulder circle, sniffing.

Her pigeon! It sat against a stone in the dark, and she wondered if it had been watching her the whole time, by the way it lifted its chin and stared down its beak. "I thought I had lost you, little one," she said.

The crystal around its neck burst into brilliant, scarlet light.

Someone had answered her message!

She scuffled closer, and settled onto her belly, inches from the bird. "Open."

And then she reached for the crystal locket, and dug out a piece of parchment with her claw. She unrolled it, her heart thumping in her chest.

She scanned her own message.

I am a stranger here. I am afraid of what I must do. I need someone to know I am not what they think. I need a friend.

Below her message, scrawled like fledgling script, and hard to read, was the reply.

You are not alone.

She hugged the parchment to her chest, and quietly cried.

CHAPTER FIFTEEN

Sela felt as though she was being called into her father's quarters for a scolding every time the dragon council collected for another discussion. There had many meetings in recent days. More than she could ever remember. She wasn't overhearing them the way she used to, hunched in a shadow, or behind a shrub. She'd been in the room, face to face with the council, the way she'd always dreamed it could one day be.

But she still felt as though she was eavesdropping. When she did speak, she was barely acknowledged. When she didn't speak, she was outright ignored. As the days passed, and the council talked circles around decisions without actually making any, Sela began to see her hope for mighty action unravel like a yarn from an old, knitted cap.

And she was still trapped as a human. All she wanted was to be herself, her whole self, as a part of these mountains, and the magic, and her dragonkind. Here, with everything she'd been dreaming of her whole adolescence laid out at her feet, where she should be able to easily reach down, think large, brave, dragon thoughts, and be free to fly.

But she couldn't. She'd strained. She'd soothed herself, screamed at herself. She'd tried everything she could think of to get back to that place of fearlessness. But for days, since her change for Bannon, she remained human. Hopelessly, perplexingly human.

How was this happening all over again?

She'd worked hard to keep anyone from sensing her frustration, but her father knew. She could hardly bring herself to look at him. And now, the dragon council collected in the Great Hall, and she would have to look them all in the eyes and hope against hope they believed she was human by choice.

Because how could she explain it otherwise?

She took a place between her mother and father, and they all watched as the council members filtered in. No Bannon, or Gladdis. No Avara or the venur. No Layce. The only other human, besides herself, was Orman, who stood at the end of the long table and impatiently tapped his toes.

Expressions were as solemn as Sela remembered them being.

"We are here to discuss what we will do with the scroll information uncovered by the wizards," said her father. "They believe the land itself is in danger, and a rift in her magic could drain our ability to defend her, and ourselves, if we do not address it."

Brownwing and Orangepaw exchanged a glance.

Yellowfang shifted on her feet.

"We do not disagree with the assessment," said Yellowfang. "But we are concerned that dealing with two issues at the same time could split our focus and our already small numbers."

"Three issues," Orman said, sticking three fingers in the air.

"Three?" asked Brownwing.

"The war, the land, and the hero."

Brownwing squinted up his eyes. "Are we considering pursuing that particular course?" He turned to Yellowfang, who looked between Brownwing and Orangepaw.

"We should at least talk about it," said Orangepaw.

Just what they needed. More talking. Time was slipping away from them, and danger lurked closer by the minute. Sela closed her eyes, and fought against the urge to scream some sense into them.

But then her father spoke. "Venur Ebouard Riddess has bonded in service to us, and believes a human and dragon together will make a large impact as we strive to assemble support against Blackclaw. He has offered to cross the sea with any dragon willing to travel."

"Leave Leland?" asked Brownwing. He shrank back, his eyes wide, as though he'd been slapped.

"Do you really think it would make any difference?" asked Yellowfang. "Leave or stay, human or dragon. We're alone in this fight, Kallon. Others have always wanted what we have in these mountains; magic, or crystals. Peace of mind. We can fight this battle now, but another will rise up to take its place."

Was Sela hearing things right? Is this what the council had come to? She looked at her mother, who hung her head, and closed her eyes.

"I will go," said Orangepaw. "I will join the venur."

Sela's eyes filled with moisture. She mouthed 'thank you'.

"Foolishness," said Brownwing. He moved off and around the great table, and then loped into the darkness of the hallway. Orman watched him go, his eyes narrowed.

Yellowfang shook her head at Orangepaw, and then turned around to exit through the archway. Greenscale hadn't even bothered to show up. So with that, the council meeting was over, as far as Sela could tell.

Now she verbalized her thanks to Orangepaw. She hurried to the dragon, and hugged her arms around her neck. "Thank you, Lin," said Sela. "I don't know what's wrong with the others, but I'm so grateful for you."

"Don't be too harsh on them," said her father. "I know how they feel. They're tired, and growing hollow inside. They're feeling—I'm feeling—as though the world is full of enemies, and in order to survive them, we must conserve our strength."

"It's the magic," said Orman, crossing his arms. "The lack of it. As it dies, all creatures made of magic are fading, too."

"Fading?" asked Sela, alarmed. She looked from Orangepaw, to her mother. To her father. "What do you mean, fading?"

"Just like I say it," said Orman. "Like a whitewashed fence, bleached by the sun. Fading, confound it all. It's happening all around us."

Sela stroked her hand over Orangepaw's neck. "But Lin isn't fading. She's as brave as always."

"I feel it," said Orangepaw. She closed her eyes. "I know exactly what Orman is talking about. I just…" She opened her eyes again. "I just can't bring myself to let it take over."

Just then, hushed talking broke through the sound in the room, from near the wide manor entrance. Everyone turned toward the sound, and Orman rose up on tiptoes to see the disruption.

Drell and Bannon stepped together through the entrance. "Forgive me," said Drell. "But it seemed as though the meeting was over."

"It is, for the most part. Come in, young Blackwing," said Sela's father.

Drell's brows shot up, and a faint smile broke out across his face. Sela looked at her father, but she wasn't sure if he even realized he'd just given Drell a tribe name.

Drell seemed to be wondering the same thing, by his hesitation. He glanced at Bannon, who smiled, and then at Sela. She smiled, too.

Drell cleared his throat. "Bannon and I were just hearing you describe what's happening to the mountains. The fading of the magic."

"It's the same thing that's been happening to the forest," said Bannon. "My people have been tired, and too easily defeated. As though the forest can't sustain us, and itself, too."

"We can't hope to defeat Blackclaw, and fend off the fading, too, Kallon," said Orman. "We have to deal with what's in front of us. Now. Not talk, not discuss, not debate. Deal."

"I agree, Father," said Sela. "If we wait for the council to decide what to do, they'll never decide."

"It's not how it works," said Sela's father. "I can't just go on without their input."

"Yes, you can," said Sela's mother. "It's called being a leader."

"A leader of what?" asked Sela's father. "A non-existent army to go after Blackclaw? A scraggly crew to drum up a hero with a boundary key? Or am I supposed to lead a contingent to heal the land, and heal the rift?" He pressed his crimson paws to his eyes. "I can only plan one thing at a time," said Sela's father, shaking his head.

Sela's mother tried to pry his digits from his face. "I think we shouldn't wait for one thing at a time," she said.

"I can't think, Riza," said her father. "I'm so tired, I can't even think."

Sela's mother gripped his paws, and tugged them from his eyes. "Look at me, Kallon Redheart."

He met her emerald gaze with his weak, brown eyes.

"You're in there, and I know it," she said. "Now wake up. You want to fly."

Sela's father blinked slowly. He drew in a sudden breath, as though remembering a bright dream. And then his foggy gaze cleared, and he smiled.

And inside Sela, something gave way. She felt it like tears from her heart, salty and cool. Realization. Whether she wanted it or not, her world was changing. No matter how hard she fought to keep things the same, no matter how she tried to recreate the safe embrace of the mountains she'd been denied as a youngling, that time had come and gone, and there would be no reliving it.

Holding on to *then* would only keep her from being a part of her *now*. And this was where she was needed. Now.

"I'll go," Sela blurted. "I'll go to Murk Forest."

Bannon came to her side, and took her hand. "You're sure?"

She was sure. She didn't know what she was supposed to do once she got there, but she would go. She wouldn't let her mountains, her friends, and her family fade away without fighting it to her last breath. She tightened her grip around Bannon's hand, and nodded. "I'm sure."

"Then so will I," said her mother.

"But Riza," said Sela's father. "I need you here."

"To do what?" asked Sela's mother. "I want to fight, too, but I'm no soldier. If my daughter will brave the forest to see if she can heal it, I can at least go with her."

"I'll go to Esra. To the desert," said Drell. "I'll find the well, and... then I don't know what. But I'll go. I'll find it."

"Not alone, surely," said Sela's father.

"My tribe will help," said Drell. "They will want to

do what they can, as well."

"But into Esra. Into Blackclaw's—"

"He won't be alone," said Layce's voice from the archway. She stepped into the Great Hall, her blue skirt shimmering from torchflame. She swept her scarf around her shoulders, and gazed down her nose at the room with all the steadfast determination of a venerated ruler. "I know Esra's secrets more than anyone," she said. "I will go with Drell Blackwing."

"Done," said Orman. He clapped his hands together, and rubbed. "Well, then. That's settled, and it's about time, too."

"Yes," said Sela's father. "It's settled." But he looked at Sela with sad eyes, and she felt the words he couldn't say. He didn't want her to go.

Orman took Sela's hands, breaking her eye contact with her father. "I wish to high heaven I could go with you. To see inside the forest? Ah, the studies I could conduct there." Then he sighed, but cut it mid-breath. "But an old barnacle like me has important matters to attend to here. To start, I've got to collect some crystals to send with you. All of you."

He turned. "Where's that friend of yours? That girl from Cresvell."

"Gladdis?" asked Sela.

"Someone find her. She's going to help me. Has anyone explained magic to her yet?"

"I've taught her dragonscript," said Drell.

"Is that so?" Orman curled his face into a frown, but it was just the way his wrinkles naturally pulled whenever he got thoughtful. Sela could tell he was impressed.

Gladdis appeared near the hallway leading to the back rooms. Beside her stood Avara and Ebouard. "Someone asked for me?" she called.

Orman hobbled toward Gladdis. She startled, and looked as though she was considering a retreat. Orman just took Gladdis's arm and drew her across the Great Hall, toward outside. "Tell me again how you got mixed up in all this. And how your dragonscript lessons are going. And what you understand about magic."

Sela leaned out to whisper into Gladdis's ear as she passed. "Don't worry. He likes you."

"How can you tell?" Gladdis whispered back, but before Sela could answer, Orman had dragged the girl halfway out the door.

With Orman, there was really no clear answer for that, anyway.

§

Jia rested her chin on the ground of her makeshift cave, and considered what to do next. She debated going back to Leland, but couldn't bring herself to admit she'd failed. Not yet. And she didn't know how she could be of any help there, anyway.

If Whitetail wasn't interested, at least Blackclaw was. And she knew the Black's plans for the next few days, as well as far into the future. Blackclaw proved easier to get him to confide in her, and she could, at the least, get that news to Leland, and the dragons.

No, she would stay, for now. For the sake of her tribe, and for the sake of her friend at the other end of their pigeon conversation. The one who sounded as lonely as Jia felt, and helped Jia remember her bravery.

She looked at her pigeon, then. And the pigeon looked back. Then Jia took out a pot of ink from a short table, and a scrap of parchment, and scrawled a new message with her claw.

You can trust me. Fordon Blackclaw will move soon on Leland. Will post again with details.

She rolled the paper, pushed it into the pigeon's crystal, and said, "Close".

Then she carried the pigeon out into the daylight, and held it toward the clouds. "You remember what to do." She released it.

She watched it fly, like a stretch of smoke, up and away, and into the horizon.

"I was hoping to find you at the end of this scent," said Fane's voice, behind her.

She curled around, her breath caught in her throat. "You what?"

His gaze was on the sky, and his brows were clenched. "What were you staring at so intently?"

"A bird," she said. "I was watching it fly." Then she faced him fully, and breathed slowly to even out her pulse. "What are you doing? I didn't even hear you approach."

"I have been on the other side of those dunes, just there." He pointed behind himself. "Debating if I should keep tracking you."

"Apparently you decided."

"May we speak?"

He seemed different, a little. She tried to find in him what was making her think it; his small, pale eyes in his colorless face seemed as empty as ever. His snout, too slender for her tastes, breathed silently, without the slightest hint of warmth. His mind was pinched closed. She almost turned her back on him, almost said no. But she nodded, instead.

He released a held breath. She finally realized what seemed different about him. He was nervous.

"You said some things," he began.

"I meant every word."

"I know." He poked his claw into a patch of reedy grass. He looked younger then. More petite, even. For a dragon so accustomed to cowering before Blackclaw, he didn't wear the posture well now.

He raised his head. "I am not going to pretend to understand what is happening here, between us. This is not the sort of situation I usually find myself in."

Amusement made her smile, but not in a happy way. "Situation? That is the best you can do?"

"You are angry. I understand that. But I am trying to say something, and mocking me is not helping."

She pulled back a step, putting space between them. She collected her thoughts, and feelings, and settled them back into the shadows. He was right. Leaking contempt wouldn't help anything. "Forgive me," she managed to say honestly. It was her best approach, after all. She'd worked her words with care, in order to always be honest, and let him read into it what he wanted to see.

"I am who I am, Jia," he said. "Who I have always been. You say you know what I am capable of, but perhaps you are unaware of things I cannot do."

"You mean, how you cannot trust someone else? Or care about them?"

He pressed his scaled lips into a downward curve, and his eyes narrowed. "Then you do see."

Now she arched her neck to gaze at the ground. She'd already realized her attempt to befriend him had come to nothing. This phase of her plan was at an end, but she would wrangle what she could from whatever she had left. "I see you, Fane."

Then he laid his paw over her digits. She lifted her head to find him staring at her, his eyes sharp and filled in with gray thunderclouds. "But I can tell you something I have never said to another being, ever."

She couldn't stop staring at his eyes.

His mouth opened, but he hesitated. She saw him swallow hard. Then, "I would like your help."

She blinked. Then she smiled.

"You mock me again," he said quietly.

"No." She stroked her claws across his paw, and shook her head. "Believe me, I do not. I am surprised, but pleased. Really, Fane."

His anemic tongue passed over his lips, and he swallowed again. "I should not have taken you to the crevice," he said.

This time, she wasn't merely surprised, she was shocked. Was he apologizing?

He regarded their touching paws. His mouth kept working, as though he was still trying to speak, but couldn't. Then he leaned toward her, and pressed his face to the side of her neck. "I will never again make you feel as though you are in danger from me," he whispered.

She was glad he couldn't see her expression, because she wasn't sure what she displayed, just then. Alarm, at his sudden closeness; disbelief, that he was reaching out; or revulsion at his dismal attempt at a romantic confession. Probably, all three.

He lingered against her, so she wrapped her forelegs around the base of his neck to keep his eyes away from her while she struggled to find a place to respond from. In the end, she chose pity. Because this was Fane Whitetail, a dragon made of emptiness, and what he'd just said likely was his highest form of promise. In his way, it really was romantic.

And pity was her most honest form of promise back.

"Thank you, Fane," she said. She meant it.

"Then you will help me?" he asked.

She broke their embrace, and set her forepaws onto the cool ground. "Maybe you should tell me your plans."

The gray in his eyes churned, and faded into a pale glint. "I want to take down Blackclaw."

She smiled. "No more puppet? Of course I will help you."

"More than that, I want to take out Redheart and the Dragon Council. I want the mountains, and the lands at her feet."

Now Jia swallowed hard. "That is a tall order."

"Is it too much for you, then?" he asked.

"That may be too much for anyone," she said. "But tell me what you have in mind."

Fane sat back, and withdrew a folded parchment from beneath his scales under his left foreleg. "I received a letter from Leland. From Shornmar Castle, regarding the land-bride agreement. The agreement is invalid, now that Vorham Riddess is dead, and dragons occupy Esra." He tapped the letter against his palm. "I carried it to Blackclaw, with his breakfast, and meant to give it to him, of course. But then he looked at me in that way he does, and I heard his thoughts about how sniveling he thinks I am, and then he..."

Jia tipped her head. "He what?"

Fane's tongue ran along the edges of his teeth. "Well. He claimed you for himself."

Jia snorted. "That is never going to happen."

"I know," he said. "I knew it then, and wanted so much to rub it in his face. To show his fat ego he does not get everything he wants, just because he claims it. I wanted to show him everything he has gotten until now has been because of me, doing those things he is too cowardly to do for himself." He looked down at the letter. "Suddenly everything you had been telling me made sense. So I kept the letter."

"What do you intend to do with it?"

"I did not know then, but I know now." Fane offered the parchment, and Jia took it, and unfolded it to read. "Lestir Grimmin is acting lord of Shornmar Castle. He is trying to appeal to Blackclaw's reasonable side, but you and I both know he has none."

"Agreed," said Jia.

"But I do. And I see that if I am to be the leader I am meant to be, I will need to use humans and dragons both toward my goal." He shifted his weight. "That is one thing Blackclaw has never been able to grasp."

"How to use humans, you mean?"

Fane nodded slowly. "They are a part of the way this world works. Humans and dragons have no choice but to move toward each other."

Jia read through Lord Grimmin's letter, and then lowered it. "So what do you want me to do?"

"Meet with him. He will think you represent Blackclaw, and we will let that happen, for now. Find out what he wants, and do not remark whether or not it is possible. Just bring the information to me."

"Sounds simple enough," said Jia.

"Yes, this is the easy part," said Fane. He laid his paw on her shoulder, and lowered his chin. "What comes after, that will get difficult."

Jia met his gaze. "Yes," she said. "It really will."

Chapter Sixteen

Jastin sucked air through his teeth. Leesa was changing the dressing on his leg, and every time she poured fresh pithberry juice on the wound, it sizzled and stung. He wondered if that stuff always hurt, injured or not, because he'd thought his leg had been improving. He'd been standing on it. Moving better.

He was just about to ask, when so many footsteps erupted into noise around them, he felt the pounding vibrations as an earthquake. People shouted, excited. He heard the zip-scuffle of braided vines being unfurled, and ridden upward.

"What's going on?" He shifted to stand, but Leesa's firm hands held him down.

She finished tying off a clean bandage, and then sat back. She listened to the activity all around them, and then rose, and hurried to the doorway.

Farin darted past, and she reached out to clutch at his shoulder. He looked back, but he just pointed up.

Jastin managed to get to his feet by bracing on the

woven wall, and he limped to the door. "What's going on?" he asked again.

People swarmed from huts like flies. Hands reached out to ropes, and feet stepped onto holds, and then were pulled higher into the treetops, disappearing, as though the trees were shooting down green tongues and swallowing the people-flies.

A vine rope slapped to the platform outside Leesa's hut. She tugged Jastin toward it, and then knelt. She wrapped the rope around the arch of the foot of his good leg, and then once around his waist, and tied it off. Then, above his head, she gave the rope a double yank.

"Where am I—"

Before he could finish the sentence, he was airborne. He startled, and flopped off balance, but the rope around his waist bound him firmly. Then he was in the fronds of the upper tree heights, and hands found him, and helped him find footing on a mass of branches so tangled together, it made for a sturdy landing. He spotted Farin among the thirty or so others that had taken up similar perches, all staring up through the sparse foliage into the sky.

He hopped slightly to find balance. More hands untangled his ropes. Within minutes, Leesa was beside him, stepping out of thin air onto their makeshift platform. She smiled at him, and slid her arm around his waist.

"They sounded the horn," called a voice across the trees. He recognized it. Jade.

"What horn?" Jastin asked. "Who did?"

Leesa pointed up.

Jastin tipped back his head, and finally saw what had caused the commotion.

A dragon passed over the treetops. A pale brown one, and young, by the size of it. It passed so low over the trees that as the high sunlight turned its wings to parchment, Jastin could see through to its thick, dark veins.

But why did one dragon make such an impression?

Leesa nudged him, and pointed west, toward the Leland Mountains. He parted some scratchy leaves to get a better look.

There were more. Several more. Too distant for Jastin to really see much, but sunlight glinted off a serpentine form that banked, or caught the edge of a flickering wing, or sent a dragon-shaped shadow down across lumpy earth.

"I still don't get it," he said.

"They've been called," said Jade, from somewhere through the trees he couldn't see. "On the ancient horn."

The branches rattled, and parted, just to his right, and Jade's face peeked through. "To battle."

"Battle?" He looked again toward the mountains. He knew, then, that Leland was gearing up to fight against Blackclaw and his greedy clutch for more power. What else could it be?

But he also realized, from what he could see from this distance, the gathering of Leland dragons didn't seem to be enough numbers. Not the kind he'd expect for a war.

"The forest has no dragons to send. We haven't had dragons here in a long time," said Jade.

Then Leesa gasped. Jastin, and Jade, and Farin, and several others all turned simultaneously. She blinked, seeming slightly dazed, and Jastin held her against him in case she was feeling faint, or something. Then she smiled.

She looked up at Jastin. And then to Jade.

Jade grinned, too. "It's Bannon," she said. "He's coming."

A shudder passed through the trees. At first, Jastin thought it was the movement of the Murkens, beginning their descent to the hut levels. But no. Each of them was still, and noiseless. Stunned.

Farin spoke. "He's bringing someone he believes is the one."

"What one?"

"To heal the forest," said Jade. "The one."

"And they're not alone," said Farin.

Jastin didn't quite grasp what was happening. The trees did, though. Jastin would have sworn on his life in that moment, those trees knew who and what was coming, and were excited.

Excited.

CHAPTER SEVENTEEN

The gathering had begun. Ebouard Riddess and Lin Orangepaw had been sending out the word, calling dragons to Leland, and they were responding.

Sela gripped her legs around her mother's strong neck, and watched, amazed, as colorful dragons from many directions appeared on the horizon. A part of her felt guilty for not staying here to join and support them. She wondered if she would be seen as abandoning them at this crucial time.

"What we hope to achieve will strengthen them," said her mother, the wind thinning her voice.

"It will work," said Bannon, into Sela's ear. He sat behind her, his arms around her waist. "I believe in you."

They flew together across the mountains, over the gray and brown fists of stone, the patches of pine scrub that had burned long ago and been reborn. She expected to feel a tug of loneliness as they passed over the last of the peaks and found themselves above the vanishing foothills and rubble. But she didn't. Somehow, as they neared Murk Forest, she felt a compulsion to go faster, to reach it sooner.

She felt magic. Weak magic, from desperate trees, that reached toward her as though she were a drink of water, and they were dying of thirst.

"They won't hurt you," said Bannon, as though he sensed her alarm. But his tone was hesitant. He wasn't really sure.

Her mother slowed just at the leafy rim. She hovered. Sela knew her mother remembered the stories, too, told to her as a child, passed on from the generation before her.

But Bannon was alive and strong behind Sela, and proof that the forest could make friends. She laid her hand on her mother's spiraled horns.

Her mother flew on. Over the bulky forest, matted together into a green carpet. Too quiet for a wood that should be filled with animal life and Bannon's people. Too angry for a land that seemed to want Sela so badly.

Bannon moved his hand from her waist, to her thigh. She rested her fingers on his.

"Where to go?" her mother called. "Where to land?"

"We'll have to land in the open and walk in," said Bannon. "The canopy has been woven closed for—"

A breaking sound burst toward them, rocking her mother back. Sela slapped her hands over her ears. The sound echoed against the nearest mountains and ricocheted. Then the sound of tearing, ripping. Leaves shot upward, outward, and cascaded as the trees peeled open from branches to ground, and invited them in.

Her mother glided into the opening.

Branches scraped over her mother's scales and against Sela's legs. Green leaves caught in the crooks of her arms, and in her hair. When they all landed gently onto solid ground, Sela looked up to find the canopy closed back over them.

"That was amazing," whispered Bannon.

"Where are we?" asked her mother.

Sela saw only gray-trunked trees behind them, and around them, to their left and to their right. So unlike the elm and ash trees of the mountains. These trees had the scent of earth and moss, as though they weren't growth planted into the ground, but emerging from it; appendages reaching up as the soil's arms.

Peering ahead, Sela thought she could see what might be a sort of clearing, just beyond a sparse patch of gray trunks. "Can you fit between those trees, Mother?" she asked.

"That's us," said Bannon. "Where the forest growth is held back by our enchantments. We live there, above, in the treetops."

"I suppose we should introduce ourselves," said her mother. She loped forward, with her wings awkwardly held at her sides so as not to smother Sela and Bannon. Sela held the edge of either wing to help them from becoming tired.

Behind her, Bannon did the same.

Her mother eased her head into the clearing, and then pushed one shoulder, and then the other, wedging through. Sela wobbled, and yanked up her legs instinctively. But then they were into the open, so to speak. The canopy above was as thick and impassable as ever, but there was a wide, comfortable expanse of openness at ground level.

Sela slid from her mother's back, onto her knee, and then dropped both feet to the earth.

"What do we do now?" she asked Bannon.

Rustling sounds. Just ahead of them, vines flopped down from branches. No, not just vines, but thick strands of growth plaited into a kind of rope. Then more leaves began to drop.

But not just leaves. People. They lowered slowly, and although Sela thought at first they were wrapped in vegetation, she realized they were wearing what looked like twisted fabric around their waists, their hips and thighs, and up around their chests, and they had braided leaves and sticks into their coverings, too.

Two men touched ground first. Their skin was sun-darkened, with yellow undertone. One wore a long ponytail at the base of his head, and the other, shaved bald except for one swoosh of dark hair from forehead to crown.

Bannon slid to the ground behind her, and took her hand. "Brothers," he said, and led her toward them.

Both men broke into wide smiles. "Bannon!"

They embraced, and beamed.

More people touched ground. Women, wearing carved beads around their necks or wrists. Other men, in only a loin covering.

And, also, colorful birds, shaped like eagles, but smaller, with scarlet or lime green crests and vivid blue breasts and wings, landed onto people's shoulders. Emerging from around some of the sparse trees in the clearing were smooth-coated felines, who twitched their whiskers and sat, watching every movement.

As Bannon reunited with his tribe, Sela spotted another person descending into the growing crowd. A woman wearing woven wrappings, like the others, with a painted handprint on her collarbone.

"Leesa!" Sela called.

Leesa smiled, and dashed toward her. They hugged.

"I didn't know you were a Murken!" Sela said, and then realized she sounded stupid. Of course she didn't know.

Leesa didn't seem to notice, though. She just hugged Bannon, and grinned like the others. Then Leesa hurried back to where she'd touched down, and looked up.

Another man lowered from a vine, with some twigs and bark haphazardly tucked here and there into his wrappings. He wore a handprint, like Leesa. A tight binding wrapped his left thigh. He was scruffy and bearded, and familiar.

"Jastin Armitage?"

"Jastin?" said her mother, behind her. "Jastin Armitage? Here?"

Sela turned, and felt a current of air as others did, too. Jastin met her mother's eyes. His throat worked to swallow. And then to speak.

"Riza?" he asked.

Her mother's face went hard. Her eyes sharpened.

Jastin stood, transfixed, for several moments. Then he eased one limping step toward her.

"I wouldn't have come if I'd known," said Sela's mother. "If this is some sort of trick—"

"It's no trick," said Jastin. "I'm only here as a guest, like you. I was wounded, they've helped me."

"More than you deserve," she said.

Sela felt her mother's anger roil toward them all, as steamy and profound as if she'd breathed a wall of flame.

"Yes," Jastin said simply.

A long silence simmered in the heated air.

"It pains you to look at me now," her mother finally said.

"Yes," Jastin replied. "But not in the way you think."

Sela had heard little about Jastin Armitage through the years, except how he had slaughtered innocent dragons, and had betrayed her mother and father both to Blackclaw's brewing war, even back then. Now, looking between them; at her mother's rage-chiseled face, and Jastin's stricken gaze, she knew there was a whole lot more to the story her parents had never shared.

Leesa came forward, watching Sela's mother, and took Jastin's hand.

If Sela's mother noticed, she didn't betray it.

More branch rustling filled the tense atmosphere. Sela heard someone lowering from the treetops behind her, and was about to turn, when she saw her mother's face wrench in confusion. Her mother's eyes followed the descent of the newcomer. She sniffed the air.

And then her face slackened in disbelief. Her green eyes blinked. Filled with moisture.

Sela whirled to see who was causing her mother so much distress, but she found only an old woman, with greenery wrapped into a sort of tunic dress. Her graying hair was bound up into tiny braids, decorated by sprays of berries. The woman stood strong and unintimidated by the new guests. She took a step toward Sela's mother.

Sela's mother recoiled.

Bannon stepped between them, and extended his arm toward the woman. "Our Shepherdess," he explained. "She comes to welcome you."

"I can speak for myself, Bannon," the woman said. She straightened her shoulders, and looked Sela's mother in the face. "I am Jade of the Murkens," she said. "I know why you've come, and I welcome you. All of you."

Sela watched her mother's jaw work. A gust of heat escaped between her ruby lips and steamed away a leaked tear. Finally, her voice came through, weakly. Pained, as though she was speaking around sand in her throat. "Mother?"

The shepherdess drew back.

"Jade Diantus?" asked Sela's mother.

The shepherdess Jade stared up at her anguished mother. "Who are you?"

Sela's mother lowered her head to Jade's level to meet her face. "I'm Riza. I know it's hard to believe, but I really am. I'm Riza."

Jade regarded Sela's mother suspiciously.

"It's true," said Sela.

Jade turned to look at Sela. "And who are you, then?"

Now Sela struggled to speak. "I... Sela Redheart."

"She's my daughter," said Sela's mother. "My daughter."

Jade gripped Sela's chin, and turned her face this way and that. She stared into her eyes. Then she turned back to Sela's mother, to stare into her eyes as well. She took in a breath. "Riza?"

Sela finally realized what she'd been examining so closely. Their green eyes.

Jade touched a hand to dragon cheek. "How is this possible?"

"How is it possible you're alive?" asked Sela's mother.

"Then he told you I died," said the shepherdess. She lowered her hand. "That would be the easy answer. We each have a lot of explaining to do... Will you start? Tell me how my only child is this magnificent dragon I see?"

Sela could hardly make the connection feel real. Her mother, a daughter. Sela, a granddaughter. A granddaughter of a Murken.

She looked suddenly at Bannon, who was smiling. He took her hand. "I told you. You are one of us."

§

Whatever welcoming ceremony had been planned turned into a family reunion. A fire pit was dug, and a small campfire started. Pots of fig stew were set around the flame, and dried passionfruit and peanuts set out by the bowlfuls. Clay flasks of fermented rumberry, a bitter, orange concoction, were passed hand to hand.

Jastin wished he could tolerate the stuff. He'd have liked to have gotten stinking drunk.

He just nibbled on peanuts. He watched the women over the low flames; or, rather, two women and a dragon, as they cried, and laughed, and touched hands and paw. As though they were old friends, not strangers. He especially watched Riza, and the joy in her eyes he couldn't comprehend. She should be angry. Offended, at least. The mother she thought was dead was alive and well! She'd abandoned Riza as a child, is all. Oh, now that it's all settled, let's have tea.

Riza. Riza Diantus. Riza Redheart. The creature whose skin turned dazzling by the campfire. Who once reminded him of a little mouse, now all grown into her teeth and claws, and gazing at Jade as though all was right with the world.

"I tried so hard in Cresvell," said Jade. Her wrinkled hands clasped a rumberry juice flagon. "I didn't even mean to get married, if you want to know. But the Leland out there isn't like the one in here. I didn't know what I was getting into when I left."

"Why did you leave?" asked Sela, who regarded Jade with some apprehension. At least that girl had sense enough to suspect a confidence scam.

"The same reason we all do, at one time or another. For the sake of the forest." Jade sipped, and a dribble of juice collected at the corner of her mouth. "Even then the forest was ill. We've been looking for help for a long, long time." She swiped her hand across her lips.

"And now you've found it," said Riza.

"You could have brought her with you," said Sela.

Jade stared down into her flagon. "It was a long journey. She was a child."

"Your child," said Sela.

"Sela..." Riza warned.

"I couldn't take care of her," said Jade. "I snapped. It was as if... after all those years of never shifting—never!" She looked up to Riza, and rested her hand on Riza's paw. "I never shifted, at all. I didn't want anyone to suspect, for your sake."

"I understand," said Riza.

"Well, I don't," said Sela.

"A bunch of superstitious old farmers," said Jade. "With wives whose tongues would waggle at the slightest thing. And I had this wildness inside me. All the time. It *is* me; the forest, the magic, everything."

"I always felt it, too," said Riza. She turned to Sela, and stroked a strand of Sela's hair between her claws. "I understood it in Sela, because I'd always had it in me, too."

"Well, and then, one day, I just couldn't control it anymore." Jade sucked down another deep pull from the flagon. "I didn't want to."

"I understand," said Riza. "It's what made *me* leave, so how can I be angry?"

Jastin couldn't stand to hear anymore. He pushed to

his feet, glaring at them all. He threw his last handful of peanuts into the fire, scattering embers.

Riza's sinewy neck curled back, and she glared at him. Eyes of lead.

Jastin stomped out of the ring of campfire light. Only when he reached the edge of darkness did he realize he was limping, and the pain in his leg had turned hot.

"What was that about?" Sela asked behind him.

"Let him go," he heard Riza say. "No one wants him here anyway."

He was just lumbering toward the edge of the clearing, when a hand touched his spine. He whirled, arm pulled back to slug whoever it was.

Leesa. She regarded his cocked arm, scowling.

He didn't hit her. But he did grab her arms. "You heard her. No one wants me here."

Leesa winced in pain, but it only enraged him. "You see why, don't you? You see me now, for who I am?"

He threw her toward a gray, bare tree trunk. She thumped hollowly, and slid down to a crouch at the roots, glaring up at him.

"So much forgiveness going on around here," he said, the words tearing through his teeth like a snarl. "But none for me. None. You know why?"

Leesa slowly stood from her crouch.

"My crimes don't get forgiven. I'm not the kind of man who deserves it."

She eased toward him, touched her hands to his chest. But he didn't want her tenderness. He didn't want her to make him feel better. He pushed at her hands.

She stepped closer, defiantly. Clenched her hands. And then she reached up, just beneath his throat, and freed the gold dragon scale from beneath the coiled fabric he wore; the pale, twisted sheet of a garment these people called clothing.

It caught just enough distant campfire light to glow like a fallen star in her hand.

He almost hated that scale right now.

Then she kissed him. He hadn't seen it coming, and when her mouth landed on his, he at first startled as though she was punching him. It almost felt like one, the way it hit him, hard and tight against his lips like a fist.

He responded just as angrily. He pushed forward to press her against the gray tree, forced her hands against her sides. He only broke the kiss when he tasted blood. He leaned back just enough to see a dark bead form on her bottom lip.

Then, footsteps.

"Everything under control here?" asked a man's voice. Jastin recognized it as Bannon's, the one who arrived with Riza. The one he remembered from Esra, and Riddess castle.

Jastin did have to breathe in and out, in and out, in long, conscious rhythm in order to answer, "Under control."

He pushed off of Leesa, and turned away. Then he limped back toward the campfire, and past it. He heard snippets of conversation. Riza and Jade were discussing the dying forest, the prophetic drawings inside swamp caves near the stream. He didn't listen in. He didn't care.

He just grabbed a dangling rope, gave it a tug, and let himself be pulled up into the trees.

CHAPTER EIGHTEEN

Drell stood outside the carved arena on Mount Gore, where eons of dragons had gathered for meetings, for celebrations, for war. His mother had always pointed it out whenever he secretly visited the mountains, but he'd never been as close to it as he'd been in these last weeks. The arena floor had long been pummeled flat by generations of dragon feet. The arena walls, slabs of mountain shale, had formed a faint inward lean, like flotus petals slowly closing against a morning frost. From this close distance, Drell could see the withering age of the place he hadn't been able to see from the sky; what he viewed as a sort of fortress in his flyovers now seemed as limp and frightened as the dragons who occupied it.

Because dragons had been arriving. Sparsely, since this morning, in tribe colors he never imagined could still exist. A few Yellows collected near the podium where the Dragon Council traditionally sat for meetings. A Green sat near them, and a Blue. A few Browns, a couple Grays. Most seemed older than him, with the wingspans and slack scales that come with age and great wisdom. But some seemed younger, too, with hardly the fortitude for fighting.

But, as impressive as the array of colors was, male and female, there was plenty of room in the arena for more. The motley collection was hardly a force to be reckoned with, especially by what he remembered of Blackclaw's supporters.

Behind him, his mother, Vaya, approached. "We have not fought in a long time," she said. She gazed through the arena opening at the collection of dragon supporters.

Large, battered storage trunks had been lined up against the stone podium. A Yellow opened one, and pawed through. Drell heard the clank of metal and smelled the mildew of years. The Yellow withdrew a set of steelclaws, metallic extensions, and examined it.

Others came to the trunks, then, and flipped them open. Pounded metal face plates, as much protection as they were intimidation tools, were handed out. Wing guards, fashioned to look like the Leland sigil flames tapered into a sharp points, were held toward the sunlight. So many battle items Drell had heard of, but never seen.

"Have you fought?" he asked his mother.

She shook her head. "I was too young for the Battle of the Vast Plain, when Kallon's father was Herald of the Reds."

That's when Drell realized there were no Reds in

the arena.

"The Redhearts are the last," she said. "We have lost many tribes and colors, even without war. Humans have stolen from us, hunted us. Starved us out, or driven us out. They do not need warfare as a reason to kill."

"That sounds like something my father would say," said Drell.

His mother regarded him. "Your father is an egomaniac who believes he should not be denied anything he wants. It makes him cruel, but it does not make him wrong about everything." She returned to watching the dragons handling armor. "How do you think he managed to collect so many followers?"

Drell hadn't thought about it until then.

"Not by his captivating personality," she continued. "But because dragons everywhere, here in Leland, and in Esra, and as far as Shan Province in the east, are weary of mere survival. We want the life we once had, full of rich lands and long tribe lines. We want back what has been taken from us."

"And you would eliminate humans to get it?"

She shook her head. "No. I do not believe in Fordon's methods. I think most dragons do not, but those that fight with him do believe that to go about it the wrong way is at least better than doing nothing."

"Except Blackclaw does not seem to be the sharing type, any more than humans have been."

His mother released a quiet rumble. "Yes, there is that."

"And maybe our dying lands and tribes have less to

do with human greed than they do our fading magic."

She turned slowly, and her golden eyes clouded. She blinked slowly.

"Our fading magic," said Drell. "Everyone keeps saying how our hunting grounds have been depleted, our tribal lands destroyed and over-mined. But what have we been doing all these years to stop it? To try to heal it?" Drell pointed out across the mountain, toward where the human village, Durance, would be. "We complain, and we blame. And in the meantime, our magic fades."

His mother's chest swelled, and ringlets of steam trickled between her lips. "You do not know what you are talking about. If you were a Leland dragon you would see—"

"I am a Leland dragon," said Drell. "I was born one."

"But you were not raised one," said his mother.

He lifted his chin. "That was your choice, not mine."

Her mouth steam evaporated, and she closed her eyes. "I was trying to protect you," she said.

"And you did," said Drell. "You also gave me the chance to see this land, and her dragons, from another point of view." He touched his paw to her shoulder. "I am not angry..." He drew in a breath, and calmly, deliberately, said, "...Mother."

She raised her gaze to his face. "You have a right to be."

Maybe he was, a little. Somewhere too deep for him to reach, or to express. But even if he was, it was pointless to expose it now. He tried to focus on the good that had come of it.

"I think it is because of my desert tribe that I can see Leland in a way you cannot. Her dragons are so full of resentment and bitterness. Perhaps because of the heritage of these mountains, so vibrant with the riches everyone wishes they had. Or, at least you all think everyone wants it."

His mother narrowed her eyes.

"Generations have been raised to see your mountains as something you must protect from outsiders. But what do you do from the inside? How many of you work to feed the land? To ensure its cycles, its renewals?"

His mother widened her stance. "We cannot undo what the humans have done to destroy it, Drell. And if we could, why should it be our responsibility to fix their mess?"

"Yes, why should it?" he asked.

His mother remained silent, and watched the dragons in the arena. Drell studied her profile; her taut mouth, her stiff neck. For the first time, he wondered if she had ever loved his father. Had she loved anyone? Was she even capable?

She swung her face toward him suddenly, startled. Sad. And Drell felt it, then. Of course she loved. One dragon, in particular. The only dragon she had ever loved, and still did. Kallon Redheart.

"Drell Blackwing?" asked a voice behind him.

Layce Phelcher hugged a fat carpet bag to herself as she came between him and his mother. "Are you ready?"

she asked.

The wizard had caught him off-guard. He was still reeling from his mother's emotional revelation. But he recovered, and nodded. "I'm ready," he said.

"Then let's be off," said Layce. "We've got much to conquer."

Layce scrabbled to climb onto Drell's back. Her bony elbows dug into his ribs, and her bare toes pinched his scales together. Either she was going to have to get better at this, or he was going to have to think of some other way for her to mount.

"Better with practice," said Layce. "Don't worry."

"I'll take the long way across, to the north of the desert," said Drell. "I don't think any dragon, Esra or otherwise, would venture that way. Too cut-off, and too risky near the sands."

"I've managed a spell or two for the heat," said Layce. Drell felt her cool hand pat his neck. "I'm as prepared as I can be."

With that, Drell pushed off to a launch. He pumped his wings, rising straight up, until the arena shrank beneath them, and he had a clear view across disheveled mountaintops toward the west.

His mother followed his movement, and hovered beside him. She didn't speak to say goodbye, but he felt her worry, just briefly, before she touched his foreleg, gave him an encouraging nod, and then closed off. She still regarded him, but he sensed nothing more from her. She was the gilt-edged, brown statue he recognized her to be.

"We'll stay in touch through Orman," called Layce into the air. "Everything will be fine."

His mother nodded again. Then she spun about, flew one circle around him, and bowed forward into a descent. She gracefully arced toward a soft landing, and Drell rowed his wings, flying slowly backward, while he watched her.

He understood her stoicism differently, now. Now that he realized they finally, ironically, shared something in common. They each loved a Redheart, in different ways, and for different reasons. It was a feeling that would never, could never, be returned. But every choice they'd made in their lives, from that moment until now, had been because of it.

CHAPTER NINETEEN

Lestir Grimmin looked up from his desk in his quarters. Had he just heard a shout? He rose and strode to the door, and opened it slightly. In the hallway, men's voices called to him, and called to arms.

To arms?

Lestir yanked open the door. A manservant bustled past, and Lestir clutched at his arm. "What's going on?"

The man pulled back as though Lestir might strike him. "A dragon! Spotted to the west!"

"Dragon?" Lestir gave the man a push, and sent him sprawling. "Idiots!" He ran through the hall, turned a sharp corner, and skidded, off-balance, into Marck, his messenger.

"Tell me the men aren't attacking the Esra dragon!"

Marck gripped Lestir's arms to steady him. "Your guard captain stayed them. They're armed, and alerted, though. It won't take much to set them off."

"Idiots, every one of them." Lestir yanked his arms from Marck's grasp and lunged toward the courtyard door. The stomp of his feet on the castle cobblestones rattled his jaw, and when he reached the door, he pushed it open so hard it slammed against the wall behind it. The sound ricocheted into the courtyard.

Twelve uniformed men stood with arrows raised toward the sky. Three more filtered onto the matted grass and readied their bows, until Lestir shouted at them. "Lower your weapons!"

The three nearest him exchanged glances, and hesitated.

"I said lower your weapons! All of you!" Lestir pushed through the men, crossing the open land inside the castle wall, and slapping at bows as he made his way to the front of the group. "Put them down, you imbeciles!"

He spotted Captain Rames, who had his bow at his side, but was tensed to raise it. "Rames," he called.

But the man stared, awe-struck, toward the sun.

Lestir followed his gaze, and spotted what the others were gaping at. It was a dragon, all right, swooping low over the castle wall and coming in fast. The wingspan reached nearly from tower to tower, and the mighty feet of the thing, curled up against its belly, looked as though they could hold three men each between its claws with room to spare. At first, Lestir thought it was black-scaled, but it turned its shoulders, and the sunlight glinted them emerald.

It lowered its legs, and gently landed. It filled the space from the front rank to the wall. It lowered its head, searching the crowd.

Lestir shrank back a step, and felt the tide of men behind him doing the same.

"I am here to speak to Lestir Grimmin," said the dragon. The voice resonated through Lestir's feet, and shuddered loose dust and pebbles from cracks in the castle wall. "You do not need your weapons."

"Lower your weapons," Lestir shouted again.

The dragon's head turned, and trained its eyes on him.

Lestir's insides shriveled.

But he straightened his shoulders. Took a single step forward.

"You are Lestir Grimmin?" asked the dragon.

"I am."

"You wish to discuss an alliance with Fordon Blackclaw, former leader of the Leland Dragon Council, and current resident of Esra's Riddess Castle?"

Lestir took another step forward. "I do."

The dragon tilted its head. "I am Jia Greenscale. I am here to suggest otherwise."

"Otherwise?" asked Lestir. He looked behind himself at his soldiers, who had finally lowered their bows and crossbows, but were as stunned and silent as before. Then he looked back to the dragon, who was studying him curiously. He supposed curiousity was better than eyeing him as lunch. "What do you mean, 'otherwise'?" he asked.

"Fordon Blackclaw is a traitor to Leland dragons," said the green dragon. "He had the Dragon Council leader murdered in order to take his place. He also had other dragons murdered in the hopes of starting a war with humans. When his plan was exposed, he fled to Esra, where he has spent the last several years campaigning for dragon supporters, and has now overthrown Riddess Castle and attacked Esra villages, bringing about the war he has been long greedy for."

Lestir glanced at his guard captain, who shrugged.

"This is the first you have heard of Blackclaw's deeds?" asked the dragon.

Lestir looked again at his captain.

"And yet you send an invitation for his visit?" asked the dragon.

Lestir bristled. "Listen, I'm just trying to—"

Movement at the back of the crowd. Murmurs. Then Lestir heard Moras's nasally voice and his clumsy steps from behind. He spun, and whispered sharply to the captain, "Don't let him through."

"I want to see the dragon!" Moras cried.

"Who is this?" asked the dragon, peering out toward the commotion.

"He's the venur. Venur Moras Shornmar, the Second," said Lestir. "But—"

"Then he has a right to be here," said the dragon.

"Yes, but..."

Moras broke through the edge of soldiers, grimacing from effort. Then, in the open space between men and dragon, he suddenly stopped. Stared. And then broke into a wide smile. "Hello."

"Hello," said the dragon.

"My name is Moras. What's yours?"

"I'm Jia."

"Jia is a pretty name. You're a girl." He inched forward, and reached his stubby fingers toward the dragon's leg.

The captain reached for his side sword, but Lestir stayed him with his hand. The dragon watched Moras openly, and without threat.

Moras patted the dragon's scaly leg. "I've never met a real dragon before."

"I've never met a real venur before."

He glanced at Lestir. "Lestir doesn't like it when people call me that."

"Oh?" The dragon's eyes glittered while they studied Lestir. He was becoming uncomfortable.

"Why are you here?" asked Moras.

"Lestir invited me," said the dragon.

"He did? Oh! Does that mean we're friends?" Moras threw his arms around the dragon's neck.

This time, she did flinch, and reared back one leg. But she smiled a large, curving sort of grin. Lestir didn't know dragons could do that. "I would like to be friends," she said.

"All right, Moras," said Lestir. He stepped in, and tugged the venur off the creature. "Stop mauling our guest."

"Guest!" Moras shot his arms into the air. "Can we have tea, Lestir? With little cakes?"

"We don't need tea," Lestir said.

But Moras charged off across the courtyard, his tunic flapping, and his eyes shining with determination.

Lestir might have taken him to task on another day, but for the sake of the moment, and the meeting, he let it go.

"He's a child," said the dragon, watching Moras hurry across the courtyard.

"A man with the mind of a child, yes," said Lestir, embarrassed by the scene, in front of his men. In front of the dragon.

"And yet he understands more about making a friend than the whole courtyard full of you," she said. Her yellow eyes swept over the men.

Lestir followed her gaze to the soldiers' weapons, held tight and tensed to raise. To their body stance, suspicious and fearful. He wondered if he looked the same.

"You do," said the dragon.

And then Lestir was embarrassed for a new reason. He cleared his throat. "Yes. Well. Shall we continue our discussion?"

The dragon lifted her chin. "I believe your venur said something about little cakes?"

Lestir blinked. And then he smiled; he made sure of it. "Of course." He turned to his captain, and snarled quietly, "Get those men out of here." And then he returned his smile to the dragon, and indicated his arm toward the castle. "Right this way."

§

The sun broke across the high canopy, spilling gold and crimson sunbeams across the carpet of foliage. Sela saw dragons in the sunrise, with the slash of the sun like a stretched wing, and tree leaves colored into glistening scales. She longed to shift, and to fly into the jeweled sky, and yet, watching Bannon as she sat with him in the upper branches of an emergent gumnut tree, she felt as alive, and human, as she'd ever felt.

He caught her looking at him, and he smiled.

She tugged at a glossy leaf as large as her hand, and then spun the stem between her fingers to give herself something else to stare at. "It's all so strange, isn't it?" she asked. "I have a grandmother. It's more family than I knew."

"Is it strange?" Bannon gripped a branch beside Sela's head and swung himself over. He crouched beside her. "To me, it seems perfectly right."

"Not just having a grandmother, though," said Sela. "I'm connected to this forest, and to your people."

"They're your people, too."

"I know, that's what I mean." She shifted, and rested her tailbone against her branch, and braced her feet in the crook where the branch met the trunk.

"All my life, while I was human, all I wanted was to be a dragon again," she said. "I just knew I'd made some kind of mistake, and I wasn't who I was supposed to be. But lately, I'm so confused. Am I dragon who turns human? Or a human who can turn into a dragon?"

"Do you really need to understand the difference?" Bannon asked.

She regarded his hazel eyes, and the bristles of sandy facial hair rimming his mouth. "Do you?" she asked.

"To me, there is no difference," he said. "You're Sela of many gifts. When you choose to fly, you do. When you choose to walk, you do that, instead. Only your form changes, not who you are inside it."

"You make it sound so simple."

"You make 'simple' sound so unpleasant."

"It's just that I need answers," she tried to explain again. "If I don't know exactly what I am, how do I know where I belong?"

He was quiet for a moment, watching her. She felt him thinking, but couldn't sense exactly what his thoughts were. Probably because he was trying to figure them out for himself. "Maybe you belong in more than one place."

"That can't be right," she said. She shook her head. "That can't be the answer."

"Why not?"

"Because if I don't belong to one special place, how will I ever know how it feels to come home?"

He took her hand, and folded her fingers over his smooth knuckles. "Maybe home isn't a place. Maybe it's the circle made by people who care about you."

Sela frowned, and opened her mouth to speak, but he held up a finger and touched it to her lips. "...but if you insist on needing a place," he said, "I can tell you somewhere you've already made a home."

"You mean the mountains?" she asked.

"No," said Bannon. He pressed her hand to his chest. "My heart."

She felt it, beating hard and fast against his ribcage. Her own heartbeat rushed in between her ears. She tried to say his name, and maybe she did, but she couldn't hear anything above the sound of her sudden feelings.

His mouth was there, against her lips. She wrapped her arms around his shoulders, and kissed him back.

Then she heard a crack. The branch beneath her jerked. Her weight tipped, and she felt gravity clutch at her back.

She only had time to yelp before Bannon's arms embraced her. They spun. She felt the brace of a soft landing, twice, before her feet hit scratchy bark again. This time, on a firm crook in a thicker part of the tree trunk.

Bannon steadied her, and then released her. His cheeks were flushed, and his breath raspy.

"Did you just reposition us? Or am I that good of a kisser?" she asked.

He smiled, despite the alarm lingering on his face. "That's not what I had in mind when I was hoping you'd fall for me."

She giggled. The sound was so light and tinny against the remnants of fear they were sharing, that it made her laugh. Which made him laugh.

The expression showed his white teeth, with one a little crooked on the top, and crinkled the bridge of his nose, and made Sela feel as though the tips of her fingers and toes were on fire.

He reached for her hand, and was about to speak, when her mother's voice called down through the treetops.

"Sela!"

"I'm here," she said, and waggled a branch.

"They're ready. Come down to the forest floor." Her mother's wings whispered a breeze through the leaves, rattling them as she moved away.

Sela was suddenly clear-headed. "I guess it's time."

Bannon squeezed her hand. "You're going to be amazing."

He found a rope she didn't know was there. Then he hugged her against himself, and they dropped. They landed on a rough platform, and he guided her down and around planks to another wooden stand. There, he grabbed another rope, and he lowered them again.

That was the best part of traveling through the Murk trees with Bannon. All the hugging.

On the ground, she turned to find Jade, the Murken shepherdess, her grandmother. She offered out a leather satchel. "Supplies."

Behind her stood several of Bannon's tribe, as well as Leesa, and Jastin Armitage. Her mother trudged into the open area from the trees.

"I'll go with you to the caves," said Jade.

"And me," said Bannon.

"From there I can't help you. No Murken still alive, as far as we know, has ever been beyond the caves." Jade put the pouch into Sela's hands.

"I'll take us all there," said Sela's mother.

Jade made her way toward Sela's mother, and Sela followed. Leesa stepped in, too, and when they reached her mother, Leesa gave Sela a hand up to her mother's shoulder. Then reached up for Sela to pull her on.

"You're sure you want to come?" Sela asked her.

She nodded. She stuck out one hand toward Jastin, and waved him over.

Sela's mother growled.

Jastin stayed put.

"I'll walk," said Jastin. "I'll have someone show me the way."

"We don't need you," said Sela's mother.

"No," said Jastin. "I'm sure you don't."

Leesa gave a sort of breathy snort. She frowned at Sela's mother. And then she tramped back through the clearing to Jastin, and took his hand. She pulled a knife and a bladder of water from the pack on her back, and handed them to Jastin. Then she pulled him toward the trees.

"Why is he going?" asked Sela's mother. "What does he have to do with any of this?"

"What, indeed," said Jade, from her seat on a dragon spine.

"Mother, can't you make him stay here?"

"He's done no harm since he's been here," said Jade. "He has every right to help, if he chooses."

"He isn't capable of helping," said Sela's mother. "He only thinks of himself."

"And you'll never see him any other way, if you can't get past the taste of your own bitterness." Jade pulled Sela into the space just behind her mother's neck. "Now let's get on with it."

When Sela leaned over to call to Bannon, he was gone. Cloth dropped onto her head, and tumbled into her lap. A tunic, and a pair of breeches. She looked up to find a golden eagle swoop low, circle back, and then let out a cry.

She smiled, and tucked Bannon's clothing into her pack.

Then they were off. Her mother carried her and Jade up over the trees. Jade called out directions, but it didn't take long before they all saw a sharp granite peak stabbing up through the canopy. Behind that, a low-slung bluff disappeared below the treetops.

Sela's mother veered toward it.

As they lowered, branches crackled and broke open to make room. Jade gasped, and gripped Sela's arm.

Bannon dove headfirst into the opening, and Sela's mother hurried in behind him. Limbs and leaves closed over them.

On the ground, Sela slid from her mother's back. Jade tossed down the leather pouch, and Sela tied it off around her waist while Jade descended.

"Riza, can you squeeze through the trees?" Jade asked.

"I think so."

Jade led them through the widest gaps between trunks, just a few feet, and to the great, gaping maw of a dark cave large enough for them all to enter, with head room to spare. Bannon brushed across Sela's hair and landed at her feet.

She tossed him his clothes.

Jade struck a flint, and lit a charred torch sconce hammered into the stone. She pulled that torch, and then walked forward, lighting torches to her left and right, looking as though she was a firefly walking the belly of a caterpillar.

"The drawings are at the widest part of the cave, toward the middle," said Bannon into her ear.

She turned to find him pulling his tunic over his head.

"They explain the prophesy?" asked Sela's mother.

"They are the prophesy," said Bannon. He waved them forward, and they followed the torchlight trail.

The cave did widen suddenly. Jade's torch barely lit one wall at a time. She pointed the flames toward a pigment-scrawled drawing of a group of trees surrounding a cave.

"This is us," she said.

Sela studied the drawing. She ran her finger over the ruts in the stone. "This is drawn by dragon claw," she said. She recognized the striations, like her own attempts at art, and the way the pigments blotched thick in some places, only to thin and stretch toward another blotch. There was a real skill to creating art with nothing but pigment and a pointer claw, and the dragon that dabbled on these walls hadn't had much practice.

"This bulge in the cave isn't natural," said Sela's mother. "It's been tunneled out."

"We suspected that," said Jade. "The pictures show a dragon entering the cave with a human. But at the end, here..." Jade cut across to a far wall, and pointed the torch at the final drawing, "...only the human exits."

"What does that mean?" asked Sela's mother, the only dragon in the cave.

"Clear as mud," said Sela, quoting Orman, and wishing suddenly he was here.

"Show us what happens in between," said Sela's mother.

So Jade circled back to the beginning of the drawings, and slowly followed her torch along the wall. The faded art did seem to tell a story, with a scrawled dragon with a bloated belly and bumblebee wings as a fledgling might draw. Sela tried to focus on the message of the art, instead of the art itself:

A dragon enters the cave with a stick figure human beside it. They reach an impasse, as a scribbled blackness. Only the dragon passes through the blackness, and into some crudely drawn trees. Then the dragon is standing at the edge of a scribble of blue pigment. In the next sequence, the blue pigment gets added colors of yellow, and the blended colors spill out through the trees. After that, the stick figure human walks out of the cave.

"A little light on the details," said Sela.

"We know a dragon finds the spring," said Bannon. "That part is obvious."

"A red dragon," said Sela's mother.

Jade, Sela, and Bannon all turned to look at her.

"Well, look." She pointed. "The dragon is drawn with red. The water is blue, the trees are green. Whoever drew this chose the colors on purpose."

Jade moved her torch closer to the nearest dragon

drawing. She squinted. Then she took a step back. "Well, I'll be."

"You mean you never realized it before?" asked Sela's mother.

Jade shook her head. "All our calling the wind, our talking to the cave, our repeating the story to generation after generation." She turned around, and her torchlight sparkled the scales of Sela's mother. "We know it's the offspring of a leader. Hidden and separate from its own."

"Which is why Leesa thought it was Drell," said Bannon.

"I don't see that in the pictures," said Sela.

"No," said Jade. "Back here." She moved further into the cave, her face a ghost in the orange, flickering flamelight. "The shepherd who first found these drawings, generations ago, spent a lot of time in this cave. Praying, chanting, studying."

Sela followed Jade, at first. But then she felt a tug; not a physical one, but just as strong as a hand on her arm. She veered deeper, where the cave began to shrink—or was that a trick of the darkness?

"He wrote his revelations on the walls. Fits of words, really," Jade continued. "Eventually, he spent so much time here, he had to be replaced. No one really knows whatever happened to him."

"How do you know he's right about this, then?" asked Sela's mother.

"He was right about a lot of things," said Bannon.

"It's an obscureway," said Sela. She turned to face the others. Daylight barely made its way this far into the carved space, and it silhouetted Sela's mother. Even the torches along the walls couldn't penetrate the inkiness near Sela, and Jade's torch did little but to turn shadows into sputtering gloom.

"A what?" asked Jade.

"She's right," said Sela's mother. She had to squeeze into this cave section, and hunch her neck and shoulders to peer at Sela. "It's right there. An obscureway."

"A what?" Jade asked again.

"Like the hidden door in the castle chapel?" asked Bannon.

Sela smiled, although she didn't think he'd be able to see it. "Yes, exactly." She reached her hands in front of her, and patted forward until her fingers found something solid. Then she traced them up and out, searching for cracks and mechanisms.

"Dragons make them," she heard Bannon tell Jade.

Sela felt dirt give way beneath her fingertips. She burrowed them deeper, and touched metal. The ground shook, and the cave trembled all around them.

Jade spun, and her torch lit dust and pebbles that rattled loose, cascaded down the walls, hit at their feet. "What did you do?" she cried.

Then, like a growl of thunder, the obscureway opened, straining to keep moving. Sela had to cover her ears against the groan of the gears. Dirt slapped her face. She coughed.

Finally, the passageway fully exposed. The gears quieted. Dust settled.

Jade inched forward, and touched the wall just

beyond the opening. "No one's ever been this far."

"Someone has," said Sela's mother.

Jade smiled.

"I think I see something," said Sela. She leaned in, and squinted through the darkness. "There, ahead. Around a corner, I think, down a bit. Some light."

"I see it, too," said Bannon. He took Sela's hand. "Onward?"

"Wait," said Sela's mother. "Please."

Sela turned. Jade held up the torch, and in the faint light, Sela could see tears in her mother's eyes.

"What's wrong, Mother?" asked Sela. She sidled closer to touch her mother's cheekbone.

"I can't go any farther," she said. "I don't fit."

"Oh." Sela looked around at the faces encircling the flame, and then toward the passage. "Do you want to wait here? I don't know how long I'll be."

"That's the thing," said her mother. She reached a forepaw to Sela's hand on her cheekbone. "A dragon enters, Sela, but never comes out. I thought it might be me, at first. But I can't even go in."

"You thought it might be you, but you were going to go anyway?" Sela asked.

"I don't know. I suppose so. It's very difficult to figure out what we're supposed to do."

"Clear as mud," Sela said.

Her mother blinked slowly, and a single tear trailed down her snout to perch on the soft skin of her nose. "I only know I don't want to lose you."

Sela dried her mother's tear with her knuckle, and

then stepped into a hug around her neck. She squeezed. "I don't want to be lost. But I've come this far, and we can't go back without at least trying."

"No, I know," said her mother. Sela felt her voice through her scales, rumbling.

Sela moved back, and her mother smiled. Tried to, anyway. "I think you're the bravest soul I've ever known," said her mother.

Now Sela felt tears prickle her eyes, and scratch the back of her throat. She couldn't speak because of it, so she kissed her mother's snout. Then she backed into the passage, her eyes on her mother's face.

"Come home," said her mother.

And Sela knew, then, what Bannon had meant about her place within a circle of those who care. Home wasn't geography. Home was love.

"I will," she said.

CHAPTER TWENTY

"Sparrow to nest. Sparrow to nest," said Layce into a green crystal. "We are on the wing."

"Blast it all, Layce," crackled Orman's voice from the stone. "You don't need to use that ridiculous vernacular to check in. And you don't need to check in every fifteen minutes!"

Drell was getting better at flying with a companion, and Layce Phelcher was a good test to it. She hardly sat still, even when sitting. She wiggled and jostled, and waved her arms. And then there was the talking. About the thickness of the clouds predicting good fortune, or how water conducted magic better than air, or how Orman was the most cantankerous soul she'd ever met. And that was just her words! Her brain thought more things than she had time to express, and Drell had to concentrate on his direction, and his speed, and his wing rhythm just to keep from being bombarded by it all.

"We are entering the forbidden zone," said Layce.

"The what?" asked Orman's voice.

"We are crossing the tawny river," she said.

"Crossing where?"

"Winging the sandy expanse."

"I have no blasted idea what you're talking about," said Orman.

"We've just reached the desert, you oaf." Layce leaned in toward Drell's ear. "He doesn't understand the intricacies of mission protocol," she said.

"Protocol?" sputtered Orman. "Layce, just deactivate the crystal until you have something important to report."

"This is important! It's very hot. And sandy."

"Layce!"

"Signing off."

Drell heard a crisp snap, like a twig. Then Layce leaned in again. "He has feelings for me, you know. Strong feelings. He's not shouting at me, he's shouting at himself; keeping himself under control."

"I wouldn't know," said Drell. He tipped north, and careened toward the Rage dunes.

The desert heat stung his nostrils. He tasted sand on the wind, felt it already scrape his eyes, collect grit in his scales. He'd almost forgotten how the grains managed to get everywhere, and be everywhere.

"Even though they're invisible," said Layce.

And he'd almost forgotten how much he missed it. Not the discomfort of the sand, of course. Just its presence.

Then he spotted another familiar sight; Tay Ambercrest slithering through the coarse air as fluid and graceful as the shifting dunes themselves. He knew his friend approached, they'd made eye contact. But he couldn't resist a shout out, anyway.

"Tay!"

Tay raised a forepaw. Drell surged on to meet him.

"We knew you would be back," said Tay, when he got close enough. "We have missed you, our Shadow."

"And I, you," said Drell. "I have so much to tell you."

"You have brought a friend."

"I am Layce Phelcher," said Layce. "We come in peace."

Tay quirked up his brow. "That is a relief."

"Her dragonspeak is out of practice," Drell said.

"Living in the Leland Mountains these past weeks has helped me remember," said Layce. "Please go about your own business and forget you ever saw me."

Tay squinted. His mouth curved upward, and Drell could see him fighting back a laugh.

"No," said Layce. "I mean to say, please go on as though you make sense. I will catch up later."

Drell shook his head.

"Funny," said Layce. "It's so much easier to understand than it is to speak."

"We do know humanspeak," said Tay.

"No, no." Layce shifted against Drell's sand-itchy neck. "The only way to improve is to keep pushing up rocks. Do not be addled."

"Very well," said Tay.

He came alongside Drell, and they descended together toward the dunes. They flew quietly for a time, until Tay glanced up sideways to Layce, and then back to Drell. "I like your friend."

Drell smiled. "She does grow on you. Unfortunately, her thoughts can be as jumbled as her dragonspeak, so she may be quite a puzzle to figure out."

"I am a growth," said Layce. "Think of me as a bump on the log of the door on the hut of your tribe's dwelling swamp."

"Do you want me to ask her to stop practicing?" asked Drell.

"No," said Tay, with a chuckle. "We must introduce her to the twins."

The sun was just arcing to its highest and hottest, so it was a reprieve to land in the shade of a low valley between two dune peaks.

Layce scrambled to slide off, her fingers digging beneath his scales, and her bony knees grinding. She smoothed her blue tunic, and then, looking around herself at the near dunes, and the distant ones, and the cliffs just beyond, she pulled up her dark, rumpled hair, twisted it around her fists, and then knotted it into a tight bulge on top of her head. "I've always heard so much about the desert, but I've never seen it. Not really," she said. "It just goes on and on, doesn't it? Like the edge of the world."

"As far as I know, no one's ever flown from one side to the other. The closer you get to the center, the hotter. And there are storms; you never know when one will rise."

"Hotter? It's already like standing in a lit fireplace."

Layce put her hands on her hips. "It really is more of Esra than I realized."

"Do you need water?" Tay retrieved a bucket from a cubby dug out of a hump of sandstone. Rage dragons took turns refilling and placing those buckets all along the northern desert route. Drell had done his share of it over the years; keeping the water fresh and easy to access. In these lands, one sip of water could make all the difference to survival.

"Yes," said Layce to Tay, too loud. "Thank you for the gift of fresh vessel." She cupped her hands into the water, and drank.

Tay curled around to regard Drell. "While we pause, you can tell me why this feels more than a simple visit home."

Drell nodded. He sat onto the warm sands and leaned his shoulder against the rise of the sandbank. "Fordon Blackclaw has moved against Esra."

"Yes, this news has reached even the desert," said Tay.

"I have spent the last weeks in Leland, in the mountains, with Dragon Council members, including Kallon Redheart. And Vaya, my mother."

"Then she has finally told you."

"I also know who my father is. Fordon Blackclaw."

Now Tay sat. He frowned. If not for that movement, he might have been a desert statue, rising up as still and solid as a sandstone boulder from the grains.

"You did not know?" asked Drell.

"No," said Tay. "But I have a better understanding

of the secrecy."

"There is more," said Layce. She nudged Drell's leg with her elbow. "Deform to him the magical well."

Tay chuckled again. "Your friend's confusion with our language has gotten even more colorful. Now she speaks of the myth of the well."

Drell ran his dry tongue over his snout. "Actually, that is the part she got right."

Tay's amusement evaporated. "I have indulged you this fairytale for many years, because you seemed to need a reason for your difference. But you are no longer a fledgling. And you have discovered the reason, Shadow."

"Our world is dying," said Drell. "From the Murk Forest, to the Leland Mountains, to the Esra greenlands. Our magic is weak, and Blackclaw's attacks only weaken it further."

"The well exists," said Layce. "We are here to bring it back to life."

"You cannot see it, Tay, because you have always known the desert and its hunger. But the lands beyond the Rage suffer. As the sands grow, our world shrinks." Drell stood, and walked several steps to Tay. "With your help, or without it, I will find the well."

Tay smiled softly. He laid his paw on Drell's shoulder. "You will never be without my help, son. I may not believe in this myth, but I believe in you."

Drell was relieved for the heat, for once, because it dried his tears in his eyes before they had a chance to embarrass him. His heart felt them, though.

"Come, have more water," said Tay. "We will discuss this more when we reach home."

"Yes," said Layce. "It is good to be the bearer of the fallen oak for the dinner fire."

"I could not have said it better myself," said Tay.

CHAPTER TWENTY-ONE

Fane Whitetail paced outside Jia's dwelling, dragging his tail into the soft dirt, making distracted ruts. She should have been back by now. Even if the meeting with Lestir Grimmin had gone well, and gave her reason to linger, accounting for travel time and discussion time, she should be back.

He would be returning to Blackclaw soon, to discuss the next phase, and he did need enough time away to make it appear as though he'd spent the last few days searching for Jastin Armitage in Murk Forest. But not too much time. Fane wasn't such a hands-on sort of tracker that he'd hunt the human relentlessly, and Blackclaw knew it. Too little time away would seem suspicious, but so would too much time. No, Fane would be tiring of the chase and the natural outdoors any day now, and would be winging his way back to Esra and civilization for a hot meal and a soft bedroll.

But he couldn't go back until he first spoke with Jia. Where was she?

It had troubled him, on and off, why Blackclaw had even sent Fane to the forest to begin with. To give the leader privacy with Jia? But then why would he so quickly agree to send Jia with Fane? Or perhaps there was a reason Blackclaw wanted Armitage distracted and running. Fane just didn't know. Not really.

It made him irritable, not knowing. Not being in control.

So when Jia finally appeared as a flapping dot on the horizon, Fane had a vitriolic speech ready to unleash upon her. But then she swooped low enough for him to see her face, and her intense, yellow eyes, and her faint smile of victory. And when she landed, all he managed was a snippy "Well? How did it go?"

"For a man meeting a dragon for the first time, quite well," she said.

"And?" asked Fane.

"And he will be easily manipulated. Lestir Grimmin believes himself venur, but he has no finesse or natural aptitude for leadership. He fears constantly it will be taken from him."

Fane softened. Smiled, even. "You seem to know exactly what kind of information is most useful to me."

"I like to think so."

"I will need to return to Blackclaw. Do you see Grimmin as a potential ally?"

"More than potential. He wants to meet with you to discuss how Leland and Esra can best serve each other."

Fane stepped back. "Meet me? You were supposed to appear as a Blackclaw representative."

"So I did," said Jia. She lowered her head. "But as Grimmin asked questions, I answered honestly, and you naturally came into the conversation."

"A dangerous tack, Jia," said Fane. His previous mood began to return. "If he sees dragons as turning against each other, he will not know which side to trust."

Jia's head lifted again, and her face tightened. Her eyes narrowed. "I informed him which side he can trust. Mine."

"Yours?"

"I would stake my life I won him to my judgment. He will side with the dragons I side with." She eased closer, and her voice went low, and steady. "You will not exchange one puppet for another, Fane. You rid yourself of Fordon, but gain me, and I have a will of my own. I did nothing to jeopardize a union with our Leland allies, and in fact, I believe I accomplished more in one meeting than you or Fordon or anyone could have."

Fane held the close distance, and breathed in the scent of her determination. She was much like himself, in so many ways. Yet, so different. "Perhaps I made a mistake sending you ahead."

"Are you afraid of me, now, Fane?"

"Not afraid," he said. But what? Even he wasn't sure. He liked seeing the parts of her that were familiar to him, but her ways unlike him were hard for him to grasp, and to know how to use.

"You have yet to make a mistake I can see," she said.

It gave him a chill, the way she said that. "This disappoints you?"

"Yes, actually." She drew in a breath, and her face relaxed. Saddened. "You think ahead in more moves than I can possibly keep up with. You see malice in everyone who does not think like you do, but no one can think like you."

Of course others didn't think like he did; that was his advantage over them. Even Jia. She did try to guess him, to outsmart his motives, to find wounds beneath his scales, but she was outmatched by him. At least she had the intelligence to recognize it, which elevated her in his eyes. "I would not be here talking with you now if I did not see such promise in you," he said.

"Thank you, I think." She smiled lightly.

He hated how he liked her face when she did that.

"I was going to be pleased to tell you I arranged a meeting with him, but the news seems anticlimactic now," she said.

"A meeting? Already?" He was unnervingly surprised.

"At Fell Lake Basin."

"Fell Lake? So deep in Leland?"

"He thinks dragons can come and go safely that distance from towns, and have the trees for cover. Plus he will need minimal soldiers. He insisted on a group of men, and I felt that arguing the point would make him uneasy."

"Yes, that was wise," said Fane. "And I can easily convince Blackclaw I will be returning to Murk to continue my hunt for Armitage." He nodded. "You did well, Jia. You have strategized quite competently, as I know you can."

"It is exhausting, trying to impress you." She made her way to the opening of her dwelling, but paused to look over her shoulder. Her glossy wings rested on the ground, and her tail weakly twitched. "I need sleep, just a few hours. You may join me, if you like."

His mind pictured it; sharing space, and warmth, and breath. He even took one step toward her. But he shook his head. "You rest. I will return to Blackclaw, and tell him I have left you searching the forest alone. He will practically insist I return to you."

She nodded. "I will wait here for you." She gracefully stepped through into her dwelling.

"Jia?"

She circled inside, and peered back out through the opening. "Hm?"

He couldn't think of the words he wanted to say. How the meeting with Grimmin had come too easily, how he had only her word that he would be there at all. Fell Lake seemed too remote to be the human's choice. He couldn't find how to voice his concerns, because she had only been away from him for a few hours, and he already figured out a way she might have betrayed him.

"Sleep well," he finally said, because he was also unable to express how he deeply, truly hoped he was wrong.

She smiled and nodded.

He turned his back, and launched into the sky.

He flew slowly, and watched his shadow beneath him as it bounced and shimmied over the sand-cracked edges of Esra's dry land. Then he circled back, and dropped out of view behind a lumpy hillock, and watched Jia's dwelling, as he'd done before.

Shortly, she emerged. She stumbled over a small rock, and caught her balance. She was at least being honest about needing sleep; she was droopy and clumsy. But then she pulled at a mound of thatch just beside one of the boulders that served as her wall. There sat an oblong wire cage. Inside it, a blinking pigeon.

He almost didn't look as Jia withdrew the bird, stuffed something into a locket around its neck, and spoke the locket closed. He tried not to watch as she lifted the bird, and then gently tossed it into the air. And he really wanted to close his eyes when the bird flew straight, up and over the sparse trees, toward the Leland Mountains.

And he desperately resisted the aching, burning sensation just beneath his ribs that told him how much, this time, he hated being right.

The moment Jia returned to her little hut, Fane swept up, caught the bird's scent, and followed.

CHAPTER TWENTY-TWO

Sela, Bannon, and Jade had been walking the back half of a cave for what seemed hours. Sela felt it descending like a spiral, but had begun to wonder if she was imagining it. Maybe the engulfing darkness was playing tricks on her. Maybe it had only been a few minutes, or it had been days. Jade's torch did little to light their way, and had begun sputtering and threatening to die out for some time, anyway.

Bannon's hand was firm in hers, though, and helped her fend off the sense of despair that had been clinging to her, as heavy and thick as the darkness itself.

Then, a pinpoint. "Look!" she cried, her voice shrill and too sudden.

"I see it," said Jade. "Daylight. Or moonlight."

"You can't tell how long we've been walking, either?" asked Bannon.

"Feels like hours," said Sela.

"Hours," Jade said. "But I think that's the end of the cave, there."

Sela found the energy to hurry forward. Her feet shuffled against pebble debris and dirt, and her right hand dragged along the cold stone wall. "I smell trees."

And there they were. She turned a corner, and the cave gaped open to reveal thick, waving branches drenched pale with blinding light. She picked up her pace, literally running toward them, and dragging Bannon along behind her.

"Wait!" he said.

But she didn't want to wait. She wanted out of this unending blackness, and into the brightness.

But just as she reached the end, pebbles skidded out from beneath her feet, and she felt her weight plunge forward. Too late, she realized the cave didn't slope gently into the trees; it ended. Abruptly. In a cliff so high, she couldn't see the valley below. She tried to stop, but sliding dirt and rocks carried her forward, and she pitched out, clawing at air.

Bannon jerked her hard. But his feet slipped, too, and so her momentum pulled them both too far. At the crest of his reach, she arced downward and banged into the cliff, dangling from his hand. Her face stung, and she tasted blood.

"Sela!" cried Jade, her voice bounding out in panicked echoes in the cave.

Sela hadn't even had a chance to scream, it all happened so fast. But she felt one lurching up out of her toward her mouth, just as she looked up, met Bannon's wide, frightened eyes above her, and realized he was already tumbling head first over the side and pulling her along with him.

"Sela!" he hollered. "Fly!" His command turned into a screech, and she felt feathers against her arm.

And she was heavy, and alone, and plunging.

An eagle screamed somewhere, far away.

And then she stuck out her arms, and closed her eyes, and aimed herself like an arrow toward the sound. She thought about the sky, and the wind that billowed her, and home. And when she opened her eyes, she really was aiming toward Bannon, who careened toward her, and she really was flying, and tasting sky, and her wings were strong and lifting her high.

"I did it!" She curled her dragon self inward, and rolled into a triumphant barrel roll.

Bannon swooped beneath her, and then above her.

"Sela!"

She heard Jade's thin voice through the night wind. She spiraled toward the gaping cave in the cliff, and hovered, pumping her wings. "If you reach out, I'll carry you," said Sela.

"No," said Jade. "This isn't my journey to take. I've gone as far as I'm able."

"It's no trouble," said Sela.

"Not for you," said Jade. "Now that you found your wings." She smiled. "You scared me for a minute."

"I scared myself!"

Jade sat at the edge, and dangled her legs over the side. She stuck her torch in a crevice between stones. "Take Bannon as far as he can go, but when the time comes, you'll have to go on without him."

"What do you mean?" Sela lowered, treading her wings.

"You will both understand. And you must both be willing."

Sela gripped the side of the cliff with her claws, and let her wings sway. "What do you mean, Jade? What are you trying to say?"

"Go on now," she said. "You must be close. The light will guide you."

Sela didn't want to go on. She wanted Jade to explain. But the woman only tucked her hands beneath her thighs, and smiled a tight-lipped grin.

Sela heard Bannon alight somewhere, and turned to find him settling into place on a high, swaying sycamore branch.

"Go on," said Jade. "I'll be fine."

Sela blew fresh flame over Jade's torch to brighten it. Then she pushed off from the cliff, soared up over the wide valley, and brushed across treetops. Bannon fluttered into place beside her, and together they searched below, while Sela worried about Jade's cryptic warning, and watched for a clue from the daylight.

§

"The sparrow has nested," said Layce's voice through the crystal in Orman's hand.

He sighed.

"The twigs are gathered," she said. "Orman? Are you listening?"

"Confound it, Layce. Speak plain, or so help me—"

"We're out of the dunes," she said. "In the sandstone caves of the dragons. They're feeding us stew. Have you ever eaten sandsnake?"

"Can't say I have," said Orman.

"We're heading out at first light, when the sands are quietest, and the heat most bearable."

"Who is 'we'?"

"Drell and me. Tay Ambercrest, Drell's guardian, is helping us plan our route to avoid the castle. Any word from Sela and the others?"

"No," said Orman. "No word." He hadn't managed to charm any crystals before Sela and Riza took off for the forest, and now he was regretting not asking them to wait. This communication crystal wasn't much help, but at least he could know what was happening.

Too much, the way Layce yammered on and on over the thing at all hours.

"The stew is ready," said Layce. "I'll check back in to say goodnight."

"You really don't need to do—"

"Signing off," she said.

The green crystal went dull.

He rested the stone on his desk, and then leaned back in his chair. The faint candle beside it barely lit the walls of his quarters; he still hadn't swapped rooms for one with a window. But soon enough, he'd get back to restoring his own little place above Wren Meadow, and he'd have plenty of windows.

If the world was still intact by then, anyway.

A soft knock sounded. Gladdis, no doubt. Her knuckles were as tentative on his door as her footsteps were on the manor floor. "Come in, child," he called.

She peered in. The candlelight found her smile, and the golden strands of her hair trapped in her eyelashes. "You always know it's me," she said.

"Have you brought me the shine stones you've been working on?"

She nodded. She stepped into the room, hands outstretched. In her palms lay shards of yellow crystal, rubbed smooth as river rocks. He lifted one, and held it toward the candlelight. "You buffed these yourself?"

"Yes," she said.

"By hand?"

"I used pumice on the very rough ones. And oilcloth."

"Pumice, you say?" Orman tilted the stone with one hand, and stroked his beard with the other. "And you didn't forfeit too much of the crystal that way?"

She set the crystals onto his desk, and withdrew a small leather pouch from a trouser pocket. "I saved the dust, in case it could still be used. I was wondering what would happen if we blended it with onyx glitter."

"Onyx is for shadows, Gladdis. For keeping secrets. Adding yellow apatite would be adding sunlight to darkness. They would just cancel each other out."

"So you've tried it before?" she asked

"No one would try that," said Orman. "Two opposing forces would need two opposing emotions to wield it. No wizard could concentrate enough to make either one effective."

"Oh, I see." She nodded, and set the pouch of dust onto the desk. She chewed at the inside of her cheek.

"You think I'm an addled old man, stuck to his ways."

She startled. "I wouldn't think that!"

"Not out loud," he said. "But if you want to keep your thoughts to yourself, you're going to need some of that onyx glitter." He tapped his index finger on her forehead. "Or you'll need to practice whispering."

Her bright eyes wrinkled up. She covered her mouth with her hand. "I'm sorry, Orman. I don't even hear my own self, half the time. I'm just not any good at this."

"Nonsense." Orman held up the shine stone. "This is one of the best darned smoothing jobs I've seen in a decade. Now speak the command."

"Alight?" she asked.

The stone burst into brightness. Prisms cascaded across his arms, his desk, his walls. It was as though someone had given him a window, after all, and had thrown it open to let in a summer day. He would have sworn the room even warmed up a little.

"Well, I'll be a nannygoat's feedbag," he said. He stood from his chair to admire the stone's reach, all the way into the farthest corner to glitter the cobwebs he hadn't noticed before.

"You have wizards in your line?"

Gladdis lifted her shoulders. "I don't think so."

"Bah, you must." He patted her on the head. "Bring

me some onyx glitter, and maybe we'll just experiment, after all."

When she smiled, he added, "Not so stuck in my ways, you see?"

She turned for the door, but paused. "Oh, there's something else."

Orman felt a shudder of something; not fear, but a shadow of it. Was it from Gladdis, or a ripple in Leland's magic? He stepped toward her. "Out with it."

She drew out a slip of parchment and offered it out. Orman studied it suspiciously before touching it, and then unfolded it, no larger than his palm, to read it.

At Fell Lake Basin, I present my gift to Leland and her dragons. Signed, your friend.

"Who is this friend?" asked Orman. "What gift?"

Gladdis shook her head. "I don't know." She regarded her fidgeting hands a moment, and then looked up at Orman. "We've been sharing letters for some time. Drell taught me dragonscript so I could read and write back."

Orman felt heat rise into his shoulders, tightening them. "Write back to whom?" he asked.

"She's never told me her name."

"She?" Orman stuck the parchment under her nose. "How do you know this friend is a she?"

"Oh," said Gladdis. She quirked her mouth. "I don't, it just seems right."

"And I suppose it feels right that this friend is also

a dragon."

Gladdis nodded. "Why else would the letters be in dragonscript?"

Orman read the words again. "Hardly a letter. This is more like passing notes in crystal memorization class." He studied the paper, held it to the light. "Utterly puzzling." Which, in his opinion, wasn't necessarily a bad thing. "Still," he continued. "I'll show this to Kallon, and what's left of the Dragon Council. A lot of betrayal and tomfoolery among dragons these days; wouldn't want to be at the wrong end of nasty trick."

When Gladdis frowned in concern, and turned a pale shade, he patted her on the arm. "I'm sure your friend means well." Then he waved his hand. "Now do you remember the way to that cove where we found the onyx? Good girl. Be off and dig us some."

He followed her into the hallway. She paused, and looked back. "I did the right thing? Showing it to you?"

"You certainly did."

She smiled then. A sweet smile in a tender face; so unlike Sela in many ways. Where Sela was waifish and unkempt, Gladdis was graceful and groomed; even wearing a tunic and trousers. Where Sela charged in, dander up, Gladdis hung back and watched. And yet, Orman found similarities in the way the girls trusted, and watched for the future with a kind of hopeful anticipation. Although Orman had lived too long and too hard to share either trait, he admired it. These days, trust and hope were rare commodities.

Especially these days. He studied the note again,

and again felt that shiver like a ripple through magic. Whomever this dragon was, and whatever he or she had in mind at Fell Lake, it did not bode well for a land trying to heal.

He didn't find Kallon in his chambers, or in the Great Hall. The Red had been downright moping with both Sela and Riza gone, and was probably off somewhere feeling sorry for himself again, dagnabbit, and just when Orman had something very important to tell him, too! Too many cubby holes and furrows in these mountains for Orman to search them all. Should have made Kallon wear a tracking stone. He would, too, as soon as he had a chance to make one.

For now, Orman would have to go on foot. Good thing he was wearing felt-lined walking shoes.

He wound his way around a patch of pin oak trees, set apart from ones ahead and taking on the faint red edge of autumn in their leaves. Funny, Orman had barely noticed a season change, but now that he stopped to contemplate it, he saw the signs everywhere. Swaying elms dangled yellow-spotted foliage, the underbrush had darkened to patches of brown. He looked up, and followed the slow crawl of gray-muddled clouds, and as he walked, he breathed in. Sure enough, cooler winds mingled with the warmth of Leland's breath. Fall crept on silent feet toward her place on stage, needing no direction from anyone.

Then something glittered at the corner of his eye, as though a mirror bounced a sunbeam. He spun to find it, but it was gone. Then, a scream. A high-pitched voice; a girl.

Gladdis!

He ran as fast as his tired old legs would carry him toward where he was sure the sound came from. His feet hit pebbles, and they skittered him down a slope toward an open area at the base of Mount Gore. The place where he and Gladdis had been excavating crystals just a day before.

He tripped once, but caught his balance, just in time to see a dragon body, as pale as sea froth, swoop up and over him. Dangling below, between razor claws, hung Gladdis, her golden hair swinging.

She spotted him. "Orman!" She reached her hands toward him, but she was too high, and too far, for him to reach back. And then she was gone, altogether, up and over the trees.

"Blast!" was all he could say. He shook a wrinkled fist at the kidnapper. Fane Whitetail. He was sure of it. That sneaky serpent had Orman's student, and all Orman had was two feet and an aching back to chase her down. "Blast!" he said again.

"Did I hear a scream?" asked Kallon's distant voice from above.

Orman looked up to find the Red scrape his belly over an oak sapling as he lowered, but he had no room to land. He circled, instead. "Orman, what happened?"

"And where in blazes have you been?" Orman snapped. "He took her, confound it all!"

"Who took her? Took who?"

"Gladdis! That devil of a white dragon, Fane

Whitetail, just scooped my student up and carried her off!"

"Whitetail?" Kallon swooped up high and frowned into the distance. "Which way?"

"Over the trees. East, I think."

Kallon sped away, and Orman spent several quiet, anxious moments at the edge of his crystal dig, wringing his hands. He saw Kallon's form swerve into view, and then away again.

Finally, after the wind had died down, and the flurry of leaves from the excitement and settled, Kallon returned. He shook his head, and coasted low. "I'm sorry, Orman, I lost him."

"You had to have found him, to lose him," he snarled. He was furious; at Kallon, for being too late to do any good, at the trees, for being distracting, at his own hands, for being old and useless, at the ground, for being cold and dirty.

"Are you sure it was Whitetail?" asked Kallon. "Why would he be in the mountains after all these years? And at a time like this?"

"I'm sure," said Orman. "I'm positive."

"What would he want with Gladdis?"

Orman shook his head. He paced. He mumbled. Then he stopped. He pulled the tiny rolled parchment from his pocket, and unfurled it. "Gladdis has been communicating with someone who claims to be her friend." He read the note with a growing illness in his gut. "A friend who had promised to deliver a gift to Leland at the Fell Lake basin."

Kallon's beating wings battered the tree limbs near Orman, scattering leaves into his hair and beard. "A gift to Leland?" he asked. "Why would anyone need Gladdis in Durance?"

"I don't know, Kallon," said Orman. "But there's only one way to find out."

"Are you going to Fell Lake?" Kallon asked.

"I am. And don't try to stop me."

Kallon swerved around a tall elm, and Orman saw him duck down to land on the opposite edge of the flat excavation site. Orman picked his way around the rim toward him.

"I'm not going to stop you," said Kallon. "I'll go with you. I'd like to see for myself why Whitetail is mixed up in this."

"And to save my student," said Orman, frowning.

"Of course. And to save Gladdis."

§

Fane Whitetail could hear the human squealing and squawking while she wiggled around in his grasp, but he ignored her. She was lucky he didn't crush her and be done with her, which was his first instinct. He was on his way to toss her into the Esra rift he liked to use for his garbage, when he veered west, instead, toward Riddess Castle. Better to keep her around for the moment, for a chance to find out, exactly, what part she was playing in all this.

"What do you want with me?" the human called.

Her tiny fists beat against his knuckle.

He just pushed his wings faster, to reach the castle sooner.

When he arrived, he swooped toward the wall, to toss her into captivity with the rest of Esra's captured. But Blackclaw was already there, glowering from his place on the wall as though he was expecting them both. But of course he couldn't be. Fane hadn't even known he was going to follow the pigeon to its receiver until the moment he took wing. And he hadn't planned on snatching the girl until she presented herself, alone and preoccupied.

So he gave Fordon Blackclaw a grin, and stuck out his claw, offering the girl. "A gift for you, Leader Blackclaw."

"A human?" Blackclaw asked dryly. "Just what I always wanted."

"This human is special," he said. He set her on the ground, where she stumbled forward, and landed on her knees. Then he dropped to a landing beside her, and folded in his wings.

Blackclaw lunged from the castle wall, watching Fane, but not the girl. Fane frowned then, feeling suspicion leak from Blackclaw like blood from a wound. "Special?" he asked. "How would you have time to find a special human while also scouring Murk Forest for Jastin Armitage and his band of fools?"

"Armitage travels with only one female," corrected Fane. "Hardly a threat."

"Wisdom from the mouth of Fane Whitetail," said

Blackclaw. "A pity I do not listen to you more often. Or, better yet, step aside so you can take my place as leader of this rebellion."

He was being baited. He knew it now. But, why? He chose not to reply. He glanced to the girl, who stayed low to the ground, and looked between him and Blackclaw with wide eyes. Did she know more about this than Fane gave credit for?

Blackclaw finally regarded the girl, too. "What is your name?" he asked.

The girl stood. She pulled her tunic into place. "I know who you are," she said, in stumbling dragonspeak.

Blackclaw's brow arched. He smiled faintly.

"I am having the strangest sense of having been a part of this scene before," said Blackclaw. "A waifling girl brought to me as an offering, do you remember, Whitetail?"

Fane remembered. "She was Riza Diantus," he said.

"No more than a wisp of a thing. Brought as revenge against another dragon. She seemed so harmless at the time, and yet... here I am, in Esra, the beggar king of a handful of rebels, still fighting for my crown."

"More than a handful—" Fane tried to say.

"Not today, Whitetail," said Blackclaw, holding up a paw. "Not now." He sniffed at the girl. "Tell me why you have brought this one to me."

Fane hesitated answering, as much for show, as anything. He furrowed his face. "As much as it pains me to say, Leader Blackclaw," he said, "...this human is proof of our betrayal."

"*Our* betrayal, Whitetail?"

"She has been communicating—"

Blackclaw cut him off again. "With Jia Greenscale? Daughter of Min Greenscale, for the taking over of Leland?"

Fane rocked back, stunned. It happened too quickly to cover, so he went with it. He tipped his head. "How did you know?"

"I was told to be on the lookout for her. For you. And for those words."

Fane was about to ask by whom, but he already knew. In his heart, somewhere, he instantly knew. And then Jia rose up from the other side of the castle wall, her long wings beating casually, unlike the rhythm of his pulse, and she landed onto crumbling stone. He'd have thought she'd look smug, or triumphant in some way. She didn't. Her thoughts were confusing, her emotions muddled. And her young face was tight with pain.

"So you see my confusion, Whitetail," said Blackclaw. "You bring the human to accuse Jia, but Jia has already accused you."

Of course she had. Fane studied her again, but her expression never changed. The dragon was curiously, mysteriously, stricken by the whole charade. It baffled him, threw him off. He struggled to take control of the conversation. "If I had been conspiring with someone," he said, "why would I bring that cohort out in the open, and directly to you?"

"My question exactly," said Blackclaw. "And yet, Jia warned this happening, and here you are." He eased close and breathed hotly into Fane's face. Then his paw darted to Fane's foreleg, and gripped so forcefully, Fane yelped. Blackclaw twisted Fane's scales, and, in a flash of movement, pulled out the folded parchment Fane kept hidden there.

Blackclaw snapped the parchment open and read it. He looked at Jia, and then to Fane. "Much like she told me I would find this letter, meant for me," he said.

"Leader Blackclaw, this is not what it appears to be," said Fane. "I have been your confidant and advisor for more years than this Green has been alive. You would trust her over me?"

"No," said Blackclaw. "In fact, I did not."

Fane glanced at Jia.

"Until this," said Blackclaw. "I thought she fabricated the letter just as a way to entice me to question you. But here it is, in my claws." Blackclaw shook his head. "A letter meant for me from Leland's venur, and you hid it from me. I laughed when she suggested it. I laughed, Whitetail." Blackclaw rapped him on the shoulder with the paper. "But it does not seem funny now. I can hear you scrambling to hide your thoughts, but there they are, all the same."

Fane felt himself wither. He couldn't find equilibrium, couldn't find words. He just looked into Jia's eyes, and found pain in them. Baffling, blinding. He tried to hate her, tried to dredge up some sort of blockade against her to keep her out of his head, but he just stood there, weak and struggling.

"I tested her, your eminence. I showed her the letter

to see where her loyalties lie." The attempt sounded desperate, even to Fane.

"Or she tested you," said Blackclaw.

"No," said Fane. "She twists what is happening here. I brought this human to you because I serve you still."

"Ah yes, the human." Blackclaw lowered his dark face into the girl's. "This weak bug, buzzing about my head. Do you know what happened last time, Jia, when I was brought a puny little human girl? I tossed her in a dungeon, and dismissed her from my mind." He turned, and strode toward Jia where she perched on the castle wall. "I gave her no more thought than a fallen rose petal on my path. But then, amazing as it is to recount, that particular human girl showed herself to be no petal. No," said Blackclaw, and whirled once again to glower at the human. "She was actually a thorn in my foot."

The girl was frightened; it rolled off her in waves, stinging Fane at the back of his eyes. Her, he could hate, and he did. "Ask the human who she talks to in secret. She can tell you I speak the truth, else why would I bring her?"

"Very well," said Blackclaw, lifting his head. "Give me your name, human."

The girl drew in a deep breath. "Gladdis," she said. She swallowed deeply, and then added, "Gladdis Thorn."

Blackclaw narrowed his eyes, but smiled again, faintly. "Now tell me, Gladdis *Thorn*, which of these dragons has been communicating with you. Mind," he said, leaning his snout close to her face, "...I will know if you lie."

The human looked at Fane, and his lip curled in disgust at the cloudiness of terror in her eyes. Then she looked away at Jia. Then she faced Blackclaw again, and spoke flatly. "I do not know."

"She lies!" said Fane.

"No," said Blackclaw. "Curiously, she does not." He tipped his head. "Now, Gladdis, in these communications, were you told political secrets or maneuvers of any kind?"

Again the girl looked at Fane. He cringed.

"I think so," said the girl. "But I did not understand what he meant."

"The human double speaks!" Fane lurched toward Blackclaw, clutching his shoulder. "Leader Blackclaw, surely you see what is happening here!"

"Oh, I see it, Whitetail. Perhaps for the first time I really understand." Blackclaw pushed Fane's paw away, and then indicated toward him. From behind the wall, a Gray and a Brown leapt up and over.

Fane didn't hesitate. He shot into the air so fast he barely had time to unfurl his wings first. He flipped up and over, and flew in a blind panic.

Until pain bit into his left wing, crippling him, making him yell. Then his right wing was wrenched. Fane felt himself drop. He hit hard, groaned with hurting and confusion. He rolled aside to find Jia Greenscale releasing his bloodied wing from her mouth.

"Jia," he whispered.

Everything went dark.

§

Jia spit the taste of Fane's blood from her tongue, wiped her paw across it to expunge it entirely. It tasted of poison; of hatred and betrayal—or that was her guilty conscience playing tricks on her?

"Well done," said Blackclaw.

Beside Jia, the Gray and the Brown, who had also wrestled Fane from the sky, turned to Blackclaw. The Gray had just clobbered Fane's head with a rock, and raised it again in question.

"No, no," said Blackclaw. "Drag him to the dungeons for now." He regarded Jia, and she thought she saw a twinge of sadness rim his eyes. The Gray heaved Fane onto the Brown's back, and the Brown struggled to bear him toward the castle.

"I am sorry, Fordon," said Jia honestly.

"Yes, me too," he said. "But we move on." He pulled himself onto his back feet, and drew in a breath, but he still seemed underinflated and limp. "Still, I think I will rest for a while."

"Of course," said Jia.

"But I will need you to take up the search for Armitage and whatever allies he has picked up along the way. Time is short, and I need him."

"Jastin Armitage," asked Jia. "The dragon hunter?"

Blackclaw nodded. "He fights for Leland now, I saw him myself during the battle for this castle."

"But I thought..." Jia began to say. Armitage killed Bren Redheart, among countless others. He had been waging his own war against dragons for years.

Blackclaw furrowed his scaly brows. "At first, I did not believe it, either. But as I said, I saw him with my own two eyes. And I saw what he wore around his neck."

"What did he wear?" asked Jia.

"A scale of the Gold," he said. "Unmistakable. And it is the key, Jia." Blackclaw stepped toward her. "The key to more than winning this war. It is the key that unlocks immeasurable power over the heavens." He cupped his paw beneath her chin. "I will have that scale, Jia. I want you to be the dragon who brings it to me."

Jia allowed his touch. And she met his eyes. "I will bring it," she said. "You can wager on that."

Blackclaw smiled, but it faded quickly to fatigue. He turned, and caught sight of the girl, Gladdis, who had begun a slow creep along the castle wall, and peeked over her shoulder just as both dragons remembered her.

"Oh, and the thorn cannot be allowed to live," said Blackclaw, almost as an afterthought. "I have learned my lesson on that."

"I will see to it," said Jia. "I know just the place for throwing unwanted things."

The girl spun around, eyes wide.

Blackclaw leapt up, caught the wind, and flew toward the castle.

Jia watched him go. Then she trotted to the girl, and without speaking, for fear of betraying herself to anyone close enough to sense it, she scooped her into her paw.

"No!" the girl cried.

Jia carried her up and away, and resisted looking

back over her shoulder.

Jia passed over the carved boulder at the bend in the path, and over maple trees, stabbed with rusting spiles. She turned east, toward the great Esra ravine full of dragon bones, and beyond it. Only then did Jia dare to speak, and quietly, to the girl in her grasp.

"I am not going to hurt you," she said.

The girl's squirming ceased.

"I am your friend," said Jia.

Then she swerved toward her hovel of a cave, and lowered just enough to set the girl gently onto the ground. She retracted her leg, and coasted several more feet into a landing.

"Is it really you?" the girl asked, behind her.

Jia curled around to face her.

"The one who wrote in the crystal?"

"You know I am," said Jia. "Somehow, you know it's me, but you managed to accuse Fane Whitetail and seal his fate." Jia smiled, but it felt as sad on her face as she was inside. "I admit, you surprise me. I never guessed I had made friends with a human."

"I never guessed I'd be at Mount Gore, surrounded by dragons," said the girl, Gladdis. "I only happened to come across the bird by chance."

"Not by chance," said Jia.

Gladdis smiled, too, just as brief and cheerless as Jia's must have been. "I think I got that white dragon into trouble. I don't want to hurt anybody."

"I don't either, it turns out." Jia settled slowly onto the cool ground, resting her belly, and tucking her legs in. "I thought exposing Fane for the traitor he is would feel better. But now, just when things were about to break loose, he still managed to think ahead of me, and I don't know what to do from here. If I hadn't seen his shadow pass over, and hadn't discovered him following my bird…"

"I don't understand," said Gladdis.

Jia shook her head. "Of course you don't. I barely grasp it, myself."

"Maybe if you start from the beginning?" She stepped closer in leather boots that slapped the ground, too big for her feet. Yet she managed a kind of grace, anyway. She reminded Jia of a white rose just catching the golden glint of an early morning sunbeam.

"I owe you that," said Jia. "Before I return to Blackclaw to let him know I've thrown you into an Esra ravine."

Gladdis stiffened. "But you'll be fibbing, right? You're not actually going to do that."

"I told you I won't hurt you. I managed to entangle you into a mess of my own making, and I'll get you out, alive and well." Jia rose to her feet. "It may be more than I can say for myself, but I promise you'll live."

The girl watched Jia's face. "Who are you?"

"I'm Jia Greenscale. Daughter of Min Greenscale."

Gladdis smiled, faint and unsure. "I know him. He's a member of the Dragon Council."

"Yes, he is." Jia's heart tugged, suddenly missing her home, and her tribe. "He thinks I betrayed him. And the dragons there."

"But you haven't," said Gladdis. "You're trying to help. Aren't you?"

Jia nodded. Then she frowned. "No, not entirely. I'm trying to give Fane Whitetail what he deserves. But, I suppose I was thinking that to do it would only help."

"What does Fane Whitetail deserve?"

"He deserves to die," said Jia, her teeth gritted so tightly she could hardly spit the words out around them. "He deserves to be humiliated, and to suffer, and then to die."

Gladdis startled again. Jia softened a bit, wondering what Gladdis had seen on her face to frighten her so. She released a long, sparkling breath. "I'm sorry. I've just been seeing it over and over in my mind for so long, and I've been working so hard to hide it from him. All these weeks. All this anger."

She breathed out again, and rested down onto her belly. She closed her eyes, and concentrated on finding control, as she'd had to do so many times now. "I've had to pretend I admire him," she said, opening her eyes. "Can you imagine? I hate him, but I've had to pretend."

"No wonder you needed someone to talk to," said Gladdis.

Jia shook her head. "I shouldn't have done it, though. I risked everything I've worked for."

"Everyone deserves someone to talk to," said Gladdis. She eased her way closer, and smiled. She tentatively patted Jia's outstretched paw. "Besides, I wanted to help, too. I wanted something for myself, and so I needed a friend, too."

Jia smiled. "I couldn't have guessed you would be human. I didn't even know there were any in the mountains."

"There have been lately. When Blackclaw attacked Esra, a group of us escaped there. Me, and Layce Phelcher, and her sister, Avara, and the venur—"

"Venur Riddess?" asked Jia, feeling a slap of alarm. "He survived?"

"Not the son," said Gladdis. "His father, Ebouard."

"Ebouard?" Hadn't he been dead for years?

"He was under a spell," said Gladdis. "But he's allied with the Dragon Council, and he's helping recruit dragons to fight against Blackclaw."

"Ebouard Riddess has allied with Leland?" Jia couldn't believe it. Humans and dragons, together. No wonder she'd been feeling ripples in the land's magic. "I was hoping to make that happen with Leland's venur, too. With one venur on our side, surely it will make the way easier for the second."

"Maybe the land's future isn't so troubled, after all," said Gladdis. "Orman Thistleby has been saying—"

"The wizard?" Jia asked.

"He escaped with the rest. He's been saying the land is suffering, because the magic is dying."

Maybe those were the ripples Jia had been sensing, after all. "I hope he's wrong," she said. "He probably isn't."

"Sela Redheart and Drell Blackwing are out there, right now, trying to repair the places where the earth's first magic has gotten sick. Or, something like that."

Gladdis drew in her bottom lip. "I'm only just learning dragonspeak, and most of the time I don't understand what's going on."

"You seem to understand just fine, to me," said Jia. "Are you just learning dragonscript, too?" It would explain the fledgling look to the penmanship.

Gladdis nodded.

"Well, of all the friends my pigeon could have found for me, I'm glad it was you, Gladdis Thorn."

She smiled brightly then, and Jia thought she could see the shine of a sunrise behind her eyes. Were more humans so delightful to watch? At that thought, she immediately remembered Jastin Armitage. She'd never seen the man, but no, she didn't think she would find him delightful.

She rose, then, gone dark inside from memories, and indicated toward her thatch-covered dwelling. "There is dried meat in a chest, and a barrel of water inside. Do you mind staying alone for a while, until I can come back and get you?"

"Wait. You still haven't told me," said Gladdis.

Jia took a step, but paused. She regarded Gladdis over her shoulder. "Told you what?"

"What did Fane Whitetail do to you to make you hate him so much?"

Gladdis closed her eyes to find her control again. Then she opened them slowly, and breathed sparks into her words. "He killed the dragon I loved."

Gladdis's face covered over in shadows. "Oh. I'm sorry."

"He didn't wield the sword, but he ordered it," said Jia. "A long time ago, when I was barely more than a fledgling."

"What happened?"

"He was Delt Bluecrest, the council's recorder, during Blackclaw's leadership," said Jia. She hadn't talked about Delt in years, and doing so now made her throat tighten, and her heart throb. "I was young, but I recognized love, Gladdis. He was so kind, and beautiful. He was a cross between blue and green, this unique shade of sky over the deepest parts of the ocean. I imagined all our nestlings as little bundles of turquoise."

Gladdis smiled.

"But it wasn't just his color, of course. He looked at me whenever I talked to him, no matter what he was doing at the time. He saw me, you know?"

"Did he love you, too?" Gladdis asked.

"I think so, yes. He never said. He never had the chance." Jia pressed her knuckles to her eyes. She refused to cry. "Whitetail sacrificed him to the war Blackclaw was stirring, even then. He had him murdered, so Leland's dragons would cry justice."

"Orman told me about how Kallon Redheart exposed Blackclaw for the betrayer he was, after that."

"But Delt never got his justice. And I swore, one day I would do it. I would give it to him."

"By destroying Fane Whitetail?"

Jia nodded. "And Jastin Armitage, the man who swung the blade."

Gladdis went pale and quiet. Jia nudged the girl's

foot with her paw. "What is it?"

"I know the man you're talking about," Gladdis said. "He does frighten me. But I've seen him…"

"Seen him what?"

"He regrets so much," said Gladdis. "I've seen it. At his home, when he burned his weapons and his trophies. I could feel his remorse as high and hot as the funeral pyre he made." She folded her hands against her stomach. "Sela told him to come to the mountains with us, when we all escaped, but he refused."

Jia snorted. "Of course he did. He has no friends there."

"That's true. I haven't spoken to anyone who believes he's changed."

"It doesn't matter to me, one way or the other, if he has or hasn't." Jia strode toward her dwelling. "What he did then, that's what he has to answer for. But first, I must return to Blackclaw, and try to salvage what I can of this jumble I've turned it all into."

She pointed into her hovel. "Dried meats. Water. Will you all right until I return?"

"How long will it take?" she asked.

"I'm not sure. Several hours, at least." She shook her head. "It wasn't supposed to happen like this. I was trying to turn in Fane to the dragons he betrayed in Leland, at Mount Gore. Not to Blackclaw."

Gladdis nodded, but she could see by the clouds in the girl's eyes she didn't understand. "I can promise to be back as soon as I can."

"I'll be fine," said Gladdis.

"I'll hurry," said Jia.

§

Fordon Blackclaw tried to keep his eyes closed, but they kept sliding back open. His bedroll was bunched and uncomfortable. A bird some distance away kept trilling obnoxiously. And the sun shone too brightly through the burned and slanted ceiling tiles.

He gave up on rest, and decided on the next best thing: confronting Whitetail. Surely he would be conscious by now, and tethered, and helpless. Would do him some good to see his advisor appropriately dealt with.

Not that Whitetail's betrayal, and denial, was a surprise, really. He had never trusted the dragon, had never completely handed his secrets to him. The White followed orders too easily; he always had. He'd acquiesce, even when Fordon knew he was internally burning with resistance. He had never grasped Whitetail's motives for his blind loyalty, and so Fordon had always known, in his heart, that it couldn't possibly be real. He'd always known, one day, it would come to this.

But now, of all times. And for the attention of a female, of all things.

Oh, the White would deny that too, of course. Whitetail always seemed to be above that sort of thing, and Fordon, for the longest time, had been throwing temptations into his path, testing. Searching Whitetail for weakness. A female had never been an issue, until now. If it was obvious to no one else, it was obvious to Fordon.

Almost amusing, really.

And if Blackclaw knew anything about his sniveling companion, Fane would be in the dungeon, gnashing and moaning, and prepared to grovel his way back into good graces. It's all Blackclaw wanted out of the confrontation at this point. Hiding a letter meant for the leader was a move bolder than Blackclaw had given him credit for, but still, it was just a letter. And the message-in-a-crystal debacle? He didn't really care who was talking to the scrawny human, Jia or Whitetail.

The two vied for position at Blackclaw's side, and whatever games they played against each other were none of his business, so long as it didn't interfere with the matter at hand; to finish what he started.

Domination.

He made his way through the cobbled halls of what was left of the castle. His footsteps echoed through empty rooms, and shook dust and debris loose from rafters. The condition of the place didn't bother him, this was temporary. Let the castle be flattened, and Leland's, too, for all he cared. His heart was set on Mount Gore Manor, the home where he once ruled. Would rule again.

The dungeon remained intact, with its sturdy tunnels and braced timbers. A convenience he didn't realize he'd be needing, and especially not for one of his own.

He reached a cavernous hollow lit by rudimentary

torches. The Brown sat lazily against a far wall, scratching his belly and lightly rumbling in a near sleep. A shortsword was strapped to his forearm by leather thongs. "Gerd," Blackclaw snapped. "Guard duty is not naptime."

Gerd startled, and righted himself onto all fours. "Right. So sorry. Only the prisoner has been quiet, and the damp chill down here—"

"Why arm yourself for a quiet prisoner?" Blackclaw pointed to the sword.

"Found a whole chest of them, just there," said the Brown. He pointed into a shadow.

"See those make it around to any dragon without a weapon," said Blackclaw. "Before our next attack."

Gerd nodded.

Blackclaw approached the nearest cell, large enough for Whitetail and another dragon, besides. Except Whitetail's forelegs were chained spread-eagle to each opposite wall, and his wings were outstretched and bolted to manacles in the floor, sufficiently using all the available space. As Blackclaw approached, Whitetail's eyes slitted open.

"That looks painful," said Blackclaw.

Blood puddled inside one of Whitetail's nostrils.

"Have they mistreated you?" asked Blackclaw.

Whitetail dragged his dry tongue across his gums, but remained silent.

"She fitted you up, I think," said Blackclaw. "The green beauty found your weakness the way I never could, and played you out to be the bad guy."

Whitetail tried to swallow, but choked in his dehydrated throat. Blackclaw nodded to Gerd, who roused to attention. He dunked an ale mug into a water chest, and carried it over. He poured it through the bars of the cell, and Whitetail stuck out his tongue to catch it like rainfall. He swallowed again, and spoke.

"Then why am I here, hanging like a gutted porker?" he asked.

"Because you had a weakness to be used," said Blackclaw. "After all this time, and all these years, you still must be taught your place. I dislike having to do it, Whitetail. I have neither the time nor patience to be dealing with your little rebellion right now."

"Then turn me loose and be done with it," said Whitetail.

"Ah, but there is the issue of an apology. And the question as to whether I could ever again trust you on any mission away. You see my dilemma?"

"She said things, made me want things for myself I have never before wanted," said Whitetail. He snorted quietly, and then winced because of it. "She came right out and told me she struggled to out-think me. Everything she ever said to me was the truth. But she let me believe her words my own way."

Whitetail closed his eyes. "I have tried to blame her, and to hate her, but I can only be awed. She manipulated me as beautifully as I have ever done to anyone."

He opened his eyes again. "But I am back now, Fordon. It is not too late to make the best out of my mistakes."

Blackclaw regarded Whitetail, trying to remember if he had ever used his given name before.

"I mean to say, Leader Blackclaw," said Whitetail. He hung his head as best he could, strung up to the wall. It flopped aside.

"I am not above forgiving a wayward fledgling his mistakes," said Blackclaw. "Go on."

"The advantage to using Jia to arrange the meeting is that she is utterly believable," said Whitetail. "This is our edge."

"Meeting?" asked Blackclaw, feeling his face go cold. "What meeting are you talking about?"

"The meeting with..." Whitetail's voice trailed. His watery eyes went wide. The blood in his nostril spilled out to dribble toward his chin. "I thought she would have mentioned."

"Well, now you really have me intrigued," said Blackclaw. "Do tell."

"You did say you would forgive," Whitetail said meekly. More like his old self. At least Blackclaw was getting somewhere with him.

"Yes, I did. Go on."

"Well, I sent Jia to see Lestir Grimmin in Leland, because of the letter. I wanted to find out what he had to say, you see."

"Yes, I see," said Blackclaw. Acid bubbled in his stomach. Steam roiled into his nostrils. "You took it upon yourself to contact him in my stead."

"Only as precaution. To find out if he had any relevance, before we went in to slaughter them all," said

Whitetail. "As I was ready to do, by your side, venerable ruler."

Blackclaw surprised himself by how much he wanted to believe Whitetail. He looked into his companion's eyes. He had never considered Whitetail a friend, but as he thought back now on his relationships over the years, Blackclaw realized Fane Whitetail was his closest thing to a friend. He also discovered he very much wanted to forgive him.

"And did he have what you were looking for?" asked Blackclaw.

"I have not met him," said Whitetail. "I only sent in Jia to set things up."

"So what did she set up?"

Whitetail coughed. His head hung again, but out of tiredness, it seemed to Blackclaw. "Fell Lake basin. He is bringing a squadron of men, expecting me alone. That means his soldiers will be split, and the castle vulnerable."

"Hm, yes. I see what you mean. Very good, Whitetail. Perhaps your little meeting will serve me, after all."

"A forgivable transgression, Leader Blackclaw?"

"By transgression, do you mean the part where you spent countless days to your own means instead of searching for Armitage like I asked? Or the part where you hid crucial information from me, and used it to puff your chest in front of a female, while at the same time subverting my authority to, what? Rebel?"

"I had only the best interests of this war at heart,

venerable ruler," said Whitetail, his voice dropping to a whisper. "My means are of questionable judgment, I agree. But my ends were honorable."

"Ah, I see." Blackclaw watched Whitetail through the bars, at the once pathetic and overpleasing runt of an advisor. Never before would Whitetail have been so bold as to fabricate his own ideas, no matter the noble reasons. "More than I thought you capable of, I confess," he said.

"Perhaps I have learned from your proficient guidance," said Whitetail.

Blackclaw sighed. "Yes, you have changed, Whitetail. In degrees, likely, without my notice. I wonder what we can do with that." He waved the Brown toward the bars. "Open them."

Whitetail revived a bit in his chains. "Thank you, Fordon."

Gerd shoved a key into the ancient lock and waggled it. It clicked, and Blackclaw swung open the ironwork. "And that is all you have to tell me? Because now is the time to confess everything."

Whitetail blinked. His tongue smacked against the back of his teeth, trying to swallow again. "I have told you everything."

Blackclaw patted Whitetail on his gaunt chest. "I forgive you," he said.

Then he lifted a cloud-white scale away from Whitetail's skin, and snatched the shortsword from Gerd's forearm. Whitetail's eyes widened, just the second before Blackclaw drove the weapon in, fast. Deep.

"I forgive you," he said again to Whitetail. "But you are of no use to me anymore."

Whitetail gasped, and choked. He went limp in his chains, and dangled.

He turned away to find Gerd staring and trembling.

"Clean your weapon," Blackclaw told him, handing over the sword. "And if I'm not mistaken, I think it needs sharpening."

CHAPTER TWENTY-THREE

Sela's wings were tired. Her legs were tired from being curled against her body, her eyes were tired from staring into the wind. She wanted to land, and to rest, especially as the day wore on, but trees were so thick below she couldn't find access to the ground.

At some point, she and Bannon had split ways. He flew off north and east, Sela searched south and west, although she couldn't recall, just now, the conversation as to why. She scoured below, but all she kept finding was the massive chasm that split off the forest from the gargantuan cliff face she and Bannon had tumbled from.

Earlier, she'd lowered enough over the chasm to find a gentle river of water deep in its gullet, and she'd tried to follow it, but the water disappeared into the trees, and was swallowed out of sight.

Then she'd tried flying up and over the cliff to get her bearings, and to find the mountains. She knew if she could see them, she could orient her position, and the mysterious cave and its tunnel would no longer be the only way to access this part of Leland. But the higher she flew, with her wing tips scraping cliff stone, the more rock there was to find. She'd pushed up, up, until her lungs burned, and the sky squeezed back at her. Still, the cliff blocked her to the west.

There was no way over the top she could find.

So she'd returned to skimming her belly over treetops. No way up. No way down. She felt trapped in this place of in-between, with the unending blue sky teasing her forward, but giving her nowhere to go.

And then she realized Bannon had been gone for hours. Or had he? Sela's stomach rumbled for dinner, and she felt the circadian pull toward sleep, but the sun was as high and bright as mid-day. Was she losing track of time? Or was time losing track of her?

Just when she felt she might drop from exhaustion, she heard an eagle cry. She raced toward the sound, but as she got closer to where she thought it came from, she heard it again. This time, behind her and farther away. She twisted about, and chased it. A third time, the cry sounded, but back where she'd originally been searching.

"Bannon!"

She hovered, watching and listening.

"Bannon!" she tried again.

Now, she was downright worried.

And her wings were cramping, her shoulder muscles seizing. She had to land, somewhere, to take a break. She considered sprawling across the treetops, but turned instead toward the sound of slowly traveling water over the rough and grizzled canyon bottom.

Hopefully, the river was as shallow as it looked.

She splashed down, timidly searching the depths. She felt rocks beneath her feet, and sand, and clamped her claws tightly for hold. Then she let her wings drop into the clear, moving water. As it passed over them, it cooled them, and refreshed her. She even took an experimental sip, and found the water sweet and satisfying.

The current did buffet her, though. Knocked her claws free, so she had to find a new ridge to grip. She'd considered changing back to human form in order to fit between the forest trees, but if she was struggling as a dragon in this water, she'd surely lose the fight as a human.

Her claws came loose again, and the water carried her several feet. She dug for the bottom, stabbed her wings toward the gritty bank. She bumped into a large boulder that paused her long enough to find fresh purchase, and there she waited, half plastered to an immense boulder, and half grabbing for her life into river bottom sand.

And she waited. And waited some more. For Bannon. Or for the sky to stop teasing her and show her what to do. Or for something. Anything, to break this weary monotony of endless nothing.

Then she saw something else, for the first time, that churned her stomach, and stole her hunger.

The clouds.

They weren't moving.

She might have burst into tears, but she was too

drained. Was she already dead, but didn't know it? Was this a place of waiting, before being ushered into her final rest? Is that why this water tugged at her, tried to carry her to her grave?

She shot straight up, out of the cold wetness, and back into freedom. She climbed past the dense forest, and followed the cliff upward. Back toward the hole in the cliff where she'd nearly fallen to her death.

Nearly. Fallen.

Maybe she'd hit, and never realized.

Panic sent her onward, flailing, flapping wings she could no longer feel, and searching madly for Jade's torch. The torch Sela had blown brighter. The one stuck into the cliffside where her grandmother waited.

It was there. It had to be.

But it wasn't.

She passed back and forth, her forepaws pounding rock. Where was the cave? Where was Jade? Where was Bannon?

Where was *she*?

§

"You seem to know where you're going," said Layce. She patted Drell's neck from where she sat on his spine. She was getting better at letting Drell carry her; she didn't lean out so hard in the wrong direction when he turned, and didn't squeeze her legs, resisting, whenever he banked or shifted.

But it was still an arduous trek across the Rage

sands, with dry heat baking his snout and turning the membrane of his wings to parchment. "How are you doing up there?" he called to the wizard.

"I have sand in my undies!" She wiggled about, forcing him to adjust dramatically.

"Thirsty? Tired?" he asked.

"Yes! But don't stop on my account." She jiggled again. "You did warn me this was going to be tough."

True enough. He flew on.

But Layce gave him too much credit. He didn't exactly know where he was going, he only knew where not to go. He'd spent so much time of his youth already searching this immense desert, he knew where not to look.

And Sela had given him a vague idea of where to start. West of Riddess Castle, at the bulge of a hem beyond a maple grove. Trouble was, he couldn't exactly fly over the castle and start from the logical place. Blackclaw used Riddess Castle as a base of operations; as far as anyone knew, and the point was to avoid it, not pass over the front yard.

Instead, Drell carried Layce the long way around, as Tay had instructed, following the desert edge from inside it, keeping his flight low, and just skimming the rim of heat. A delicate dance between using the desert as cover, and being eaten by it.

"Do you sense anything?" he asked her. She'd brought along a handful of crystals, a couple of them to help track any kind of magical vibrations coming from any mysterious place from beyond.

"Nothing," said Layce. "You?"

"Me?" he asked.

"Who else?" She patted his head, between his nubbed horns. "You're as magical as any crystal. More than," she said. "What do you sense?"

He didn't want to say it aloud, because it seemed, somehow, that keeping it to himself made it less real. But what he sensed, what he smelled in the desiccated air, was a storm. A Rage Desert storm of sand and wind that could flay the skin off both of them before they hit the ground from falling.

"I don't see it," called Layce. "Which direction?"

That was the worst part of Rage's storms. They brewed constantly, frothing about just below the surface, and only exploded into view just in time to attack. "We won't see it," said Drell.

Layce's legs gripped him. "Not until we're in it," she said, finishing his sentence.

"Want to turn back?" he asked.

"No," she said. "No, whatever happens, we have to keep going. We have to find it."

He swerved left to keep the desert edge in sight. "But we still don't know what to do once we get there."

"If a magic well is broken, it will need magic to heal it," said Layce. "How hard can it be?" He thought he heard her laugh, but maybe that was a whistle of wind past his ear.

And then they reached the bulge of sand, gnawing at the grasslands of Esra the way Sela described. Drell paused to treadle his wings, hovering.

"Yes," said Layce. "That's got to be it."

"That means we go in now," he said.

She gripped his horns. Her knees pressed against his neck. She didn't even have to say what she was thinking, Drell felt her trepidation loud and clear. And her determination.

He faced the churning heat of the desert, and pressed on, headfirst.

He felt the tickle of something going round one of his horns. "These are the crystals, on strings," said Layce. "If anything happens, you go on. You take these to that well and heal this desert."

He didn't know if he'd be brave enough to push on without her, but he nodded, anyway.

Flying into the desert was like passing through live flame. A few yards deep, and Drell could already feel his scales wanting to curl. They tugged at his skin, and scratched the sand trapped beneath them. Layce's breathing tightened. He couldn't imagine how long a human being could withstand the torture. He pumped his wings faster, trying to cover more ground in less time.

And still, always, was the fetid stench of an oncoming storm breathing across them.

He was suddenly very glad he wasn't alone.

Chapter Twenty-Four

"He is dead?"

Jia stared at Blackclaw, trying to keep her grip on the castle wall while sparkles danced around her vision. "You killed Whitetail?"

"What, no applause? I would have thought removing your rival would bring at least bring a smile to your face." Blackclaw lunged out and off the wall to the ground.

True, the news should have made her happy. Wasn't her plan all along to avenge the death of her love? And hadn't she told herself over and over that Fane's death was the highest result she could hope for? But she hadn't seen the dragon, hadn't looked into his eyes while she gloated at her victory, and told him to his face why she, of all dragons, was the one to have defeated him.

After all her efforts, and her anguished ministrations, he was simply dead. Quietly. Suddenly.

"I see," said Blackclaw. "You would have liked to be

the one, yourself."

"No," she said, quickly. Which was true. Wishing for Fane's death was a different thing than bringing it about. Had she a weapon in her paw and the dragon's legs in chains, would she have been able to go through with it? She would never know, now.

Perhaps it was best. She wasn't sure she wanted to know, exactly, who she was that far inside.

"A matter of needing to be careful what you wish for?" asked Blackclaw.

"Yes," she said. "Exactly that."

"And with my wispy advisor out of the way, you need a new goal to focus on."

She blinked slowly at Blackclaw, realizing she'd been too stunned to be careful about controlling her thoughts. "Yes," she said, regaining her conscious use of honesty the way it had always worked for Fane. "Yes, I have been more focused on a single thing than I before realized."

"That," said Blackclaw, beckoning her from the wall with his paw, "...is the sure sign of a strong will headed for greatness."

She hopped out toward him, using her wings to balance a soft landing.

"And I have your next goal. Find me Jastin Armitage. Bound and gagged, or semi-conscious. I want his key."

Jia tensed at the name. If there was anyone she'd be able to kill with her own two paws, it was that human.

"Ah, but you have strong feelings about the man,"

said Blackclaw. "And not the charitable kind."

"You could say that."

"Any other time I might let you turn those feelings loose on him." Blackclaw strode closer, and studied her eyes. "But for now, I need him alive. I suggest you keep your personal feelings out of the way."

"Of course," she said. Trouble was, her personal feelings were what fueled her this far, and now she was cut loose. What she'd hoped for, had lived for, all these years had come to pass. Fane Whitetail was destroyed. She never aligned with Blackclaw, except to get closer to the White.

She really didn't care what Blackclaw wanted.

"You will deliver him to me," he said. "I am sure of my victory now, but I have been overconfident before and will not allow for that mistake again. The magic of that golden scale will be mine, and seal Leland's defeat."

Jia was listening, though. She would have no part in Leland's defeat. "How do you know the significance of this thing?" she asked.

"I was leader of the Dragon Council for years, remember? I had access to every scroll in the library of the time. And I am not unaware of the work the Redhearts have put into the documentations in Wren Meadow. I have my sources; the fact of which you should by now be quite aware."

Jia's bones turned cold inside her. "Someone in Leland has been helping you?"

Blackclaw smiled. "Do you think you are the only one with a friend in the mountains?"

"But," Jia stammered. "But that was Fane's—"

"Look," said Blackclaw. "Whatever roaring contest you had with Whitetail, that is over, obviously. Do not insult me with nitpicking over who started what. I could have just as easily had you dragged off and executed. Whitetail is dead because he made a play for *my* power. *My* position." Blackclaw leaned closer. His sulfuric breath stung Jia's nostrils. "And he was dried out and useless. He was from an old time, and had no place beside me in Leland's new future."

Blackclaw smiled again, but the expression clashed with the iciness behind his eyes, and for the first time, Jia sensed the danger in his soul. The dark, malevolent danger. "You will be beside me, Jia Greensale. As the one who orchestrated my victory."

Jia shrank back, tried to swallow. "What do you mean?" Her voice sounded weak and too high-pitched.

"Leland's human forces will never be so divided as during this meeting you maneuvered with Lestir Grimmin. I will easily dispatch the small contingent, while my fighters finish off those at the castle." His smile turned hard as stone. "And I will take no prisoners this time. Humans will burn until there is nothing left to bury."

Jia's lungs squeezed dry. "But you... but I..." She tried to make sense, but her words didn't work. Her thoughts couldn't organize.

His paw suddenly clutched her throat. Her breath pinched off. She coughed, scratched her claws at his knuckles. "Whatever you saw in Whitetail that made you support him," he said, his breath and his eyes searing through her scales and into her blood, "...it isn't even a shadow of my strength. Of what I can do to you."

"Please," she tried to say, the word choked beneath his grip. Dots danced around her eyes.

He released her.

She dropped to all fours, head hanging. Her eyes burned and watered. She wheezed, air trying to pull in and push out at the same time. She fought back a convulsion to retch.

Blackclaw lifted up, his onyx wings outstretched. He pumped them once, twice, and then landed himself onto the castle wall and hunkered over like a gargoyle, his face fierce and snarling. He sucked in a deep breath, his chest filling, and then he blasted a stream of orange flame toward the ground, on the other side where Jia couldn't see.

But she could hear. Human screams erupted. Footsteps turned to panic. Chaos.

And she could smell. Roasted flesh.

Now she did retch.

He expelled until he had to breathe again. Behind him, black smoke roiled outward and upward. Men howled. Women cried.

"Bring me Jastin Armitage, and his golden scale," said Blackclaw. He drew in another breath.

"Stop!" Jia shouted. "Please!"

He did.

"I will find him," she said. And then she launched, eyes blinded by the sting of smoke, and the blur of her tears. Her wings faltered once, and she dropped, almost hitting ground, but she recovered enough to shoot off and away before he changed his mind and attacked his prisoners again. Before she could hear it.

She flew in a panic for several yards before she even knew where she was going. Then, she realized she was heading toward her makeshift little home. She drove on, faster and faster, until she saw the drooping thatch roof. She dove toward it, and skidded to a landing, too weakened by horror to rouse to her feet.

The human, Gladdis, hurried outside. Jia had nearly forgotten the rose of a girl was still there.

"What happened?" Gladdis asked, hugging her frail arms around Jia's neck.

The tender move broke her. Jia burst into tears. "What have I done?" she wailed. "What have I done?"

§

Sela clung to the cliff face until her claws ached. Her legs trembled. Her body sagged.

She couldn't fly up, she couldn't fly across. Wherever she was, she knew her only option was down, into the river, and at this point, hungry and tired and scared and feeble, she wouldn't be able to fight the current. If she gave up and let go, the water would carry her off to wherever it wished.

Sela had an idea of where that would be, and she wasn't ready to die. Not yet.

Even if she was already dead, but didn't realize it.

She wasn't ready, yet, to accept it.

So she clung.

Pebbles gave way under her back foot. She slipped, and stabbed her toenails into a fresh spot.

Her eyes closed. Her head nodded downward to doze, but she snapped back awake, and blinked herself alert.

Her left foreleg cramped. She flexed her knuckles to break it up, but when she reached to re-grip the cliff, she miscalculated and scraped scales off her digits. The pain startled her, sent a ripple across her shoulders, and blazed a trail for the cramp to follow. Her neck and spine seized. Her head snapped back.

She felt the cliff sliding up away from her.

She was falling.

She thrust out her wings. They trapped air, buffeting her upward, but too fast. She whipped around. She felt her head crack against stone, and she went sick and dizzy.

Then she splashed.

She submerged, found air, submerged again. She gulped, struggled. But in the end, she felt her body betray her. It went limp, and refused to obey her inward screams to fight.

She was dragged into darkness, and she closed her eyes to meet it.

§

Drell's eyes were so dry he could barely blink. Now

and again, Layce would squirt a water bladder over his brow, and whenever the water trickled down into his eyes, he would squeeze them shut in relief. But the bladder was getting lighter, and the desert hotter, and no matter how many times Drell swept low to find a blot of darkness to shade Layce, he found none.

"You're the only shadow in this desert," said Layce, her voice a croak.

"Maybe that's the answer," he said, having a sudden thought. "Instead of riding my back, let me carry you in my paw. My body can shelter you."

"I'll try it," she said.

"Let me land," he said. "Then slide down my wing, and I'll scoop you up."

But the moment his paws touched sand, like lava, he yelped, and retracted.

"Sorry, Layce," he said. "I'll try again."

He felt her shift her weight, and lay out toward his wing, so he opened it, and flattened it as best he could. "Ready?" he asked.

He turned his head to smile at her, to encourage her more than he felt it himself, but saw her staring off, eyes wide, sunburned mouth dangling open.

He followed her gaze to an erupting spout of sand. Yards away. Bearing down on them.

"Drell?" she asked, almost silent.

"Layce! Let go!"

She whipped her head toward him, her eyes even wider, if it was possible. Wider, and bluer than he'd ever seen them.

"I'll catch you, I promise! Just let go!"

She did.

He curled his wing like an ocean wave, slanted it forward, and then gave her a light bounce. She went airborne, arms flailing. Then he rolled, and swung his feet.

He felt her weight in his claws, just as the sandstorm engulfed them.

A wall of wind slammed his wing against his own ribs. He heard a crack. Pain wrenched him. He couldn't tell what broke, ribs or wing, but just as he shifted, adjusting, a second wave blasted across him. Sand scraped over his scales, grinding them, and slammed under his scales, cutting him.

He pulled up his head to get his bearings, but saw ground coming up at him. Too fast. He hugged Layce to his underbelly, wrapped his wings around her, and turned his shoulder to bear the weight of the crash.

He hit. Sand sprayed, and his shoulder furrowed the grit. On and on he slid, until he thought his scales would erupt in flame, or flay completely from his skin.

He slammed into something solid. It knocked him, splayed him out. The wind coughed backward, pulled itself into a funnel of sand, like a writhing serpent, and growled.

He looked down into his empty paws. No Layce.

"Layce!" he shouted out into the churning storm.

Then the funnel slapped toward him, sent him rolling. He tried to pull himself into a bundle, to cocoon himself beneath his wings, but he went akimbo.

"Layce!" he called again, knowing she couldn't hear.

And then he dropped, suddenly.

Darkness.

294	JACKIE GAMBER

"Layce!" he called again, knowing she couldn't hear.

And then he dropped, suddenly.

Darkness.

CHAPTER TWENTY-FIVE

"What did you do?" asked Gladdis again. Jia felt her soft hands on her face, tugging her chin to find eye contact. "Jia, what happened?"

"I've killed them," she said, unable to open her eyes, to face the light of Gladdis's countenance. "All of them. Blackclaw is going to destroy every Leland human, and I've helped him do it."

Jia felt a rumble. At first, she thought it was the breaking of her heart, but then the vibration rolled outward, away toward the south. Jia shot to her feet, cocked her head to listen.

"Did you feel that?"

Gladdis nodded, wide-eyed. "Like an earthquake?"

"That was no earthquake," she said, feeling ice form in her stomach. "That's our magic. It's cracking."

"Just like Orman said it would. If we don't hurry."

"Hurry and do what?" asked Jia.

"All I know is that Sela and Drell are trying to find the places where the magic first erupted, in Murk Forest, and in Rage Desert." Gladdis opened her hands. "He says the scroll says 'heal the rift, and heal the land. Heal the land, heal the rift.'"

"So if they're trying to heal the land, who's trying to heal the rift?" asked Jia.

"What do you mean? Orman says the rift is the tear in the magic, so fixing the land will heal it."

Jia clutched Gladdis's shoulders. "Don't you see? Whitetail was only ever right about one thing. One thing. Humans and dragons have nowhere to go but toward each other, the way it used to be. The way it's supposed to be."

"I don't understand."

"Heal the rift, Gladdis," said Jia, giving the girl a gentle shake. "Heal the rift between dragons and humans! We have to go toward each other, the way it's meant to be!"

"Heal the rift, heal the land," said Gladdis, breaking into a wide grin. Then her expression clouded over. "But how?"

"I only know where to start. Believe me, I wish I didn't know, but I do," said Jia. She knelt down, and beckoned Gladdis to climb onto her back. "We find the man with the Gold's blessing, just as Blackclaw made me promise to do. We find the man who holds the key to the boundary."

Gladdis grunted, and then swung herself over Jia's spine. "What man?"

"The last one I would ever choose for a champion," said Jia, as she vaulted up and into the air. "The last one any dragon would choose. We have to find Jastin Armitage."

§

Sela became aware of the bouncing of her head, and cold splashes against her eyes. Her first realization was she wasn't dead, apparently. Her second? Hands beneath her chin were trying to hold her head steady.

"Bannon?" she asked, peeling her eyes open.

She squinted at her helper, and her focus pulled together. Dark eyes. Dark, wet hair and beard. Graying.

Jastin Armitage.

Sela pulled back, fully aware. She lay on soft grass at the edge of the river. Willow trees bunched together along the bank, and caressed their branches over her ruby feet. The air was thick and warm, and smelled of leather and hyacinth.

Jastin trudged in knee-deep water toward her on the bank.

"Jastin?" she asked, blinking as though it might wake her from whatever strange dream she was having. "Where's Bannon? Is he all right?"

"He's fine," said Jastin. He crouched, and pulled himself, dripping, onto land. A pendant around his neck dangled loose, and glittered so bright she squinted. "He's wondering what happened to you. They all are. Jade, Bannon, your mother. They said you disappeared."

"Disappeared? Bannon is the one who flew off somewhere. I never found him."

Jastin bunched his brows together. "Flew?"

"When we fell out of the hole in the cliff."

"What hole in the cliff?"

Was she speaking the right language? Jastin was staring at her as though she wasn't making any sense. Maybe she wasn't. Maybe Jastin was just as confused in her dream as she was. She tried again, but slower.

"At the end of the cave. Jade and Bannon and I walked to the place in the cave where it suddenly opened up, and I fell out. So did Bannon. And he shouted at me to fly, so I shifted, but I couldn't find anywhere to land."

Jastin slowly shook his head. "There's no cliff. They said you did reach the end of the cave, but you stepped through and disappeared." He turned to look over his shoulder, and pointed somewhere to his left. "That's where I came through. But I never saw a cliff." He faced her again. "Just a riverbank, and then you, splashing down so hard I thought you hurt yourself."

"But Bannon shouted at me! He came through with me!"

Jastin eyed her. "He's back in the cave, waiting with the rest. There's an invisible wall or something. He can't get through, and neither can Jade."

"I don't understand," she said. Was everything after the obscureway a dream? Or was this part the dream? Could she be having a dream inside a dream?

Then she blinked. "Wait a minute. Then how did you get here?" Sela asked, studying Jastin, trying to figure out if he was telling the truth. If he was even real.

"Honestly? I don't know."

So much for that. She didn't know where she was, how she got here, and why Jastin Armitage, of all people, was with her. "Well, for someone who's supposed to be figuring out a way to save our magic, I'm not doing a very good job."

Jastin looked around them, at the river, where it slivered down into a thin stream and pooled against smooth rocks, and at the willows, that waved in a light breeze along the bank, and at the sky, and its endless blue. "It's like a hallucination," he said. "It should be night."

"Feels like that to me, too. As though I've been here for days, but it never changes."

His eyes lingered on her, and his hard-edged face relaxed, took on a sort of shyness. "You're the girl," he said. "Riza's daughter. I saw you change... into that..." He waved his hand at her, "...back in Esra."

"It's a long story," said Sela.

"Does your, ah, does your mother change back and forth like that?"

"No," she said. "Just me. First of a new Kind." She felt a little silly saying it, as though she was the dawn of a new age, or something. But, in a way, she was. Wasn't she? It's what the Gold had told her.

And at that moment, Sela recognized the pendant around Jastin's neck, and pointed at it. "That's what you're wearing!"

Jastin touched the scale with his fingertips. "It's a gift."

She roused from her position, half-sprawled, half-sitting, to alert and perched. "From whom?" she asked, even though she hoped she already knew.

He hesitated.

"You met the Gold, didn't you?" she asked. "That's a scale. The Gold's scale."

Jastin lowered his hand. "Jade called it a key of some kind."

Now Sela rose to all fours. "A key? Did she say to what?"

Jastin pushed to stand, too, following Sela's lead. "To the boundary, whatever that is."

"The boundary!" Sela clapped her forepaws together. "You're the one! All this time, right here in front of us! Wait until my father and mother..."

Her voice trailed. She regarded Jastin, who stood hunched and uncomfortable, almost ashamed of the gift, instead of celebrating it. At the mention of her parents, he'd turned downright sullen. "You have a lot of history with my parents," she said.

He gave a dry laugh. "I don't know what I'm supposed to do with this thing, but if has anything to do your father, you can forget it."

"You hate him that much?"

"He hates me that much," said Jastin. His voice went quiet. "I don't blame him."

Sela frowned. "Well. One thing at a time. You're here now, and I think that scale, that key, has something to do with it. Which means, maybe this weird little space where time stands still is somehow related to the boundary. Maybe it isn't only above us, in the sky, but all around us, all the time. And somehow, we crossed through." She tapped a claw against the scale against his collarbone. "Except I don't have one of these, so I don't know."

"Maybe you don't need a key, because you are one," said Jastin.

Sela smiled, and shrugged both shoulders. She liked the sound of that.

Then she circled, searching around them to get her bearings. All she saw was willow trees, most of them green and unmoving, except near the riverbank, where the water flowed and the trees waved. "I fell into the water. The only thing that acts normal around here. And it carried me here."

Jastin turned around, and looked down at the river. "I swam after you. You had washed up onto the bank."

"Because the water collects here, against these rocks, and turns into a brook that goes off, through the trees, there." Sela pointed toward a patch of more willows, blended with speckled birch trees.

"Except it's flowing toward the river, and the river's flowing toward it," said Jastin. "That doesn't make any sense."

"It doesn't make sense in our world, but maybe it makes perfect sense here." Sela stepped down off the bank into the trickling pool of river water, and then back up and out, a few feet away, where the gentle stream joined the water. She followed it against its flow, along a green and waving path of foliage.

She couldn't shake the feeling that she was walking

with two feet in one world, and two feet in another; straddling planes, and magic. Where one world was dying, and the other was being blocked from saving it.

"I feel it, too," said Jastin, and she heard the faintest tremor in his voice.

The smell of the place changed; moldy. As she followed the water, it turned dark. She closed in on the patch of trees, and found their roots buried in a cesspool. The water stank of death; a layer of scum had grown over the water and was reaching putrid arms of moss out over the ground around it.

"If that pond is supposed to be magic, it's no wonder I can't stand the stuff," said Jastin, coming along beside her. He pinched his nostrils shut.

"Yes, I think that's what I'm looking for. But now what?" she asked.

Jastin just looked at her over his hand on his nose, and shrugged.

§

Drell rocked back as though he'd been shaken. But there was no grip on him, no one with him at all. He was engulfed in darkness, and utterly alone.

And he remembered Layce, and losing her. He curled forward, seized with pain. He'd let her down. He'd let her go.

He wanted to lie out on the ground, wherever he was, and grieve her. To give up on himself, too. And, for a moment, he thought he might. He was tired, thirsty, and utterly defeated. Maybe it was time to admit he'd lost.

But then, he heard whispers. He stilled his breathing to better hear them.

No, not whispers, but definitely voices. Voices so quiet, they might have been miles away, except he heard them near his ears. Words of conversation. A male. A female.

He spun around to stare at the dark where he thought they were coming from. Then he opened his mouth, and gently blew flame into the air, lighting the spot.

He found a well. A stone-walled, circular well, butted up against a slab of stone, covered in brown vines. He was inside something? A part of an ancient building? Whatever it was, it had long been gobbled by desert.

No wonder no one ever found the place by flying over it. It had been buried by generations of sand.

But here he was, standing beside a well in the Rage Desert. He had made it. Somehow, he'd survived, and he'd found it. The well was crusted over with filth, and slimy green moss, but it existed.

And it was talking to him.

At least, it was talking about him. He heard his name.

He blew more flame, this time across the water, and it singed the floating growth, and cracked it, and the growth withered off to the sides of the stone. Small, mossy fires cast more light around the room, and he could see a maze of broken walls in the near distance, scrawled with drawings beneath more parched vines.

But he focused on the water, and the voices.

He could see a halo of daylight in the murky depths. Two figures hovered against a blue background; two faces. As though they were peering at Drell, while Drell peered at them. A human, and a dragon.

A Red.

"Sela?" he called.

The dragon face startled backward. Then she smiled, confused. "Drell? Is that you?"

"I'm here," he said, gripping his paws around the well's stone edge. "I found it!"

"So did we!" she said. "Jastin and I found the water. So strange, we were just talking about you."

"I heard," he said.

Jastin poked his finger toward Drell, and made a ripple. Then he wiped sludge across his garment, scowling. "How do we see him in there?" he asked.

"How's Layce?" asked Sela.

Drell felt a stab in his gut. "There was a storm," he said. "I lost her."

They were both silent a long time. Then Jastin said, "Maybe she just couldn't get through."

"I thought I lost Bannon, too," said Sela. "Turns out, he never passed through at all. But he's fine. Maybe it's the same with Layce."

"Maybe," said Drell, although he didn't think Layce fared any better outside, in a desert storm all by herself, even if she was still alive.

"I'm sure she's all right," said Sela.

"Yes," said Drell, because it was easier than arguing he was certain Layce was not all right. "So what do we do?" he asked.

"We've been talking about that," said Sela. "We've been wondering about the drawings in the cave that leads to this place. As vague as the message is, some things are very clear. Like how a human enters, but a dragon comes out. And how the dragon's color is red."

They must have understood something Drell didn't, because it didn't sound clear to him at all. "Layce said we had to heal broken magic with magic," he said, reaching up to his horns, to the strings of crystals she'd entrusted to him. "She gave me her crystals..."

He found nothing. No strings, no crystals attached to his horns. He slumped forward. "I've lost them, too."

"It's all right," said Sela. "We knew this wasn't going to be easy, but we're closer than ever to an answer." She smiled, but it wasn't the water clouding the expression. "We have plenty of time," she said, her voice tight, nervous. "We have plenty of time."

CHAPTER TWENTY-SIX

It had been a long time since Lestir Grimmin had needed a contingent of soldiers for any reason, let alone leading them across Leland toward Fell Lake for a discussion of a dragon alliance.

Dragon. Alliance.

The very words sent a shiver down his spine, but would draw more than that from his citizens, if they guessed his agenda.

Bodily harm came to mind. Grievous bodily harm.

It's why he hadn't explained it to anyone. And he'd tried to keep the soldier group small, both because he wanted to gain the dragon's trust, and because he didn't want the attention of Leland farmers as he trudged his men across their fields and into the Leland woods. But, attention they got. Dusty children pointed and waved. Sweaty men set down their implements to gape, as troops passed their front gates.

"No eye contact," he reminded the men over his shoulder. Quietly.

He and thirty men, ten of them on horses, stomped over Leland's graveled and tilting lands toward Fell Lake and its dry basin, and tried to pretend they weren't there.

He'd left his captain, Rames, behind with the rest of his men, and had settled for Marck, his trusted messenger, as aid to the proceedings. Rames was too quick to draw, and Lestir's memories still stung from his last meeting with the green dragon.

The meeting where he had served a dragon tea, and had discussed an oncoming war over sweet cakes. The meeting where the green dragon, Jia, explained Blackclaw's treachery, and had promised Leland help from dragons that opposed the black dragon. The meeting where they were both too suspicious of each other to let down their guard.

Today, though, he was ready. Practiced. He'd stripped his soldiers of all weapons but their most basic blades, as proof this was a peaceful mission between his people and the Leland Mountain dragons. He would show the green dragon, and the authorities she brought with her, just how peaceful and trusting he could be.

They finally reached the edge of Fell Lake, just as his boots were beginning to rub a sore spot into his left foot. "Line them up," he said to Marck, who arched his brows. Right, Lestir reminded himself. Messenger, not captain. "Just figure it out."

"Horse and riders to the back," said Marck. "Give me five rows of four."

Lestir stared down at the dry lake. It had once been a wide expanse of crackled, orange clay, but over the years, green growth had managed to sprout. It criss-crossed the clay, turning the basin into a green and orange plaid quilt. Although, today it looked more like a giant had just gotten out of the bed and left it rumpled and unmade.

A shadow blotted the sun above them all. Lestir shaded his eyes, and looked up. No, not a shadow, but a black dragon, who soared in from beyond the trees, and lowered himself onto the curved edge of the lake bed. He folded in his wings, and stared across his snout at the men.

Lestir gulped. Not the dragon he was expecting. How was he supposed to tell them apart from each other?

"Good day," said the black dragon. "Fane Whitetail is not available, I'm afraid."

Lestir heard men behind shuffle their feet. Horses shied. Lestir held out his hand, silently steadying them. "I am Lestir Grimmin, here as a show of good faith by the people of Leland for a mutually profitable future."

"Mutually profitable?" asked the black dragon.

"As discussed with your green dragon," said Lestir.

"Her name is Jia Greenscale," said the dragon.

Lestir swallowed again. Not going well, he sensed. He tried again. "We are here, as agreed, to discuss the alliance of Leland and her dragons against the forces of Fordon Blackclaw."

The dragon roared, quivering the ground. Lestir's legs nearly gave out. He heard shuffling feet of his men behind him, trying to keep balanced.

The dragon shot up like an arrow, and swelled out to cover them all under the darkness of his hovering form. "I am Fordon Blackclaw."

Betrayed. Now Lestir's legs did give out. He felt the ground come up to jar his spine. "To weapons," he tried to say to Marck. He couldn't tell if the words came out.

"Now!" snarled the dragon.

Behind him, from the ragged depths of vine and clay at the base of the lake, dragons erupted. Yellow ones, blue ones, some gray and some brown... more than Lestir could count in those moments. He saw them burst from the ground like an explosion of stones, and everything around him went quiet and slow.

"To weapons," hollered Marck's voice.

And then came the insipid whisper of his soldiers unsheathing their only defenses. Daggers.

Betrayed. They were all dead. Here, and at the castle, and everywhere. He couldn't think past the looping hopelessness.

He looked up, into the ferocious face of a yellow dragon, who snarled at him from the sky before pulling in a long, deep breath.

He heard Marck shout again. "Take cover!"

And then he saw flame, and smelled the burning of his own hair.

§

Kallon careened over the mountains, watching his shadow below him as it darted forward and back, catching on a high spot, and then dropping to scrape over a round, low boulder. Orman sat on his neck, and Min Greenscale and Hale Brownwing flanked him. They were taking the long way around to Fell Lake, using forest cover as long as they could, both to avoid entanglements with any local humans, and to surprise Whitetail, and whatever his plans for the human, Gladdis.

This was a part of Leland he hadn't visited in a long time. Didn't want to see.

Orman dug in his heels. "Can't you go any faster?"

"Only if you can hold on tighter, old man," said Kallon.

Kallon pushed forward, but then suddenly slowed. He heard a shout. A dragon roar. The scrabble of feet and fighting. He looked at Brownwing, who pulled up in surprise. Greenscale also hesitated. Collective confusion.

Then the three dove toward Fell Lake, nostrils steaming. Wings pumping.

Trees gave way to open land, and Kallon immediately saw Blackclaw.

Blackclaw?

He was pointing and shouting orders to other dragons, who spat flame into trees, and swooped low, clawing and biting at men who kicked, and crawled, and stabbed tiny knives toward dragon noses.

A squat, brown dragon stabbed a shortsword into a man's gullet.

Kallon's brain didn't have time to process the why, or the how, but he grasped the 'when'.

Now. Blackclaw attacked now.

"Greenscale, get back to Mount Gore! Bring what dragons we've got, and hurry!" Kallon pointed to Brownwing. "Fly on to the castle and see what goes on there, if they need help."

Brownwing looked out over the fighting. "You can't tackle this alone, Redheart."

"I'm not alone," said Kallon.

"If you mean me, I'm not much with a sword," said Orman. "But let me get my crystals out!" He dug his heels into Kallon's throat. "Come on! Before the brute gets away with it!"

"Go, now!" Kallon said to Brownwing and Greenscale, who both sped off like flashes of lightning.

Kallon lowered behind a copse of sycamore trees, and Orman stepped off onto a short branch. Then, before Blackclaw even had the chance to realize he was there, he pushed with all his strength away from the tree, and jettisoned himself.

He lowered his head, and aimed his horns into Blackclaw's throat.

CHAPTER TWENTY-SEVEN

"The drawing in the cave is red," said Sela, sprawled on the ground beside the festering water. "My mother thought it was important. Of all the colors of dragons that could come here, why red?" she asked.

"Because you're red?" said Jastin.

"But they couldn't have known it would be me. That drawing isn't *me*."

"There are drawings here, too," called Drell through the water. "Old and faded, I can barely make them out. There's a black dragon sitting in the well."

Sela pushed up with her paws. "A black dragon?"

Jastin crossed his arms.

"*Sitting* in it?" she asked. She looked at the murky water near her feet, and then at Jastin.

"Don't look at me," he said.

"Tell me again what Layce said about healing broken magic," said Sela.

"She said to use magic to heal magic," said Drell. "She brought a lot of crystals."

Jastin crouched beside the water and peered down into it. "Look, I don't know anything about this, and I've hated magic my whole life, so you two are the experts here, not me."

"But?" asked Sela.

"Aren't dragons supposed to be made of magic? That's what Jade said, anyway. Something about crystals being pushed out into the sky to fly. I figured it for a bedtime story."

"What else did she say?"

"I wasn't really paying attention." He scowled, and his whole demeanor shifted, closing off. But he added, as though the words stung his mouth, "But why would you need a crystal, if you *are* a crystal?"

"You mean, I don't need a key, because I am a key?" asked Sela.

Jastin shrugged. "Like I said, you're the expert."

"He's right," called Drell. "He's right! I'm getting in."

Sela eyed the filthy water. She dipped a toe.

And as soon as she touched it, she knew. As sure as she knew the sky was up, and the earth was solid, she knew who she was, why she was here, and how the magic had been waiting for her to come home.

"I'm a bloodstone," she cried. "I'm a wish!"

Already, the water began to clear. She dunked her forepaws into it, splashed it over her face. "I'm a wish!"

Then she submerged, and made the best possible wish she could think of, for today.

§

Sela, a wish?

Drell lowered himself into the well, and waited for the water to settle. He couldn't feel the bottom, even with the tips of his wings, and he wondered if he reached far enough, would the black tips find Sela Redheart at the other end?

But even as he thought it, he knew she was too far away to actually touch. In another province. Another world, really. She would never be his to touch.

It was the story of his life. Hovering at the edge of worlds, never quite being a part of one. He was expected to live with mystery and never ask; to live with questions and have no answers.

And then it dawned on him, as the water began to clear around him, and churn against his shoulders.

He was onyx. He was a secret.

And he had a secret, one he could never, would never tell. So he pulled his whole self under, and spoke into the magic.

He told the water he was in love with Sela Redheart.

§

Kallon reeled back, and hit the ground. He felt claws at his shoulders, wrestling him to turn belly up. He roared, blasted fire.

Somewhere at the edge of his blurred vision, he saw a bony figure, waving arms. Orman. Light grew out from where the wizard stood, bulging toward a group of dragons closing in on near soldiers. The light burst, blinding them, skewing them off course.

Kallon leapt forward, and grasped a Blue careening toward him. He flipped mid-air, and launched the Blue at Blackclaw, who tried to dodge, but couldn't shift his bulk fast enough. Both dragons collided, and in a tangle of wings and feet, dropped from the sky.

But so did Kallon. His stamina drained faster than he could sustain it. Every lunge, every sweep, every dive into the fray took more and more of him. He landed hard, and his legs crumpled.

"Kallon!"

He looked up to find Min Greenscale bearing down, adorned with steelclaws. Behind him, a hoard of dragons dressed for a fight, with leather and metal face plates, and wing cuffs, all bearing the glint of Leland's flaming sigil. Like a stream of fire, they propelled into the action, knocking Blackclaw's fighters off kilter, and clutching up singed humans to throw them into the safety of the nearest trees.

Kallon saw them, and raised his fist to cheer them. But he couldn't even stand up to join them.

Then, off in the distance, so far away Kallon could barely hear it, a detonation. Like the hiccup of a volcano. Just as he was squirming around to get a look, a gout of light shot up beyond the trees, stabbing into clouds. Colors bubbled up from the base of the light, and spilled out, turning gray cliffs into sharp browns and blacks; over treetops, brightening foliage into chartreuse and deep emerald; over open ground, boiling outward as a lava flow, but carrying only vibrant life and light.

And then it hit him. Like wind, except there wasn't any. Like an explosion, except all was quiet. He had to grip the ground to keep from being bowled over by the force, and he saw Leland dragons and Blackclaw's dragons and weakened humans fall, tumble, and roll.

An invisible storm opened out across them, and saturated the earth with its unseen rain.

But Kallon felt it. Inside, in his bones. In his heart. Magic.

He lunged upward, renewed. And he spun around, eyes searching for Blackclaw.

Then, a second explosion. Farther away, in the west. Magic boiled across the land, lighting and replenishing.

They had done it. His daughter, Sela. And Drell, the mystery. They had really done it.

"A-ha!" cried Orman. He hopped once, twice, his gangly legs kicking, and he pointed up at Kallon's face. "Those kids, those foolhardy, wonderful, blasted kids, they did it!"

And then Blackclaw swooped. He breathed out a gust of fire straight at Orman.

"Orman!"

Leland dragons bloated upward, and pounced Blackclaw, cutting off his flame stream. Kallon was hit in the shoulder, and knocked away.

If Kallon was invigorated by the indwelling of this fresh magic, so were the others. The fight took on a newly vicious bite. A Yellow gouged claws at Kallon's eyes, and Kallon barely had time to turn his head, let alone defend it. He trotted along the ground just a few steps to get his bearings, and then he spun back and threw his weight into the Yellow's midsection. He snapped at waving legs, felt claws in his teeth, and then yanked. The Yellow slammed to the ground, and went still.

But all around him, as his valiant dragons fought back against Blackclaw's scourge, they struggled. They were too few in number, no matter their fortitude. Blackclaw had twice as many dragons in the sky, still fighting, besides the ones on the ground, chasing after the handful of human soldiers that were left.

And Brownwing hadn't come back from the castle, so Kallon could only imagine the worst of what was happening there.

He spotted Orman, though, finally, as a haze of burning vines cleared. The old man was brushing ashes off his trousers, completely unsinged, and glowering with annoyance. He dug a clear crystal from his pocket.

And found Kallon staring at him.

He knew, too, they were losing.

A horn bleated.

He heard a voice call out, and, at first, he wondered if he was imagining it.

But no! He twisted around to find Riza, surrounded by a flock of colorful birds, flying to meet him, wings pumping hard. "Kallon!" she called again.

"Stay back!" he hollered.

A golden eagle veered high over the treeline, and then plummeted head first toward the rumpled rim of the basin. Just as it skimmed over the clay dirt, more animals burst through the trees behind it; furry monkeys, white faces screeching, swung out on vines. Mottled cats emerged, running so hard and fast their mouths frothed.

And then, men and women, with branches and vinery twisted, wrapped, and wildly flailing from their arms and legs, looking more forest than human, lunged into the fray, swinging sharpened sticks and flinging rocks from sling-shots.

A cat leapt from a rock onto a surprised Brown, and sank its teeth into the back of the scaly neck.

A pebble cracked into the left eye of a Blue, bloodying it. The Blue yelped, and then roared, and, just as it spun and sucked in a breath, a stockpile of monkeys leapt out, scattered across its face, screeching and clawing.

"Kallon," called Riza again, and clutched at his paws. They met mid-air. "The Murkens knew you needed them."

"You shouldn't be here!"

"I want to help!"

Kallon pulled Riza up higher, away from the chaos below them, as best he could. "I can't. I can't have you here, in the danger."

"But I want to help!"

He didn't have time to argue. He barely had time to think. "Then help the wounded. Burned humans, bleeding dragons. Can you tend to them?"

"I will," she said, and spiraled down into the

billowing smoke of scorched earth.

Then he drew up his wings, but, just as he was about to throw himself back into the fray, he spotted a wavering flicker of movement on the far horizon, toward the west. He squinted.

The movement grew into a shape. A black shape, undulating toward him. A dragon. Drell!

And he wasn't alone. Behind Drell flew more dragons, careening forward like a tawny spray of desert sand. More dragons, reflecting the high sun off their Esra-emblazoned face masks and chest plates. More dragons, for the fight.

But Kallon's hopes didn't raise very high. What had seemed at first like a reprieve was just a motley few. He counted twelve. Twelve dragons, altogether. Still, as Drell pulled in closer, Kallon rose up and out to meet him, and the brave, willing others.

Drell didn't look as triumphant as Kallon was expecting. And then he saw why.

Drell carried Layce Phelcher in his forelegs. She sprawled ominously limp.

"She is alive," said Drell, when Kallon got close enough. "But she needs…"

"I will see to it," said Kallon. He reached out, and Drell carefully rolled Layce into Kallon's paws.

"These dragons are my tribe, plus others. From the desert," said Drell. "They wish to join us."

"We need them. Blackclaw has attacked."

Drell nodded, swallowed.

"You found the well," said Kallon. "We all felt it."

Drell nodded again. "Sela?"

"She was successful, too." Kallon ran his dry tongue across his mouth. "I need to ask more of you," he said.

Drell waited, his wings slowly treading.

"I sent Brownwing to scout Shornmar Castle, but he has not returned. Will you go? Take your contingent to find out what is happening?"

Drell looked behind himself at his tribe; Tay and Lena Ambercrest; Orus and Rasp Ruddyhock, the twins. Each bobbed their heads in a nod, along with the others.

"We will go," said Drell. He rested a single digit on Layce's pale brow. Then he dropped, flew beneath Kallon, and led the desert dragons to the east.

§

Drell's flying faltered as Kallon Redheart returned toward where he came, and disappeared from sight. He should have stayed with Layce, in the desert. He should have stayed with Layce now.

He was still looping the memory around and around his mind of finding her there, just at the entrance to the ruins of the well, sprawled and weak.

She'd talked, though. Smiled at him, knowing they'd healed the magic. "Been here the whole time," she'd said. "I just couldn't get through."

And then she stopped talking, and had been silent since.

That was what worried him the most.

He should have stayed with her.

But it wasn't over yet; this battle. It had turned from a fight for the land, to the fight for life. Blackclaw still had to be defeated, and the best way for him to help Layce, and the rest of his friends, and his tribe.

His tribe. Flying behind him, supporting him, and willing to risk to make things right. He owed them strength and courage. And so he drew himself inward, pulled his fear into a corner of his soul, and tucked it away. And he led them onward, steady and true, toward the castle.

But he saw—they all saw—before he even fully approached the castle's courtyard that Redheart was right to be worried. Brownwing's body lay across grass and cobblestone where it appeared to have been felled. Blackclaw's dragons, at least twenty of them, hung like stormclouds over the parapets, blasting steam and flame at any humans who dared to expose themselves by trying to fight them back. Seared soldier bodies sprawled in the courtyard, outside the bailey, and even out in the fields to the south.

Whatever battle had happened here, it had been over in minutes.

Drell looked backward at Tay. "I have no fighting experience," he said.

"No," said Tay, his facemask rattling. "But you have survived a Rage storm as none of us have."

A Rage storm. Of course. "Follow me," he said.

Drell swept up, leading the others into an arcing mass. And he twirled, beginning a slow spin. His tribe and the rest instinctively mimicked, and Drell barely had to think his plan before the others knew what he was doing.

At the highest part of his flying arc, Drell pulled his wings against his belly and dove. Continuing his spin, he drilled right into the heart of Blackclaw's collected dragons, splintering them. Surprising them.

And the desert dragons followed suit, in a dizzying funnel of blinding speed and wind.

He felt dragon bodies topple aside before they even had a chance to blink.

When his speed slowed enough, he stretched his wings to catch himself, and spun about. The ambush had worked. Blackclaw's dragons laid out, stunned, on the ground, or flopped clumsily about in the sky, trying to recover.

The nearest dragon, a small Brown, jerked beside Drell, startled and dizzy. Then she yelped, and dove under a stone overhang, hiding out of sight.

But the next one, a larger Brown, didn't shy so easily. He bore down on Drell, nostrils blasting steam. Tay divebombed him, and stabbed his claws at the base of his brown tail. They wrestled together, veering off.

Then a cry, a human cry, came ricocheting up from somewhere in the courtyard shadows. It grew in volume, screeching fiercely. Drell just pinpointed the sound when he saw a man, sword raised high, racing across the courtyard, tunic flapping. His face was round, like a child's, with slanted eyes. But he ran with all the determination of a soldier.

His scream pitched higher, and when he reached

one of Blackclaw's stunned dragons, twisting about in matted grass, the man plunged the sword to its hilt in the dragon's neck. "Bad dragon!"

The dragon howled, and swung his foreleg. The man was knocked flat.

But others appeared, then, and swarmed out from castle doors and hallways. More humans, dragging swords, or awkwardly swinging shields, looking more like a flock of peasants than an army.

And his tribe dove, and slashed claws, and wrestled with Blackclaw's fighters. Drell swept his tail at legs, gnashed his teeth at wings, and blasted flame at unprotected faces.

Somewhere in the midst of it all, he realized another human had joined the fumbling group below, and was organizing them, rallying them.

Venur Riddess. From his seat on the back of Lin Orangepaw, Ebouard Riddess was leading.

Drell shot downward to communicate. "We need help!"

"We have dispatched more dragons to Fell Lake," said Orangepaw. "But we do not have enough here, either!"

"We will work together," said Ebouard. "Humans are not weaklings!"

"Not weaklings," echoed the voice of the man from earlier, who had defeated a dragon, himself.

"Indeed," agreed Drell.

"Venur Shornmar," said Ebouard, indicating the man. "We've explained that Leland dragons are here to help."

"Here to fly!" called Venur Shornmar. He leaped at Drell's legs, scrabbling and clinging.

Drell fully rested on the ground to steady the man. "Are you sure you're able?"

"Not weaklings!" said the venur. He pulled up and over, and settled in behind Drell's neck.

"Then let's fly," said Drell.

§

Riza waited at the edge of the treeline, watching over the human soldier at her feet, while Avara dug out roots from a nearby patch of eyebright. Avara hurried back, and helped Riza pound the plant into a waxy poultice, and to smear it across his scalded eyes. He moaned softly.

"We have lost too many," said Riza.

Avara glanced up. Then she looked over at Layce, her sister, where the wizard rested, unmoving, beside a charred elm trunk.

"I should have made Orangepaw take me back to Mount Gore for more supplies," said Avara. "How can we heal these fighters without more supplies?"

"How can we win a battle without enough fighters?" asked Riza.

"I didn't see it ending this way," said Avara. She knelt beside Layce, and lifted a cup of cool water to her mouth. The water collected in the cracks of her lips, and dribbled down her cheeks. "I just didn't see it."

Then Riza felt a stirring. Inside her soul, at the base of her heart, she felt a ray of hope. She gasped, and clutched her paw to her chest.

"Sela!"

Avara stood, eyes widening.

"She's coming!" At first, Riza burst into a wide smile. And then, she clutched at her chest for a different reason. "She can't come here! Not to this!"

Riza leapt upward, slicing through the miasma of smoking trees, smoking bodies. She cut left, and northeast, following the tug of her heart. She'd barely gotten beyond the sound of the combat before she felt Sela, and then saw her, just yards away and careening closer by the moment.

"Sela!" she called. "Wait!"

And at that moment, she also realized Sela had a rider. Jastin Armitage.

Then, behind Sela, another dragon rippled into view. A young Green, with the girl called Leesa, and Gladdis, Sela's friend.

But her eyes snapped back to the dark human on Sela's back.

"Mother!" Sela cried, with a crackle of emotion.

"Stay back!"

Sela drew up, and caught the wind with her wings to pause, giving Riza the chance to catch up. Riza circled, glaring at Jastin, and then led them all to a smooth patch of short growth to land.

With her feet on the ground, Riza immediately turned to point her claw at Jastin. "What do you think you're doing?"

"He's with me, Mother," said Sela, pulling back, and lifting her wings, thrusting her chest.

The fool girl didn't know what she was saying. Riza's anger at Jastin bubbled over into anger at Sela, and at all of them. She leaned toward the Green, too. "And just who are you?"

"Jia Greenscale," she replied. "Daughter of Min—"

"Yes, I recognize you now. Seems your waywardness has influenced my own daughter, and I just won't have it." She vented her feelings to Gladdis, next, scowling at her. "I should have thought you would learn to keep better company."

Gladdis, on Jia's back, winced. Leesa, ever silent, glared.

Jia scowled, too. "Now wait a—"

"Mother!" Sela stepped between them, her brow tightened into ridges, her green eyes dark with pain.

The expression stopped Riza cold. She tasted the bitterness of her words in the air between them.

"I am taking Jastin to where he needs to go," said Sela. "To my father. We will need him when the fighting starts."

"It has already started," said Riza, pain flashing through her gut.

Sela and Jia exchanged looks. Even Jastin seemed more somber at the news.

"Then we must hurry," said Sela. "We can't win without Jastin."

Riza snorted. "He is the embodiment of all the

reasons we are fighting. He is a greedy, self-absorbed human. A murderer. Not only has Blackclaw used him for vicious acts, but Blackclaw has enraged other dragons into violence because of the likes of him."

Riza breathed heat into her words, and leaned forward to sizzle Jastin with them. "Our fight *is* you, Jastin."

For his part, Jastin lowered his eyes, and remained silent.

"I know how you feel," said Jia Greenscale. "I have my own reasons to despise this man." She pushed forward, and met Riza's gaze. "But I have put it aside, for now."

Riza shifted her feet, parted her mouth to object.

Jia held up a paw. "For now, Riza Redheart. Because something bigger than my own pain is going on right now. This man is our champion."

Riza fell back a full step. Her blood stopped flowing in her veins. She looked from Jia, to the man on her daughter's back. "Are you insane?"

"Show her, Jastin," said Sela.

He drew out something tucked beneath the twist of fabric near his neck, and then laid down his hand. There, resting against his chest, was a golden amulet.

No, not an amulet. A scale. The Gold's scale.

"Where did you get that?" she asked.

"He gave it to me," said Jastin.

Riza felt her nostrils flare. "You expect me to believe that?"

Jastin squared his jaw. "No, actually. But it's true."

"It's the key, Mother," said Sela.

Riza shook her head, again and again. She couldn't seem to stop.

"Mother," said Sela.

"Heal the rift, heal the land," said Gladdis, quietly.

All eyes turned to her. She startled, but then looked at each face, in turn. "What stronger magic can there be, but his forgiveness?" she asked.

Riza's hatred faltered. She felt it fracture, deep inside, like a gash in a frozen lake, weeping iciness. It was still there, frightening her. Confusing her. But she did know, now, what had to be done.

"You want this forgiveness?" she asked Jastin.

The man's eyes dampened. Riza wouldn't have believed it if she hadn't seen it for herself. And his voice cracked.

"I do," he said.

She wouldn't have believed that, either. She regarded him for a moment, trying to sort out too many emotions at once.

No time for it. She'd have to figure it all out later.

"Come on," she finally said, and arched her wings to fly. "If you think I'm a tough sell, wait until you talk to Kallon."

§

Jastin couldn't think of anything else he hated more than the thought of facing Redheart. He might rather dig out his own eyes, even. Riza was right, it had been difficult enough to face down her accusations, even though nothing she'd said was untrue.

That's what made it so tough.

But Kallon Redheart?

He was more afraid of looking into that dragon's eyes than he'd ever been chasing one through the trees, hunting it down.

He felt Leesa's warm presence in his mind, though, and he turned to find her smiling, encouraging.

Maybe that part of magic—having her comfort him without his being able to ask for it—wasn't so bad after all.

Riza, in the lead, slowed. That's when Jastin realized he heard the unmistakable groans of warfare, and smelled the gruesome scent of death.

Sela jarred to almost a full stop. The green dragon beside them did the same.

The trees had opened up before them, and offered them full view of charred earth littered with blackened bones, of humans, of dragons. More dragons filled the sky, slashing at each other with teeth and claws, some stabbing rusty weapons. Smoke was so thick Jastin couldn't see through it to the other side. A group of glassy-eyed men sat bleeding at the Fell Lake rim.

Jastin could feel Sela's heart break, right through her scales and into his legs around her neck.

Near a broken tree, Layce Phelcher laid out, pale and limp.

Was she dead?

Her sister Avara knelt beside her, pressing a cloth to

Layce's brow. Hope yet.

Jastin couldn't find Blackclaw in the confusion, but he did manage to recognize Leland's fighters by their protective armors.

Blackclaw's fighters outnumbered them three to one.

One Leland Yellow fell out, hard, and wavered toward the ground, dead or dying. One less.

"Mother," Sela moaned.

Riza rowed backward, and took Sela's paw in hers.

And then Redheart was there, suddenly, lurching toward the group, his wings torn. His mouth bleeding. One eye swollen shut. "Riza," he whispered, as though he was too tired for even a full voice.

"Kallon," she whispered back. They touched snouts.

Then he looked from Jia, to Gladdis and Leesa. To Sela, and to Jastin.

Whatever Jastin had been expecting, had steeled himself for, it wasn't this: the Red met his eyes with gratitude.

It gave Jastin the courage to speak. "I'm the champion," he said. He wasn't even exactly sure what that meant, but it felt right.

"Somehow, I knew you would be," said Redheart.

"I thought you would resent it," said Jastin.

"I probably will, later. For now, my friends are dying." Redheart circled, and then came alongside Sela. "You have the key?" he asked.

"Yes." Jastin showed him the Gold's scale.

"You know what to do with it?"

"Not really."

"Well, it's never stopped any of us before. Climb on."

Redheart stilled his wings enough to spread them out. Sela matched the height and stiffness with her own wings, planking them together. Jastin eased over, stepped across the membranous walkway, and then settled onto Redheart's back.

The last place he thought he would ever find himself.

"I can hardly believe my eyes," he heard Riza whisper. "Kallon Redheart and Jastin Armitage? Saving Leland together?"

"Believe it, Mother," said Sela. "It's what I wished for."

Redheart dropped briefly, and Jastin wondered if he even had the strength to fly. But then the Red soared upward, straight into the clouds, beyond the stench and smoke, into clear blue brightness.

Jastin had never been so high up his whole life. The wind stole his breath. He felt a little dizzy, especially when he glanced down, and saw treetops as faint and tiny as shrubbery. "How far do we go?"

"Until we can't go any farther," said Redheart.

Jastin felt the sky pushing back at them. His body chilled from the inside out, and he began to shiver uncontrollably. He struggled now to breathe at all. He collapsed to Redheart's spine, unable to sit up.

He flattened against the Red, invisible pounds of weight trying to iron him out, trying to squeeze him right through the dragon's skin. "How far?" Jastin tried to ask again, his mouth unwilling to move right.

The Red's wings gave a final thrust, and then stilled. Jastin could feel his wing muscles ripple, trying to move, but the sky fought back. The only place they had left to go was backward.

"Now!" called Redheart.

Jastin's fingers were stiff and clumsy. He managed to wedge his arm between himself and the dragon, and gripped the scale. He gave the leather thong a yank, breaking it. And then, with a grunt of fight left in him, he shoved his fist into the sky's gritting teeth.

They broke. Something broke, anyway. The sky cracked, oozing golden light. It suffused Jastin's hand, warming it.

The crack split wider, bathing Jastin and the dragon both. Jastin heard voices. Whispering. He heard his name, heard Redheart's name.

Then the sky burst. Filled with so much warm, glittering light, it pulsed outward, knocking Redheart back. Jastin fumbled for hold.

The Gold launched out through the gaping fissure, and shot past them both, his wings unfurling, blinding, and crackling with strands of pulsing energy. A stream of white light blazed a path behind him.

The white light broke apart into shards, grew transparent wings, and flew.

Dragons. Hundreds of them. Spilling out through the sky with radiant slashes of translucent bodies, wings, faces. They spiraled downward, following the Gold, fixed on their purpose.

Redheart charged after them.

"What are they?" Jastin called.

The illuminated bodies surrounded them, carried them both with a speed the Red couldn't have mustered alone. Redheart passed under some, over some. Jastin even reached a hand, curious, toward the nearest blue-white form to his right. His fingers passed through, but tingled. And he knew everything was going to be all right.

Then the ghostly face of the shimmering dragon turned, meeting Jastin's eyes. Jastin knew him.

"Bren Redheart," Jastin whispered.

He felt Kallon twitch. He rolled aside to look up, his brown eyes startled.

The shimmering dragon tilted his head at Kallon.

"Father?" Kallon asked.

The dragon face smiled.

Kallon rolled the other way, and searched the face of the specter on his left. "Mother?"

This dragon smiled, too.

Kallon's wings skipped rhythm, but recovered quickly. Jastin saw, too, that his wing wounds had healed over.

They dove onward, back toward the trees. Back toward the smoke, and the reek. But as the waterfall of light reached the battleground, the whiteness bleached the sky, dissipating the haze, and obliterating the stench.

Speeding, dazzling dragon forms passed over Blackclaw's fighters, one by one, or in rushing groups, and when they retreated, the fighters were left weaponless, dazed, and dropping like autumn leaves to the ground. A second spout of light broke off to the south, toward Shornmar Castle.

And Kallon found his family. Riza joined him in the sky, followed by Sela, and the three watched, with Jastin, in silent wonder, as the boundary spirits spun out, over, and around the entire scene, dancing a graceful ballet through the bloodshed.

Bringing an end to it.

Other Leland dragons joined the Redhearts in staring, amazed. Jia Greenscale flapped silent wings. A second Green came beside her, larger, and took her paw. A Brown flitted upward, tears in her eyes.

"My father was with them. I saw my father," she said.

"I saw mine, too, Vaya," said Kallon.

Below, monkeys collected into a group, and colorful tree birds settled onto their shoulders. Jaguars and other ground walkers joined Murkens in standing, watching. A golden eagle swept up and landed on Sela's back.

Eventually, Jastin realized the growing crowd of staring dragons wasn't just Leland fighters anymore. Even Blackclaw's troops gathered; the ones capable of moving, anyway. They lowered their heads, and drooped in the air. Jastin could feel their shame emanating like the stink of spoiled milk.

Jastin saw Layce where she lay on the ground. She stirred. Sat up. Her sister embraced her. Orman Thistleby limped into Jastin's view, and hunkered down to hug them both.

From the south, more dragons flew across the horizon into view. An orange dragon, with a rider—Venur Riddess. And the black dragon, Drell, with Venur Shornmar. Other dragons, colored with the mottled blends of desert clay and sand, followed, each with human riders on their backs.

And then, as the last vestige of glimmering white light funneled back off through the sky, toward the unending distance, and a final breath of smoke pushed off to clear away from the battleground, Jastin finally saw Fordon Blackclaw.

Just as Redheart saw him, too.

He was spread-eagle, dangling over the crumbled edge of the basin, his tail split in two near his rump. Bleeding out.

Redheart lowered, and landed beside him. Jastin swung his leg and slid off to the ground.

"I would have won!" Blackclaw shouted. He thrust his closed fist toward Redheart.

"You would have lost everything," said Kallon.

Blackclaw growled. Coughed. "I will be remembered," he said.

Kallon nodded. "Yes." He opened his paw toward a near Murken, a woman, who held a bloodied, sharpened javelin. She carried it forward, and laid it in Kallon's paw.

"Mercy," whispered Blackclaw.

Kallon used the point of the weapon to lift away a scale over Blackclaw's heart, and pressed the tip to his skin. "That is what I am giving you," said Kallon.

Then he drove the weapon home.

CHAPTER TWENTY-EIGHT

Torches blazed around the Mount Gore arena in the early, breaking light of a new dawn. On the carved podium sat the surviving Dragon Council members; Kallon Redheart, Lin Orangepaw, Min Greenscale.

In the audience were the ragged, assorted collection of Leland fighters, including those who had flown in from across the sea to defend her. As well as the first human guests in many years; Jastin Armitage, Orman Thistleby, Bannon Raley, Jade and a handful of Murkens, as well as Venur Ebouard Riddess, and Venur Moras Shornmar.

The latter of which seemed unable to keep still. Sela watched Moras wiggle, staring around himself at all the dragons, and occasionally petting one on the neck or leg. When his irresistible roaming found Drell, and he scratched the black dragon behind the ear, Drell just winched up his face in patient amusement, and let Moras scratch.

"We have come through a dark time in Leland

history," said Sela's father from the podium. "We have interred our brave dead, and reclaimed our broken land. This is a new Leland from out of the old, and we step into a wholesome future from our shattered past."

He swept his foreleg toward Vaya Brownwing, waiting just off the edge of the raised platform. "We come to rebalance our rule, and our council. Welcome Vaya Brownwing, newest member of the Dragon Council, and Herald of the Browns."

Vaya stepped forward, as humans clapped, and dragons slapped their wings to the ground in support.

"Thank you," she said to the crowd. "I only hope I am worthy to fill the immense role, and to make my father proud."

Sela knew just what Vaya meant. Sela's father looked at her then, and she smiled.

One day, he whispered into her thoughts. *You will stand here, in my place.*

Sela Redheart, Herald of the Reds? Maybe. Just maybe.

Then Layce Phelcher burst through the arena opening and called out, "Kallon Redheart!"

There was a collective shift to look.

Sela gasped. It had happened! She beamed at Bannon, who smiled, but shrugged. And then she pushed her way through the crowd, using her wings to part bodies and make room. "Excuse me," she said. "Excuse me, please."

"I..." her father stammered behind her. "Uh. Dismissed!"

Sela just made it into the open to join Layce as her father swooped over and landed beside her. They all rushed into the manor, through the Great Hall, and down the hallway, jostling for room on their way to her parent's room.

Layce opened the door, and Sela squeezed through first.

Then she stopped, and stared at her mother, who lay out across her crumpled bedroll, panting, but grinning. Avara Phelcher knelt beside her, hugging a blanketed object in her arms, and then gently set it into the arms of Sela's mother.

An egg. A smooth, oval egg as richly crimson as bloodstone.

Her father brushed past, and drew his digits over the egg. He made a purring sort of sound, and they nuzzled their snouts together.

"My little brother," said Sela, with a giggle in her voice.

Her mother looked up. "How do you know that?" she asked.

Sela gave a little shrug, and a smile, looking between her parents. "Oh. I just do."

Then Jade burst through the door, twigs scattering from her hair to the floor. "Move aside and let me see my new grandbaby!"

She trotted toward them, and dropped to her knees to admire the glittering egg. She passed her hand over it. She pursed her lips.

She looked up to Sela's father. "Hm. Looks like it

takes after you."

§

Jia Greenscale stood at the edge of the sandy Esra crevice where the bleached bones of Fane Whitetail's mother and father tumbled together, forgotten.

Nearly forgotten.

Gladdis stood beside her, with her soft hand on Jia's shoulder. "I wish I would have understood this idea of forgiveness sooner," said Jia. "I wish I could have managed it."

"Would you have made different choices?" asked Gladdis.

"Yes, I think so." She lowered her snout to look into Gladdis's face. "I would have." She regarded the girl for a time, resisting what she was about to do.

But then she turned to the body of Fane Whitetail, which she'd carried from the Esra dungeon to here. She'd thought, early on, what a satisfying act it would be to throw him into the wastes where he once threatened to toss her. Now, she stood here with him for a different reason. "He belongs," she said. "He should end up with those he began with."

She crouched, and gave his pale body a hefty push. It rolled, bounced, and then came to rest on the same lumpy outcroppings where the other bones waited.

She straightened, and stared down, and surprised herself with tears in her eyes.

"I should have known better," she said.

Gladdis's hand came to her shoulder again. "Your next lesson on forgiveness will have to be how to use it on yourself."

Gladdis looked down at the girl again. "I'm very glad to have you as a friend."

Gladdis smiled softly, and patted her scales.

"Are you ready to go back?" asked Jia.

"We'll stay as long as you need."

"I think I have given Fane Whitetail plenty of my time already," said Jia. She lowered to give Gladdis a place to step up, and the girl gracefully settled into place behind her neck.

Jia looked once more into the cleft. Then she pushed up, turned her back, and headed for home.

§

Jastin stood aside at the entrance of Mount Gore Manor, as the contents of the arena funneled out. Some dragons flew off in all directions, presumably home. Some lumbered forward into the Manor, toward the scent of roasting meat and vegetables emanating through the giant arch. Others stepped inside to the feast, too; the Murkens who'd joined the council ceremony filed past, mumbling and smiling, and pointing at the intricate statue artwork on either side. The venurs, who had already agreed on an alliance between provinces, especially since Moras Shornmar was in need of trusted guidance.

Ebouard Riddess paused, just as he was about to go

in. He turned, instead, and stuck out his hand toward Jastin. "Few words have been said to you for your part in all this. We thank you."

Jastin didn't know what to say, so he just gripped the venur's hand.

"Leland and Esra guards will need restructuring, recruiting, organizing. Moras and I are looking to bring them under a joint chain of command. We could use a captain with your experience."

Jastin released the handshake. "It has been a long time since I commanded anyone."

The venur smiled. "Not as long as you think."

Kallon Redheart lumbered outside and down the manor steps, parting those straggling few going the opposite way. "With the Dragon Council as a fixed part of Leland's new government, we will need to relearn how to liaise as soldiers, as well."

"Now, now!" called Orman Thistleby, hurrying to join them all, wagging a dribbling drumstick in his hand. "You have perfectly capable wizards for that, Kallon Redheart. Don't be giving away all the best posts." He bit off a juicy slab of meat and chewed, eyeing Jastin. "Besides," he said around his food. "This scallywag has a lot answering to do, yet. Key or no key."

"Orman," began the venur.

"No, the wizard is right," said Jastin. "I've got a long way to go before I'll ever earn the trust of Leland's own, human or dragon." He regarded Redheart.

The Red nodded faintly. "I will not deny there's a lot of confusion, just now, about what to do with you,

Armitage."

Now Jade appeared, followed by Sela, whose claws clicked delicately as she stepped down the sweeping marble stairs. "We'll be happy to take him off your hands," said Jade. "Man's got somewhere to be, anyway. There's a pretty maid, decorating herself in the finest foliage Murk has to offer, and waiting on you to make that handprint official." She rapped her knuckles on the cracked and faded print on Jastin's chest.

Leesa hadn't even given Jastin a chance to propose; she'd informed him at the first opportunity after the chaos that they would be wed. Not in words, of course, but Jastin was beginning to understand her, all the same. "She's not going to patient with me much longer, I think."

"Well, the least I can do is get you to your ceremony on time," said Redheart.

"Oh, Father," said Sela. "I want to go, too. Mother will understand."

"I'm sure she will," said Redheart. He knelt forward, offering a climb.

Jastin hoisted a leg, and slid into place. He was getting better at it already.

Jade pulled herself onto Sela's back, just as a golden eagle soared around the corner of the manor, and brushed past Sela's face. She laughed, and jumped off after the bird, with Jade still scrabbling to hold on.

Redheart seemed to hesitate, just before he coiled back, poised to leap.

"Second thoughts?" asked Jastin.

"I've been carrying you often lately," said Redheart.

"Don't worry, I won't get used to it."

Redheart gave a snort of a laugh. "I don't think either of us ever could." But then he did lunge up, quickly, over the arena, over the pin oaks and scrub pines, toward the east, and Murk Forest.

Kallon and Jastin flew.

Own Them All!

Redheart

Book One of the Leland Dragons Series

Make sure to read the first entry in the Leland Dragons Series!

"Marvelous! Jackie Gamber has created a wondrous, enthralling world of adventure, mystery, and richly crafted characters. Dragons soar--and so do we! This is high fantasy at its most extraordinary."

- T. A. Barron,
New York Times bestselling creator of
The Merlin Saga and *The Great Tree of Avalon*

Find *Redheart* online and everywhere you buy books!
Print and digital versions are available internationally.

Own Them All!

Sela

Book Two of the Leland Dragons Series

Make sure you've read the second entry in the Leland Dragons series!

"Fast-moving action adventure with dragons, mystery, and heart."

- Sheila Deeth
Author of *Wind and Snow: A Triptych of Triptychs*

Check your favorite book seller to see if they already have *Sela* in stock, or if you can request a copy!

Fantasy

Liminal Space

Fiction from the Slipstream

"Jackie Gamber's world and character building are astonishing. The stories are so vivid they leap off the page and transport you into the middle of the story with the characters."

- Robin Blankenship
Librarian, freelance editor, and literary blogger of *Robin's Book Spot*

Find *Liminal Space* online, or print and digital versions are both available wherever you buy books!

MORE FROM BIG IMAGINE

Science Fiction

Living Things
Short Tales of Science Fiction and Dystopia

"*Living Things is about aching to be, striving to embody our best selves, and remaining optimistic in the face of adversity; success not guaranteed.*"

- Anthony Taylor
author of *Voyage to the Bottom of the Sea: The Complete Series - Volume 2*

Find *Living Things* in both print or digital versions online, and wherever you buy books!

www.ingramcontent.com/pod-product-compliance
Lightning Source LLC
Chambersburg PA
CBHW072044190726
48294CB00005B/1398